DETECTIVES WITHOUT GUNS

Unarmed and Unofficial
Book 1

CLAIRE HARRISON

Acknowledgments

This book was a long time in the making, with many halting moments along the way. But I have my beautiful friends Chez, Sharon and Janet T to thank for inspiring the characters and for always being those wonderful people who stick with you, hold you up and keep you going.

Thanks to Janet Townsend and Nick Clarke for reading the manuscript twice and providing valuable feedback. To my treasured family Clayton, Lauren, Reece and William, for being my absolute rock and allowing me many hours of alone time to write.

Thank you Liat Kirby from Lynk Assessment for editing the manuscript and providing sage advice, and to Next Chapter for taking a chance on me as a new author.

To Diane Clarke, without whom, there would be no book. Thank you for your continued support, encouragement, advice, and many, many edits. I could not have done this without you. You are a great friend and yourself, a talented author.

Finally, to you the reader. I am humbled that you have given up your precious time to read the book. As an author, that brings the greatest joy.

To my Dad – for your love and always believing in me.

Chapter 1

Lou slammed the door on her way through it, just for effect. Mel felt sure, that somewhere in the pit of his belly, Campbell's gut contracted.

The meeting room he'd booked was the nicest in the Treasury building. Wood-panelled bookcase in the corner, polished parquetry table in the middle – oval in shape so no one felt left out and a dozen high back, leather-look chairs to complete the picture. The view from the half-wall window was breathtaking – lost on a public building.

Lou sat in the chair at the narrowest curve of the table with her back to the window. Always assume the power position in a fight where you're going down.

Campbell, from HR, hesitated between two chairs to Lou's left, unsure what to do. Luckily, he wasn't a poker player. He finally chose the one furthest from her and beckoned Sharin to take the seat between them. Mel took the one to her right, whilst Jill, their new manager, sat at the opposite end of the table.

Campbell fidgeted with the cuff of his shirt sleeve and cleared his throat.

'Thanks for meeting so early, Unfortunately, I do have some

bad news.' He slid a sidelong glance at Lou and rushed on. 'Um, it appears they're expediting the changes. We have eight weeks to finalise the roles, which means your decision about redundancy, redeployment, or resignation, needs to be made next week.'

'For God's sake!'

Campbell sighed in what sounded like a huff. 'Lou, please. This is not my decision.'

'Bollocks!,' said Lou, heaving her ample bosom onto the table as she leaned over it. She was sliding into full flight.

Mel settled back to watch. She was listening, just not quite. Her mind drifted back to the drive into work and the news on her radio. It hadn't really focused on anything else since the story broke some weeks before.

'Detectives are appealing for community assistance as they continue investigations into the recent deaths of two young women. Police discovered the bodies of 22-year-old Kristen Bell and 17year-old Erin Delaney at separate locations in March and May this year. The two women disappeared a month before their bodies were found in nearby laneways in inner Melbourne. Both women were raped and brutally beaten and forensic psychologist, Daton Burke, believes there could be a pattern to the killings. Police are yet to confirm if the two are related.

Investigators are piecing together a timeline of events and are seeking public assistance to fully understand the circumstances leading to their deaths. Kristen disappeared in February and Erin in April...'

Mel jumped as Lou's palm slapped the table. She looked up to see Campbell flush pink and work his cuffs so hard Mel feared a button would snap off.

Jill stood up. She'd been silent until now. 'Lou, we hear you, but this is happening so we just have to get on with it.'

Jill was a recent addition to the management team and her motives were not yet clear to the girls. They didn't know if she was friend or foe.

Lou paused a moment longer before flopping into the high back chair. A whoosh of air squeezed out around her. Thankfully the lamb's wool of her jumper softened the sound. The tension was thick and claustrophobic. It clung to them, until the tiny breeze that was Sharin, spoke up and cleared it.

'If we redeploy, how long do we have the first option on new jobs?' she asked.

'Six months,' said Campbell.

'And if we don't get one?'

Campbell hesitated. 'Um, you're let go.'

'With no option for the redundancy,' said Mel.

'No,' said Campbell.

'And how much do we get paid if we take the redundancy?' asked Sharin, as her slender fingers wrestled each other. Campbell started with the HR speak.

Mel drifted again to the warmth of her faithful red Wolseley and the dulcet tones of the newsreader. The story was familiar. She'd heard it all before. Twenty-seven years ago. But not through a radio. In her face. Full frontal.

She'd been at university all day, wandering in and out of classes she had little interest in. She was in the first year of her second attempt at a degree and that wouldn't last either. She came back to her room in Ormond College at Melbourne University to find a note under the door asking her to see the Chancellor.

Forty-five minutes later, with the Chancellor hovering in front of a heavy mahogany bookcase and the tick-tock of a clock recording the seconds before her life spun off its axis, a modulated voice informed her that the body of Peggy Hilliard was found, beaten, raped, and murdered, alongside a skip behind a restaurant off Lygon Street.

Mel later described the moment as feeling like she'd been hit in the face with a cricket bat. The tick-tock of the clock stopped. The modulated voice hummed on somewhere in the distance. The firm hand of the Chancellor reached out to hold her upright.

And the image of a body lying by a filthy skip, cold and battered, left her gasping for air. She knew she screamed out, but she had no recollection of thoughts and words.

Her reaction was to get away. To go to Gran. To find out the truth. To beg for a different answer. But the answer was always the same. Her mother was dead.

Chapter 2

ANNIE SLID OFF HER HEADPHONES AND PICKED UP THE iPhone.

'Hellooooo,' said the voice on the end of it.

'Hi Aunt Rosa,'

'Darrrrling, are you coming to see me so we can make that beautiful dress?'

'Yes we are. Me and Mum. Is there anything we need to bring?'

'Thank you darling, put it there,' said Rosa.

'Sorry?' said Annie.

'Darling, just Marcus with the mail.'

'Oh, that's nice. How is he?'

'Always lovely.'

Annie giggled into the phone. Everyone was lovely until they weren't. Rosa Rebello was a force of nature. A Sicilian force of nature.

'So, should I bring anything?' asked Annie.

'No, darling. Everything is here. What colour are you wanting?'

'Silver.'

'*Bella*. I have a silver silk. *Exquisito*.'

'I have a picture of the dress too. Is that, ok?' asked Annie.

'Of course.'

'Thanks, Aunt Rosa. See you .... Hang on! Will Uncle Eddy be there?'

'Of course, darling!'

'Great. I want his opinion on the shoes.'

'Well, he'll give it. Ciao darling.'

Annie hung up the phone and smiled at it.

'You seriously want shoe advice from Eddy?' said Mel, standing in the doorway to Annie's room.

'Yes, mother. He only runs a shoe emporium.'

'Hmmm.'

'He can't win with you, can he?'

'Nope,' agreed Mel, wandering into the room and flopping on the bed.

'You're unfair.'

'You don't know the half of it, Annie.'

'I am sure I know enough.'

'Righty-ho. Let's just leave it,' Mel said.

Annie opened, then closed her mouth. She knew better. Mel might lie down and die for her, but some arguments she wouldn't win. Eddy was one of them.

Annie averted her eyes and fiddled with her earphones. Mel watched her and let the moment pass. She wondered in awe, at the way time could so quickly transform a child into an adult. She felt she'd missed some of those moments in that transition.

Mel had fallen pregnant with Annie after a weekend of gastro. Six months after she'd met Annie's father Ricky in a noisy bar in Rome, Mel travelled back to Italy to make it official with him, before he immigrated to Australia to make a life with her. She spent the first weekend in his bed, the second meeting his parents, and the third with her head in a toilet bowl following their drunken nuptials. Contraception doesn't work effectively at the bottom of a sewer. Eight weeks after she arrived home, she discovered she was pregnant.

Mel never wanted children. She'd been carer to her sister Lexie since she was twenty years old and feared she couldn't love any child as much. More overwhelming was the paralytic anxiety that a child may experience what Lexie had, and Mel couldn't face it. But Annie came along anyway. Mel fell instantly in love with her but the fear of losing that love made her rally against motherhood for a time. Fortunately, Ricky guided her gently and confidently through it and by the time Annie was eight months old, Mel had settled into an acceptance that things might be all right. But the specter of fear remained.

Mel stretched out on Annie's bed, pushing Big Ted to one side. Even at sixteen years old, she couldn't part with Big Ted. He'd been with her since birth – a gift from her great-grand-mother. Tattered and tired, he was a constant in her short life.

Annie settled cross-legged on her chair. 'You're getting comfortable. This must be serious,' she smiled.

'Am I that obvious?' asked Mel.

'Always,' said Annie.

'How did you get to be so smart?'

'Dunno. Must've got it from Dad,' said Annie.

Mel threw Big Ted at her.

'Ok, maybe some of it came from you,' she conceded. 'Watcha wanna talk about?'

Mel twiddled the quilt cover between her fingers, trying to choose her words carefully. She fluffed the pillow behind her head. 'I was thinking I'd pick you up after school on Wednesday. Save you riding to Rosa's.'

'You never pick me up.'

'I'm making an exception,' said Mel.

'Why?'

'Just because,' said Mel, not looking at her.

'I'll be ok, Mum.'

'I want to.'

'All right.'

Mel picked at a thread on the quilt.

'Mum, what's the matter?'

'I know I sound overprotective, but these murders are worrying me. I really need to know you are being cautious when you're out. Like, don't walk alone – anywhere!'

'MUM! Seriously. I'm ok.'

'You say that, but these people are clever. They manipulate, play on your kindness. I don't know, they....'

'Mum... please. We're all careful. Promise.'

'It's only that you are the most important thing in the world to me. Nothing scares me more than losing you.'

'You worry too much.'

'It comes with the territory, Annie.'

'It's not necessary, I'm sixteen!'

'Honey, I will be worrying about you when you're sixty.'

'Um...no offence, but not sure you'll be around then.'

Mel smiled. Then didn't.

'Please, Annie, just be careful.'

Annie sat Big Ted on the desk, uncurled her legs, climbed onto the bed and into Mel's arms. She lay her head on Mel's shoulder. 'I'm not Peggy, Mum. Lightning doesn't strike twice,' she whispered.

Mel wrapped her arms more tightly around the only thing whose loss would cause her to give up on life. She stroked Annie's hair but couldn't speak. Lightning may not strike twice but the odds on this one seemed somehow greater.

They held each other as the hum from Annie's headphones filled the silence. Annie was the first to break it. She pulled away, turned into Mel, and hugged her. 'Right young lady, off to bed with you,' she instructed.

Mel kissed her. 'Ok, Mum.'

Annie slid away and off the bed, extending a hand to help her mother up. She didn't give Mel a chance to say more as she picked up her headphones and rolled them over her ears. Her little wave indicated the conversation was over.

Chapter 3

DAN HILLIARD TURNED OFF THE IPAD AND SLID IT onto the bedside table. The light from the screen still illuminated the corner of the room.

He ran a finger gently along the shoulder of his sleeping wife before falling silently back against the pillow. He stared into the gloomy light and recalled the article he'd just read. The journo was thorough, but there was nothing new. He'd even phoned Dan for comment, but Dan refused to speak to him. He didn't trust journalists. They'd burned him when it first happened. How long before they dredged up more old stories and theories that dragged him back there again.

He'd been away at a car show when the police came to see him. She'd been dead a whole night and half the day. He shivered again at the thought.

There were investigations and accusations. He weathered it all. Badly. He oscillated between grief and anger, confusion and clarity. Tried to hold it together for Lexie, the longed-for baby he'd waited a lifetime to share with the woman he'd waited a lifetime for. He succeeded until that miserable Thursday morning when he opened the door to Mel, and saw the reflection of his Peg, in her beautiful face. He howled in pain and she held him. He never truly recovered.

Sarah stirred beside him. Far off the sounds of night echoed around their cattle property.

It seemed forever ago and really, it was. He'd had three lives. One with Peggy when they first met, another when they got back together and had Lexie, and this last one, with Sarah. Life had settled with Sarah. He hadn't known how it could be, until he met her. With Peg, it was passionate and chaotic. Somehow, the sameness and predictability of the routine he now had, soothed him.

He picked up his phone and began a text. It had been too long. He was leaving his calls longer and longer these days. The stabs of guilt were deep. Deeper with each contact, opening wounds he'd worked so hard to conceal.

But he texted anyway. He knew Mel would want it. Knew her thoughts had ventured where his had. He owed her. It was time to see Lexie again anyway. The guilt stabbed him harder. He'd run away. Left everything of Peggy behind, including Lexie. He couldn't cope and he couldn't move on. Sarah saved him. But he was a coward. And he'd sacrificed the greatest love of his life for the numbness of predictability.

Mel's phone lit up. She ignored the beep. But it kept reminding her every 30 seconds. She smashed her hand over it and dragged it to her face. 'Who the bloody hell texts at 11p.m.,' she thought.

'Hey Mel. Guess you've read the news. Know you will have. Those poor families. No one should go through this. How's Lexie? Thinking I should book to come down soon. Thoughts?'

Mel smiled. She loved Dan. Apart from Pop, he was the only dad she'd known. She was the product of Peg's shag in the back-seat of a car with a Swedish backpacker named Lars. By the time Gran confronted Peg about her pregnancy, Lars was long gone, and fifteen-year-old Peggy was nowhere near ready to be a mum. So, Gran and Pop built the nursery and helped Peggy by becoming surrogate parents to Mel. When Dan came along three years later, he swept Peggy and Mel off their feet. For six years they were a family. And then they weren't. Dan wanted more children but Peg was restless. She found ways to avoid it happening and Dan discovered it. The lies and deception tore apart whatever love they had for each other. And they did love each other, but for Peggy it wasn't enough. In the end, Mel went back to Gran and Pop, and Peggy went off into some neverland. Then Dan came back into her life ten years on and they made a real go of it. Mel was living away at Uni. Lexie was born. And life was as happy as it could be. Until it wasn't.

'Hey Dan. Yep, all over it. Shit show. You ok? Sarah well? Lexie would love it. I'd love it. Send me the details soon. I'll tell Lexie tomorrow. And send you the pic of that crazy smile she gets. Love ya.'

The phone vibrated in Dan's hand. He cried silent tears. He didn't deserve either of them. Or their love. But there it was. He'd left Mel alone to care for his severely disabled daughter. He gave money in lieu of being there. He was a coward and he hated himself for it.

He sent back a quick note with several kisses and a heart. An emoji to show how he felt. It was pathetic but it was all he had.

Chapter 4

MEL WAS TYPING 'ANNIE 13' INTO THE PASSWORD BOX as Lou drifted in, wearing what could only be described as a tent. 'What the hell are you wearing?' asked Mel.

'A kaftan.'

'Yes, I can see it's a kaftan. Why are you wearing it?'

'It hides the fat.'

'Jesus, Lou. You don't honestly believe that three metres of royal blue nylon is going to make you look slim?'

'No. But it hides the fat.'

There was nothing else to say. You could hardly argue with logic.

'I think it's quite pretty,' said Sharin, who'd followed her in.

'In a Demis Roussos meets *Cirque du Soleil* kind of way,' suggested Mel.

'This is not making me feel better!' said Lou, flopping into a chair. The hem of the kaftan floated to the floor like a deflating balloon.

'Sorry, Lou but the Kaftan is clearly a cry for help.'

'I need *help* to lose weight,' said Lou.

Sharin leaped across the room and hugged Lou. The kaftan

enveloped them both. 'You don't need to lose weight. I think you're perfect just as you are.'

'You do need to lose that Kaftan though,' said Mel.

That afternoon, with a diet shake under her belt, Lou was in a better frame of mind. 'Any thoughts on our casino visit?' she asked.

Every few months they made a trip to the casino in Melbourne. Occasionally they ventured interstate.

'Yeah,' said Mel, 'it might soon be our primary income.'

'That is too true,' agreed Lou.

Sharin fidgeted with her mouse. Of the three, she was the most concerned. 'At least you both have partners with incomes. Maybe my Julia will have to turn tricks.'

Lou nodded. 'And not the ones with a stick.' She hesitated then added 'although ...'

'Wash your mouth out!' said Mel.

'Well,' said Sharin, 'you never know.'

'Sharin Pentagast,' said Mel, 'I will pay you from my own pocket before I allow your precious cocker spaniel to prostitute herself.'

'But, to be fair,' said Lou, 'it could be a thing. Redhead Goddess with Redhead Doggess might make you some real cash.'

'Or maybe we'll keep counting cards and screw the casino instead,' said Mel.

Sharin nodded. 'Yep, agreed'

Lou looked disappointed.

'I'll see what's coming up. Time our visit with some major event,' said Sharin firing up Google.

'There's bound to be plenty on. It's the start of the Spring Racing Carnival. There'll be bookies, jockeys, and punters all over the place,' said Mel.

'Ooh, hello' said Sharin wiggling in her seat, 'I've got a kiss.'

'A what?'

'A kiss,' repeated Sharin. 'It's when someone wants to meet you. I've joined RSVP – thought I'd give it a go.'

'Perhaps you and Julia won't have to do tricks after all,' said Mel as she and Lou gathered around the screen.

'Let's have a look then,' said Lou.

Few decisions were made in the office, which weren't collective. And very little information was sacred. If Sharin was going to date this guy, Mel and Lou would have a say in it.

Sharin was blessed with beauty and brains but lacked the confidence to use either to her advantage. As a result, she attracted her fair share of losers. Left alone, she was too sweet and naïve for her own good. Fortunately, she had Mel and Lou.

Sharin clicked on the 'kiss' and a picture with an accompanying profile popped up. Mel and Lou pushed closer to the screen.

'Not bad!' said Mel.

'Good jaw,' nodded Lou.

Mel and Sharin looked at her. 'Good Jaw?' repeated Mel.

'What? I like jaws.'

They returned to the picture. It showed a man, tall by all accounts, with a number two haircut, high cheekbones, and forearms tattooed to within an inch of their lives. Most striking were his eyes. Even from the grainy photo, you couldn't fail to notice them. They were ink black. He was leaning up against a boat, shirtless, looking relaxed.

'I'd do him,' approved Mel.

'Mmmmm, me too,' said Sharin.

'Let's read the details first,' advised Lou.

The description read like a page from a James Bond novel. Lou skimmed the page and summarised the vital statistics.

'Thirty-seven years old, 183 cm, slim, non-smoker,' she paused sucking the air in between her teeth, 'has a kid.'

'No, it's ok,' she continued, 'it doesn't live with him. Phew.

What else? Doesn't watch TV, enjoys the opera, (she rolled her eyes), and travel, fencing, surfing, sailing, karate, blah blah.'

'Oh, and look,' exclaimed Mel, 'he's French. How exotic!'

'Sounds too good to be true,' said Lou, 'but probably worth it for a shag.'

'Definitely,' agreed Mel.

'You never know,' said Sharin, 'maybe he's the real deal. Maybe he's 'the one'.'

Snorts and scoffs echoed around the room.

'Well, someone has to be 'the one',' said Sharin folding her arms.

'I've had five of 'the ones',' said Lou, 'there's no such thing. It's all about what you're prepared to put up with. And for how long. But give him a go anyway – what have you got to lose.'

'Absolutely nothing!' she said defiantly, clicking the 'accept' icon. Secretly she wished him to be the one.

Ever since her failed marriage, Sharin had looked for a replacement. She wasn't needy, she just loved being loved. When she'd married Ethan, in a gala extravaganza at the impressionable age of twenty-one, she believed it was forever. He swept into her life, swept her off her feet, and swept right out again. He'd promised so much and delivered so little, but she never gave up the dream of 'happily ever after.' Mel blamed the Piscean in her; Lou blamed Mills and Boon.

'So now that your love life is sorted, what's on at the casino?' asked Mel.

Sharin found the page she'd searched for and read out the upcoming events.

'Ok, we're looking at sometime in September,' she mumbled to herself, as she viewed the Crown Casino Events section. 'Mid-September is perfect! There's a photo exhibition on Friday the twentieth. Or better still, is the Racing, Fashion and Entertainment Gala on the Saturday. Now that would be perfect.'

'It would indeed,' said Mel, 'and we can dress up.'

'Done,' agreed Lou.

Chapter 5

It was close to 6 p.m. when Mel poured the first of two glasses of wine. She'd chosen a cheery little Alicante from the recently arrived wine delivery, and a glass the size of a small fishbowl. The house was quiet. Ricky would be heading into peak hour traffic and Annie was at dancing. They'd both be home by 7 p.m. with an expectation and an appetite. It gave Mel one hour to prepare something delicious.

Mel could cook. It was the thing that relaxed her. Whilst Peggy was trying to get an education or laid, Grandma did most of the parenting. Mel learned to cook from her grandmother. And Rosa Rebello. They could make a leather shoe melt in your mouth and they'd taught Mel well. Her husband, Ricky, was evidence of it. He'd gained a kilo for every year they were together. After seventeen years, he was well upholstered.

One hour and a glass of wine later, a bunch of baby pink roses wrapped in layers of lavender tissue appeared from around the bench. Mel closed, then opened her eyes, taking in a deep breath as she did. She was being spoiled.

The arm carrying the flowers wound around her waist, pressing the roses gently to her chest. Their perfume mingled with the warm, faint smell of aftershave as Ricky leaned in and kissed her neck.

'Well, hello,' he mumbled against her skin as his lips moved knowingly from her neck to her ear. She shivered and giggled, turning slowly in his arms.

She slid her fingers under his shirt collar, opening it to reveal the groove between his collar bones, and kissed him there. She blew a raspberry and laughed, drawing his face to hers and kissing him fully on the lips.

'Ew, get a room,' groaned a voice behind them.

Ricky pulled Mel more tightly to him and kissed her with passion.

Annie made puking noises. 'Can you stop?! Hello, children present,' she complained pointing a finger at herself.

They stopped. Scarring their child for life was definitely on their 'to-do' list, but the pasta was starting to bubble over.

'Thank you!' said Annie throwing her school bag under the bench. 'I am starving, what's for dinner?'

'Your favourite. Sheep's brains,' replied Mel, 'so set the table please.'

Annie grumbled as she rounded the bench and opened the cutlery drawer. Ricky flicked on the TV, then poured himself a glass of wine and another for Mel. The bottle was empty.

'So how was your day?' he asked.

'Well, the redundancy is progressing rapidly. Campbell moves quickly. One day we're having a meeting and the next we have a full-page email with all the options.'

'Oh,' said Ricky. 'And the deadline is when?'

'End of September. But we need to decide what we want to do, by next week.'

Ricky puffed out his cheeks and let a slow whistle form. 'Not much time,' he said.

'I know,' she said moving toward him. 'But it'll be ok. Promise.'

Ricky let her hold him. His body was tense. Mel rubbed his

back. 'I promise,' she repeated pulling away to look him in the eye.

She changed subjects and asked about his day. They traded stories, interjected by Annie and her considered opinion on the topics being discussed. The conversation ambled its way to Annie and her upcoming formal.

'You still going to drive me to Aunt Rosa's tomorrow?' she asked.

'Yep, all good. Have you found any more dresses you like?' asked Mel.

'Nah, I've made up my mind. I like the silver one.'

'It better cover everything,' warned Ricky.

'It's the 21st century, Dad.'

'I don't want all those sweaty boys perving on you,' he said.

'Oh my God. You are such a boomer!'

'A what?'

'Apparently you are old Ricky. He is not a boomer, Annie. Wrong generation.'

'Whatever. I'm wearing the silver one,' she said. 'The one with no straps!'

Ricky threw his napkin at her.

The voices on the TV provided background noise, until the music heralding the start of the news came on. They all stopped to look and listen. Ricky took up the remote and turned the TV up a little louder as an ABC reporter with a clipped tone began recapping a story:

'Police are yet to confirm if there is any connection between these cases and that of Fitzroy woman, Lisa Harding, who was reported missing on July 5th. It's been almost a month since her disappearance and police are concerned for her whereabouts as both Kristen Bell and Erin Delaney vanished a month before their bodies were discovered in inner city Melbourne. It is believed they were dead for less than 24 hours when they were found. And joining us now is the head of the Macro Taskforce, acting Superintendent Gerald

Turner. 'Superintendent, do police have any theories as to what happened to these women?'

'We deal with evidence, not theories. But we have several leads we are following up.'

'Can you give us further details about the two recent murders?'

'At the moment we are appealing for anyone with information to come forward. We hope the $100 000 reward posted by the family of one of the victims will help in this investigation.'

The images of two young women, both smiling into the camera, flashed onto the screen as the news reporter took up where the detective left off:

'Circumstances surrounding the disappearance of all three women remains unclear, but it is known that both Kristen and Erin were raped and strangled at the time of death. An unnamed source revealed that both women had their hair cut off at the nape. Forensic Psychologist......'

'Turn it off!' said Mel, 'It makes me sick.'

The images burned on the screen a moment longer as Ricky pressed buttons on the remote and changed the channel. Their innocent young faces, full of promise, happy in the moment. Erin, dressed in her school uniform, blue eyes rimmed by moon-shaped glasses, fair hair caught up in a ponytail, and Kristen, gazing just left of the camera, her pink fringe brushing the tops of her eyebrows as her long blonde hair disappeared down her back.

'I do look a bit like them, don't I,' said Annie.

Ricky squeezed Mel's thigh under the table.

'And that's why I worry,' said Mel.

'To be fair, Mum, I also look like you.'

'And that's why I worry,' said Ricky, squeezing Mel's thigh again.

'But I'm not the demographic,' she said looking at Annie.

Annie shrugged. 'Had you heard their hair was cut off. I reckon that's new?' she said.

'Yeah, it is,' said Ricky.

'Peggy's hair was cut,' said Annie.

'Ripped, really. Honestly, I wish you didn't know any of this,' said Mel, pressing the heels of her hands against her eyes. Ricky reached over and took both hands in his, bringing them to his lips.

'It's good I know,' said Annie. 'I wish I knew more. I wish I'd known her.'

'Mmm, I wish I'd known her too. I mean better. So much better,' said Mel.

Annie leant across the table to touch Mel's arm. 'I bet she wished she'd known you better too. She'd have been so proud.'

Mel felt a rush of emotion flood through her with a force she couldn't suppress. Tears welled up and she squeezed her eyes hard shut to prevent them spilling over. She'd never contemplated her mother's feelings for her in that way. The sense of loss she felt again overwhelmed her.

Chapter 6

THE PHONE ON LOU'S DESK RANG.

Lou continued to stare at her computer as fingers flashed across the keyboard in fear of making sparks. And the phone kept ringing.

Finally, she answered.

'Department of lost souls, Delores speaking.' She smirked to herself as she waited for the awkward silence to follow.

'Oh sorry, my mistake. Department of Grants and Funding. How can I help?'

Lou held the phone at a forty-five-degree angle and tipped her head toward Mel. 'For you. Some bloke?' she said holding out the receiver. Lou did not transfer calls.

Mel slid out from behind her desk, hitting her thigh on the corner as she reached for the phone. She winced but gritted her teeth against the words forming on her lips. 'Fuck' was a great word, but not for unknown ears on the end of a phone.

'Mel Cooke speaking,' she said, taking the phone. As she listened, Mel's shoulders slumped. 'Oh ... it's you.' More silence followed. Mel switched the phone to her other ear. 'Really ... are you serious? How did you get this number?'

Lou stopped typing and straightened up.

'Just STOP calling me,' Mel growled and hung up the receiver with a thud.

Lou leaned back in her chair. 'Ok, spill.'

Mel twisted around to sit on the edge of the desk then dropped her head into her hands.

Sharin was on her feet and heading toward her. Nothing shouted 'hug' like a head in hands. Mel let her wrap her arms around her shoulders and pat her back. She rested in the pillowy softness of Sharin's cashmere cardigan for a few moments before Lou repeated, 'Spill.'

Sharin stopped patting and Mel lifted her head. 'It's this bloody journalist. He's driving me nuts,' she said.

'Why?' asked Lou.

'He's interested in my mother.'

'Your mother's dead.'

'Lou!!' shrieked Sharin.

'Well, she is.'

Sharin vigorously patted Mel's back.

'It's ok, Shaz, I know she's dead,' said Mel squeezing Sharin's free hand.

'So, what does he want to know?' asked Lou, fixing Sharin with a cautionary glare.

'He wants to know more about her. He reckons there might be a link between her murder and the girls who have died recently.'

'But she died nearly thirty years ago.'

'Yeah, I know. It's crazy.'

'How could they be linked?'

Sharin stopped patting. She pushed aside a tray of files and sat on the opposite edge of the desk. Lou wheeled her chair back a few inches and relaxed her arms.

'He reckons there are lots of similarities. He's doing an investigative series on serial killers and he found out about Peggy. She looks similar, same MO and same city.'

'Yep – but 27 years apart. That's a long time between drinks.'

Mel sighed. 'That's what I said. But they never did find who did it.'

'Maybe whoever did it, went to prison for something else and got out recently,' Sharin chimed in. 'Or perhaps,' she started to stand up, 'someone was in jail with him and has copied him.'

'Or, its two different people and this is just some new sick fucker,' suggested Lou.

Sharin slid down onto the desk again.

'I don't know,' said Mel, running a hand behind her neck. 'I guess it's possible it's the same person but ...'

'Winning the lotto is possible,' interrupted Lou, 'but unlikely.'

Chapter 7

ROSA WAS IN THE DOORWAY WITH THE SCREEN DOOR ajar as Mel and Annie stepped out of the car. At exactly five feet tall, she should have looked tiny. But her girth, the teased-up Jackie O hairstyle, and the aura that surrounded her filled the entrance. No-one ever saw Rosa at home without her Laura Ashley country rose's apron and paler than pale pink lipstick, and today was no exception.

Annie ran straight into Rosa's open arms as Mel locked the car. Annie was a little taller than Rosa but still managed to look small and childlike in her embrace. She held Annie out with two hands and studied her. She smiled at what she saw and pulled her close again before leading her and Mel into the hallway.

Stepping into Rosa's home was a step back in time. Her husband Gino purchased the building in the late 1980s to expand his shoe shop. It was an upstairs, downstairs arrangement decked out in the finest 1970's brown and orange that was refreshed but never refurbished. Gino loved the colours and the shop. He used the rooms upstairs for storage and converted the four large rooms downstairs into 'Gino's Shoe Emporium.' The first of the Rebello emporiums.

For ten months, business boomed. Gino and Rosa were happy. Five of their boys were working or studying trades, and Eddy, the youngest, was learning the retail business in between finishing his last year of school. Then Gino died. An aneurism that lay dormant in his brain for fifty-one years, exploded, shattering the veneer of a future that was bright and enduring.

The house next door to Mel's Grandmother, where the family had lived for twenty-five years was sold; the boys moved out and Eddy went with Rosa to live in the apartment above the shop. She turned the downstairs rooms into a dressmaker's salon and went to work, transforming devastation into a dream. Twenty years later she retired, comfortable and well off. But she never changed the décor.

As they ascended the stairs, Mel slid her hand along the dark wood of the rail and reviewed the photographs that lined the panelled wall. Gino with his arm around Rosa leaning against their first car – a green valiant with cream roof; Rosa balanced daintily on the edge of a wingback chair, surrounded by her six boys solemnly staring down the lens of a camera; pictures of family, of friends, of memories, fading into hues of sepia, and a final one; of Rosa, her sister Maria, Mel's Gran and Peggy. A cloudless sky was watery blue behind them as they posed in short summer dresses, sunglasses reflecting little stars of sunshine and drinks decorated with colourful paper umbrellas held high in salutation.

She loved that photo. It reminded her of a time, real or imagined, that was free and heady. Of a summer, hot and long. BBQs, cricket and slip n' slide. In the days when her mum was present. In the days before she wasn't.

'Hi Uncle Eddy,' called Annie as she stepped off the top step and into the brightly lit living room, which served as both the dining and living area.

'Hi my Annie,' he replied leaving the glassware he was laying on the table and moving toward her. She hugged him with her arms wrapped around his waist and her face pressed sideways into his chest. Eddy gently ran his hand up and down her back. Over her head, Eddy glared at Mel and pulled Annie a little closer. Rosa stood between them with her hands on her hips, flicking her gaze back and forth until one of them spoke.

'Mel.'

'Eddy.'

'Tsk,' scoffed Rosa, shaking her head.

Behind Mel, the soft tread of a footstep on a creaky board made her turn.

'Hello, Melinda ... Annie,' he waved into the room, 'thought I heard you guys come in.'

Rosa's face softened and Annie let go of Eddy.

'Hi Marcus,' Annie and Mel said in unison. Both flushed a little.

'Wondered if you needed a hand, Ed?'

Marcus Kirby was Rosa's boarder. He'd been living in the rooms downstairs for almost a year and fitted into the place like a hand in a glove. He treated Rosa like gold and Eddy like a brother. In turn, they provided him with a place to call home five days a week, before he returned home on weekends to help his parents on their vineyard.

After Rosa retired, she didn't need all the rooms so turned the downstairs space into a bedsit with a shared entrance hall for them both. Eddy moved out for a short time but moved back in again so she wasn't alone. Several boarders came and went over the years, but Marcus was the only one to fall into step with Rosa and Eddy, soon becoming part of their daily ritual.

'All good thanks, Marcus. Just finishing off. Unless you want to open that wine you have in your hand?'

'Happily,' he said.

'Oh, the perks of a wine merchant,' sighed Mel.

'That is true. Would you like a glass?'

Annie coughed.

'Umm, I would but I won't,' said Mel. 'Gotta be the responsible adult here.'

Eddy coughed.

Mel glowered at him.

Eddy inclined his head. Across his cheek a tiny rash of glitter flashed under the overhead light.

'Right, time to work on this dress I think,' said Rosa, catching Annie's hand and leading her toward the spare room at the back of the house. Mel followed.

The spare room was all chintz curtains and Queen Anne furniture. The tones were more subdued than the living area, in pastel peach and beige, but the sheen on the curtains caught the glint from the tiny chandelier, giving it a more upbeat feel.

Laid across the bedspread was a rivulet of silver silk that didn't so much shimmer, as sparkle. 'Wow, I feel like it's flirting with me,' said Mel as the light winked off it this way, then that.

'Oh, Aunt Rosa, it's beautiful!' gushed Annie running her fingers along the delicate folds of fabric.

Rosa shifted her weight from one hip to the other and clapped her hands together. 'I knew you would like it, darrrrling.'

'I LOVE it!'

'Pick it up, wrap it around you. See how it feels.'

Annie did as she was told, wrapping it in a cape around her shoulders and pinching it in at the waist. She spun one way, then the other. The fabric flowed seamlessly with her movements.

Mel couldn't take her eyes off it.

'Perfect,' said Rosa.

'Definitely the one,' agreed Mel.

'Now, the picture?'

Annie stopped spinning. 'Mum, it's in your bag.'

Mel pulled out the folded sheet of paper and lay it flat on the bed. Rosa hovered wordlessly over it, but the tiny movements of her head and hands indicated she was working out how to make it. 'Hmm,' she finally murmured. 'I can do that. Let's get some measurements.'

Rosa left to find her tape measure and a notepad. She'd kept one of the other bedrooms as a sewing room and at least once a month produced a piece of couture art for the women, or their daughters, who'd previously been her customers. Neither Rosa nor her clientele quite embraced the full meaning of the word 'retirement'.

'... not even spaghetti straps?' Mel was asking as Rosa came back into the room.

'What you want straps for darrrling?' asked Rosa.

'Thank you, Aunt Rosa. Exactly.' Annie looked smugly at her mother.

'I don't, but Ricky wants her covered from head to toe.'

'Pfft.'

Mel raised her eyebrows. 'I guess no straps then,' she said, smiling at Annie.

'Right, no straps!'

They finished up the measurements and came back into the living room, leaving the silk lying on the bed in a pool of its own light. Only when the chandelier was switched off did it look like a dark stain on the pale coverlet.

Eddy was reading the paper at the table. Marcus was sitting in a lounge chair doing something on his iPad. They both looked up as the women came into the room.

'All good?' said Eddy to Annie.

'Better than good! Gorgeous!' said Annie.

'You or the dress?'

'Uncle Eddy!'

'What?' he said.

'The dress of course,' said Annie.

'And you, darrrling,' added Rosa.

Annie blushed a happy blush and changed the subject. 'What are you reading?'

'Stuff that is the reason you need to be careful,' said Eddy.

'I have my chaperone,' replied Annie, tossing a look at Mel.

'Dead right,' said Mel.

Eddy ignored her and spoke to the room. 'They think this latest missing girl might be connected to the others.'

'Let's just hope she doesn't turn up in the same way,' added Marcus.

'It doesn't bear thinking about, I mean ...' But Mel was interrupted by the doorbell.

'Shall I get that, Rosa?' asked Marcus, pushing himself up from the chair.

'Yes please, darrling.'

Marcus moved across the carpet and onto the stairs.

'... Anyway, at least nobody's turned up in a skip in Lygon St,' continued Mel.

Rosa clasped her hands together in prayer. 'Thank heavens, and we hope they never do.'

'Don't want history repeating,' added Eddy.

'Quit it, idiot,' snapped Mel.

'Just saying Mel, you never can be too ...' but voices echoing up the stairwell drowned him out, followed shortly after by a door being firmly closed. Marcus returned moments later with a broad smile and a booklet promising to deliver 'the truth that leads to eternal life'.

'Ah well, you gotta admire them for trying to convert an atheist,' he said, dropping the booklet on the table.

'No, no, no ...' muttered Rosa, making a sign of the cross and blessing the room.

'Sorry, Rosa,' he said, coming to her and hugging her. 'I'm not afraid of hell.'

'Oh la ...' she said, making a sign of the cross again.

Marcus laughed. 'Only your spaghetti putanesca can save me!'

Rosa gave him a gentle shove. 'You lucky we have it for dinner then,' she said.

'Speaking of dinner, we should get going. Ricky will have it ready,' said Mel.

'I'll walk you out,' said Marcus, 'before I'm sprinkled with holy water.' He ducked as Rosa lent in for another thump.

Mel, Annie and Rosa made plans to meet in a fortnight for the first dress fitting, and said their goodbyes.

As they made their way down the stairs to the front door, Mel looked into the face of her mother as she passed her photo on the staircase wall and thought of the dark stain on the pale coverlet.

Chapter 8

On Saturday afternoon, Mel and Annie sat on the study floor, surrounded by albums and photos, sourcing a baby photo for a classroom competition.

As their only child, Ricky was obsessive in his quest to capture every moment of Annie's life. She was their one shot at immortality, and he wasn't missing a moment of it. Besides this, Ricky's parents in Italy had an insatiable appetite for their absent grandchild and insisted on weekly updates.

The earliest photos were mostly of Annie on her own – lying on a blanket, asleep in her cot, cuddled up to Big Ted, or in the arms of Gran and Mrs. Rebello.

The few of her with Mel showed the love but also the fear and uncertainty Mel felt at the time. Her smile in those photos was always close-lipped and never reached her eyes.

But Ricky was patient and the women in her life took her gently by the hand and showed her what to do. She'd had some counselling from a social worker and by the time Annie was eight months old, Mel was a constant in the photographic timeline of her life.

Annie chose a picture of herself grinning into the camera, a dandelion chain sitting crooked on her head and a chunk of grass in her chubby little hand. It didn't worry her that her chin was shiny with dribble or that her fine blonde hair stuck straight up. She laughed when she saw it and decided there and then, it was the one.

Mel sat for hours after Annie lost interest, going through albums of history no one would care much about when she was gone. It saddened her that the number of photos gradually diminished as digital replaced film and gave the impression that life stopped somewhere in her late thirties.

'Want the light on?' asked Ricky coming into the room with a glass in each hand.

Mel glanced around at the gloom and nodded. 'I didn't realise the time.'

'Wine?' said Ricky, handing her a glass and easing himself onto the floor beside her.

She leaned in and kissed him on the cheek. 'You need to ask?'

He shrugged before picking up and putting down several of the photos laid out on the carpet.

Mel was flicking through pages of an album that belonged to Gran. When she died, Mel inherited a chunk of cash, some jewellery, and the photo albums. The open page displayed three 4 by 6-inch colour photos.

'You and Eddy seemed to get on in those,' said Ricky.

'Yep. Not for much longer though.'

'I particularly like this one,' said Ricky pointing to the second photo on the page.

Mel took a sip of wine as she studied it. 'He was great fun back then. We did a lot together. That was taken at Gran's. Playing dress-ups.'

'He does look good in a frock,' said Ricky.

Eddy was pouting at the camera in his outstretched hand, as Mel tied his hair into pigtails. The boho strappy dress in faded paisley hung loose on his thin frame while the coral lipstick highlighted soft full lips against skin that was smooth and tanned. The dark stubble that would come to torment him wasn't yet evident.

'If I'm honest, I regret what happened. But he never let it go.'

'Do you think he ever will?'

'Not now. I tried for a while to make it up to him. But ... he just hates me.'

'And you don't hate him?' asked Ricky gently. He was looking at Mel and she knew it. But she didn't look at him. She stared at the photo. 'I hate that he isn't honest about it. What I said was true. He hates me because he knows it's true. It's easier to blame me and that's not fair. He can't ... won't face the truth.'

'Sometimes eets not so easy.'

'But if he was true to himself, he'd be so much happier.'

'Or maybe eet makes things even harder.' Ricky wrapped an arm around Mel's shoulder 'Not for him. For everyone he loves,' he finished.

She took another sip of wine and let him stroke her hair. The tip of her fingernail picked at the corner of the page, as she let the thought of that sink in.

She and Eddy were inseparable growing up. They'd lived next door to each other all their lives. He knew her secrets and she knew his. But he was more careful with hers.

One afternoon, they'd been in the living room of his house, with two of his brothers, Alex and Mario, when his eldest brother Nick came into the room twirling a bra in his hand. 'Hey, Eddy, who's the lucky girl?'

Eddy froze on the spot.

'More likely he stole it off some clothesline,' laughed Mario grabbing it out of Nick's hand and pretending to strap it on.

Eddy launched at him and grabbed the bra, ripping it from Mario's hand before hiding it behind his back. Mel joined in, snatching it out of his hand. 'Hang on, this is mine!!'

'Ahh, so you two are at it. Good one, Eduardo,' sneered Mario, rubbing his crotch.

Mel flushed red. For months she'd had a crush on Mario and the last thing she wanted was him thinking she liked Eddy in that way. It was him she wanted to 'be at it' with.

Before she had the sense to think, the words were spilling out of her mouth. 'No way! Eddy doesn't want to be *with* a woman, he wants to *be* a woman.'

In that moment, everything changed.

A look, fleeting but unmistakable, crossed Eddy's face. The pain of that truth was evident for only a moment, but everyone in the room saw it.

The look of betrayal and howls of denial followed but nothing could unhide what was seen.

Both Mario and Nick took to Eddy like a punching bag. Mel, driven by shame and guilt desperately tried to intervene, but it took Mrs. Rebello and a leather strap she'd used on them as children to end it.

No one spoke of it again.

The bitterness between Eddy and Mel grew, fueled by humiliation and regret.

For Mrs. Rebello's sake, they kept it civil when she was around. If anyone had explained the situation to her, then she made no mention of it. She had six sons. And Mel was the daughter she never had.

Chapter 9

MEL AND LOU ARRIVED TOGETHER MONDAY MORNING to find Sharin slumped over her keyboard. She was sliding her fingers from temples, through her hair, and back again, pulling long strands around her face, before burying herself in them.

'What's wrong?' they asked in unison.

'Check your emails. They want an answer today.'

Mel dropped her bag and phone on the desk. 'Damn. Still weighing up options, but reckon I'll go with the package.' Lou agreed with her. 'Me too.'

Sharin shook her head. 'I can't afford to lose my job,' she mumbled.

'None of us can,' said Mel.

'No point worrying. We just need to make decisions and move on,' added Lou.

Sharin rested her head on the desk. 'Worry is my middle name.'

'If it all goes to shit, we have the casino.'

'Until we get busted.'

'It's not illegal.'

Mel was right. Card counting wasn't strictly illegal, but casinos made your life impossible if you got caught.

'And there's always the new boyfriend,' said Lou giving her a wink.

Sharin didn't move. 'He's hardly a boyfriend. We haven't even had a date yet.'

Lou threw an eraser at her. She caught it in one hand.

'Great reflexes,' said Lou.

'Softball.'

'And when *is* the date?' asked Mel.

'End of next week. Agostino's.'

'Another week! What is wrong with him?' said Lou.

'He has a job that takes him interstate and he's working away 'til then.'

'Like fly in, fly out?' asked Mel.

'Not sure. Guess I'll find out more when we catch up.'

'I have a lovely flowing blue silk dress you can borrow,' smiled Lou.

'You do not want to take advice from a woman who wears kaftans, Sharin,' said Mel. 'You *are* looking to get laid I take it?'

'There is nothing wrong with a good kaftan to get a man excited,' said Lou. 'It keeps him guessing.'

'What? If you're stuck in a time warp?'

'It's retro.'

'It is not for a first date,' said Mel.

In the end, they agreed on a forest green halter neck to set off her auburn hair and a pair of slim-fitting jeans, with heels. As they argued over the choice of underwear suitable for a first date, Mel's mobile vibrated on the desk. She pulled it close to check the number. It was the journalist. She hesitated, her finger over the red dot, but then decided it was time to put an end to it once and for all, so she hit green instead.

'The answer is still no and if you keep phoning me, I'll take out a restraining order.'

Sharin was watching her from across the room. 'Journalist,' mouthed Mel.

'I have nothing to say that ...' she paused.

'No. What news?'

Mel gripped the phone more tightly in her hand and caught the ribbon on her blouse with the other. She pressed the blouse hard against her - heart pounding against it.

'I have to go,' she said and hung up.

Lou was up and moving toward her.

'What happened?'

Mel dropped the phone. Tears pricked her eyes. She stabbed them back with her forefingers.

'MEL!'

'They found Lisa Harding. In a skip off Lygon St.'

'Fuck.'

'Oh my God, Mel,' whispered Sharin, who was rounding her desk.

Mel stood, the chair propelling backward behind her. 'I have to go out for a minute,' she mumbled.

She made it to the bottom of the stairwell, deep in the basement of the building, before she let the tears flow. Sobbing was an indulgence she seldom allowed herself. But at that moment, a void of twenty-seven years closed. The same story was being repeated. Not just familiar, but the same.

Chapter 10

SITTING IN THE STAIRWELL, MEL WRAPPED HERSELF tighter around the railing and let the reality of what was happening flood through her. Feeling the cold hardness of the step against her legs was strangely comforting and she cried freely. It stunned her that pain this old could feel so new.

She didn't hear footsteps, but felt the warmth and familiarity of Lou, as she sat down on the step behind her. She rested her chin on Mel's' shoulder and pressed her head against her cheek.

'Wanna smoke?'

Mel hiccupped between sobs.

'You know it's good for you,' whispered Lou.

'I thought you gave up.'

'I did. But I have emergency supplies.'

'In case of what?'

'Emergencies.'

Mel turned her head to look at her. 'And this is an emergency, right?'

'Yep.'

'You're the best, Lou.'

'If you say so,' she said, as she pulled two cigarettes from her pocket. She slipped them both between her lips and lit them simultaneously.

'Wait! There might be a fire alarm down here,' said Mel.

Lou let the cigarettes dangle and looked around. 'Uh uh,' she mumbled, shaking her head. The sound came from somewhere deep in her throat.

When the cigarettes were glowing, she took one and gave it to Mel, who hadn't had a cigarette since before Annie was born. She took a small slow inhale and let the smoke ease its way into her lungs. She held it for a few seconds too long, before exhaling. It made her head spin, but it felt good.

Lou moved a step lower to sit next to Mel. She drew hard on her cigarette, before blowing little rings into the air.

'How do you do that?'

'Skill my dear.'

'There is no limit to your talents Ms Barnes.'

They sat silently and smoked until the butts were the only thing left. Lou flicked hers down the steps while Mel crushed hers with the toe of her shoe.

The space around them was cool and quiet. Blank walls painted in dirty cream hemmed the staircase but the cavernous shaft leading up sixteen floors prevented it from feeling claustrophobic.

'I don't mind it down here,' said Mel.

'Well, if we weren't being roasted in this departmental amalgamation, this is likely where we'd be setting up our desks.'

Mel's laugh echoed off the walls. 'So true!'

Lou twisted on the spot, using the wall to push herself up. Mel used the railings. As they turned to move up the stairs Lou asked her, 'so now what?'

Mel leaned into the railing with one foot poised above the step.

'I'm gonna call the journalist.'

Mel rolled the phone back and forth in her hand, trying to decide how best to approach the conversation. She needn't have bothered. The phone rang only once before a coarse, gravelly voice answered. 'Wondered when you'd call.'

'Screw you', thought Mel but instead said, 'I don't want to be doing this, but I figure I have no choice now.'

'Yep, shit just got real close to home,' he said.

'So, what do you want to know?'

'Everything.'

'I don't know everything.'

'Then anything 'ya do know. Just start at the beginning.'

Mel was standing at the office window staring at a murky view and seeing nothing.

'I didn't see her much before it happened. She and Dan, that's her husband, had a place in North Carlton. She always caught the bus because it was close to town. Dan was away and she'd hired a babysitter for a few hours to watch Lexie. Joanna was one of the neighbour's kids who used to babysit occasionally. Peggy said she'd be back at ten o'clock but when she wasn't home by midnight, Joanna called her mum and she later called the police. Dan was working away at a car show, so it wasn't until the next day they got hold of him.'

'Did she say where she was going or if she was meeting anyone?'

'Nope. Dan had no idea and Joanna said Peggy didn't say. She only told her that if there was a problem to call her friend Kathleen. Which was odd, because Kathleen lived in Ballarat. She didn't leave a number for Dan or me.'

'Did Kathleen know Peg was meeting someone?'

'No. She said Mum had called the weekend before and they chatted about all sorts of things. Just everyday things. Nothing out of the ordinary, except Mum seemed a bit ... um ... edgy, or scatty. I dunno.'

'What d'ya mean?' he asked.

'Like ..., she'd start to say something and not finish it. Just a bit all over the place. And Kathleen said Mum got all nostalgic at one point talking about things they'd done together and her past. She could be sentimental like that. Said she'd seen a 'ghost from the past' but laughed it off. Peggy was a bit crazy anyway, so I guess Kathleen didn't think much about it.'

'She didn't mention who the ghost was? No planned meet-ups?'

'None, that Kathleen remembered. There were so many ghosts in Mum's past, it could have been anyone. Or no one.'

'Mmmm. Do you know anything of the man she met the night she died?'

'The first we knew about it was during the investigation. They spoke to a waitress who recognised Peggy. But there wasn't much to tell about the guy she was with.'

'Yeah, doesn't say a lot in the files either.'

'You have files?'

'A couple. But bits are missing. Crap note-taking. Or they've sanctioned parts. I'm actually trying to find the waitress. Keen to have a chat with her myself.'

'What have you found so far?'

Mel could hear pages flicking back and forth. She heard a drink drain.

'Mainly notes taken at the scene. I guess you know those details anyway,' he said.

Mel shuddered. She'd allowed herself few occasions to imagine her mother lying dead in a dark laneway. The feelings of panic and pain that bubbled up threatened to overwhelm her. Whenever her mind wandered down that path and nausea rose in her throat, she would shake her head, speak aloud to herself and force her thoughts in another direction. Over the years, she'd trained herself well.

'I know what they told me, but what does it say?'

Whether the journalist was sparing her the graphic details or he just wanted to cut to the chase was unclear, but he only gave a summary.

'Says, she was lying behind a skip. Had a coat on, but it was loose, with two buttons ripped off the front. Her blouse was torn. She still had her skirt but no knickers. And she was wearing shoes.' He paused. Mel didn't interrupt. 'Interesting. She still had her bag, earrings, but no wedding ring. Did she wear one?'

'Yeah. But whether she wore it that day? Who knows?' said Mel.

'Mmm, guess that helped fuel the lover angle,' said Dave.

'Yep. Anyway, read on,' said Mel.

He cleared his throat and coughed. Shuffled the page.

'She'd put up a fight. Nails torn, scratches on her hands, bruises on her wrists. Her face was crushed around the eye and cheek. Her lip was swollen. Cuts and deep bruises on her neck and chest. Blood on her shirt and coat. Her hair was pulled out in places.'

Mel dry retched, covering the phone with her hand. She pressed her head against the cold window to take the fire out of her face. Bile rose in her throat.

'And she was raped. Says her thigh was broken too.'

Mel tapped her head back and forth against the glass and said nothing. The agony of knowing what her mum endured, alone in some dark place was devastating.

'Ya right?'

'No.'

'Why do you think she was there?'

Mel stopped moving. How often had she asked herself that?

'I don't know. An affair maybe. Or debts or some other trouble she'd got herself into. Who knows?'

'Were you and Peggy close?'

'She was my mother.'

'Yeah, but were you close?'

'What, are you my psychologist, now?'

'Huh!' He laughed with a roar that surprised and startled her. 'I don't give a fig about feelings, love, just facts. '

'So why do you care if we were close.'

'I don't. But the closer, the more you know.'

'How about you buy me a coffee and we can talk about how close Peggy and I were.'

'Sure. When?'

'Tomorrow, 10.30 a.m., Flour n' Fruit, on Spring Street.'

'OK,' he said, and hung up.

Rain started to trickle down the window. The cold crept in and wrapped itself around her.

'Were Mum and I close?' she thought. 'I wish.'

Chapter 11

TAIL LIGHTS FLICKED RED AND AMBER IN FRONT OF HIM, as Marcus drove along Punt Road. It was late. His last wine delivery was to Ziggy's. A boutique bar in St Kilda. His regular drop offs had led to regular conversations with the owners. Then to conversations with a drink and now to a few drinks with the addition of a cheese plate. It wasn't every week. Maybe twice a month. But he liked it. Liked the owners. He hadn't meant to stay so long tonight, but the conversation was interesting and he had nowhere else to be.

A cheese plate isn't enough for a healthy adult male, so he pulled into Macca's. Two burger meals later and he was back in his car, waiting for the lights to change.

His headlights stretched across the intersection to the National Storage Units piled high on the corner of Wellington St. He thought about the dingy warehouse he used now and considered the possibility of the storage units as a cheaper option. 'But would they be cool enough?' he thought.

He was contemplating the humidity and air temperature when a figure loped out of the dark from the side of the building. Something about the gait was familiar. He focused his thoughts and flipped the headlights to high beam. The figure raised a hand to cover its eyes and Marcus recognized him immediately.

The lights changed from red to green. Marcus slid the van smoothly across the intersection and slowed to walking speed, alongside the figure, which hesitated for a moment as if deciding to turn back or run ahead. Instead, he stopped.

'Hey Eddy,' called Marcus as the window lowered on the passenger side, 'what are you doing out?'

'Umm. Just been to my umm, class,' he said.

'Late finish?'

'Yeah, had some questions I needed answered.'

'Right,' nodded Marcus, smiling. 'Want a lift?'

'Ah it's all good. I can catch the bus,' replied Eddy.

'Don't be stupid! We live at the same address. Hop in,' he said, leaning over to release the door.

Eddy looked around him, and moved the bag he was carrying from one hand to the other.

'Umm,..' he mumbled, hesitating again. 'All right,' he said, pulling the door further open to climb in. As he did, the light from the cab glinted on something in the bag and Eddy pushed it in deeper with his free hand. Marcus caught a glimpse of gold mesh.

Eddy quickly dropped the bag into the footwell, sliding it away with his foot. 'So how was your night?' he asked as he pulled the door shut.

Marcus's eyes flicked from the floor to Eddy. 'Yeah, good thanks.'

Eddy forced a smile.

Marcus cocked his head. 'Is that lipstick on your top lip?' he teased.

'What? Uh, no,' he said sliding his hand self-consciously across his mouth. 'It's just lip balm.'

'Right,' winked Marcus.

Eddy ran a hand across his mouth again and looked away.

'Don't worry mate, your secret's safe with me!'

What secret?!' said Eddy spinning back to face him.

Marcus thumped him lightly on the arm. 'Some lucky girl had all her questions answered, I'd say.'

Eddy looked away but said nothing.

Marcus smiled, turning back to the road and the trail of lights he would follow home.

Chapter 12

As she pushed the glass door open, it occurred to Mel she didn't know what he looked like.

She scoured the pretty white wrought iron tables for lone men and spotted two. One sat at a table with a spare chair in the corner by the window, whilst another spread out at a table for four, partially hidden behind a pot of red geraniums that decorated a pillar in the centre of the room.

She took a chance on the man by the window. On the table in front of him was a takeaway cup, so either he'd arrived early or ordered to save himself buying her one. He had a large Romanesque nose, thick curly brown hair, and the ugliest shirt she had seen on a man in some time.

He turned toward her as she approached. He didn't stand but looked up and smiled. His mouth was broad and full-lipped. 'Either my luck just changed or you're Mel,' he said.

'Not both?'

He bowed and gestured with both hands toward her. 'Of course,' he said, extending one hand to shake hers. She took it, firmly.

'Dave. Dave Ferguson,' he said.

She sat down and pointed at his cup.

'Addicted. What would you like?' he asked.

Mel watched him as he moved to the counter to order. He reminded her of an old cat she once owned.

When he returned, he placed the table number by the sugar shaker and pushed his notepad across an inch.

'That's old school,' said Mel.

'Prefer the feel of a pen over a keyboard,' he said.

'I get it.'

He drew a sharp line under the jumble of illegible letters on the page. 'So, tell me more about Peggy.'

'I will, but do you really think there's a link?'

'Dunno. Sure, starting to look like it.'

'Whoever it is has to be old. Is that likely?'

'Not necessarily 'past it', kinda old. Could be as young as fifty, even a bit younger.'

'It's possible it's a coincidence though?'

'Yep. Could be,' said Dave.

'Do you have a theory?'

'Plenty,' he said.

The coffee arrived before he could tell her about them. Dave's arrived in a takeaway cup.

'I don't trust the dishwashers in these places,' he said by way of explanation. He was happy to sacrifice Mel's health. Hers arrived in a china mug. Mel spooned a teaspoon of sugar into it and said, 'tell me them.'

'I'd prefer to hear yours,' he said.

'Well, I want to hear yours.'

Dave smiled. 'Fair enough,' he said. 'I guess I have one main theory. These new murders have pretty much the same MO, and now location, as your mum's. So, if it's a coincidence, then it's a big one. And I'm not a fan of coincidence. To my way of thinking, it's the same person. And I reckon it's likely one of two suspects - the mystery man Peggy met on the night she died, or Dan.'

Mel shook her head. 'No way. It's not Dan.'

Dave held up his hand. 'He was a suspect at the time too, but he had a pretty tight alibi, so we can drop him down the list.'

Mel sipped her coffee and shook her head. 'We can drop him off the list. It wasn't Dan.'

'Ok, Ok. For now,' he agreed. 'But the bloke she met, he's another story. He's my pick. The problem is there's nothing on 'im. She must've known him or if not, had met him before. 'Ghost from the past',' he said shrugging his shoulders.

'Or it wasn't him either, and she was attacked on her way home.'

'Yes, that's a possibility too but I prefer my theory for now,' said Dave.

Mel set her cup on the table, rested her elbow beside it, and ran a hand across her forehead.

'Any ideas as to who he could be?'

'Could be anyone.'

Mel sat back and folded her arms. 'That's helpful.'

'But,' he continued, pointing his finger at her, 'I reckon it's one of two pieces of scum who were around at the time.'

'Who?'

'A guy named Robert Lang.'

'And the other one?'

'John Coreman. But he's pretty much a vegetable, so it's not him. Well, not now anyway.'

'What happened to him?'

'Beaten senseless in jail, with the bar of an exercise bike. Strangely no one saw anything.'

'How convenient,' agreed Mel.

'Mmm ...'

'So, Lang. Why do you think it's him?'

Dave flicked back his hair, crossed his arms, and tucked his hands under his armpits. His belly was round so his arms rested comfortably across it. He settled in for what looked like a long explanation.

'Lang and Coreman were mates and hung around together

from the early 1980s. They were convicted of the murders of four young women killed in '93 in inner city Melbourne and Geelong. All blonde, all pretty.' He raised an eyebrow.

Mel chewed her lip. 'How young?'

'Seventeen to twenty-five.'

'Peg was thirty-four,' said Mel.

'Still possible.'

'Were they raped and strangled?' she asked.

'Yep.'

'Christ.' Then she added 'Wait, but Peg died in '92.'

'Yeah. I know, but she might have been the first and there could have been others. It's common for these psychos to work their way through different scenarios until they find their 'thing'. They become more brazen. Take risks. Each of the murders they were charged with were ritualized, but the last of those four murders was extreme.'

Mel hunched her shoulders before looking up. 'God. Peg's murder was carnage, so I don't want to imagine what extreme looks like.'

'No, you don't,' agreed Dave, resting his chin on his chest. 'No one should see that.'

For a moment he was very still and quiet.

'Is it something you've seen?' asked Mel.

Dave turned his head toward her. 'My sister, Kitty, was the fourth of those murders. The things done to her are unspeakable.'

Mel reached a hand out to stroke the sleeve of his shirt. 'I'm so sorry.'

He patted her hand and straightened up. 'Thanks. It was a long time ago, but that bastard didn't pay for it. He needs to pay.'

'What do you mean? I thought you said they went to jail?'

'They did,' he said, 'But on different charges. Coreman for murder and Lang as an accessory. The wrong one was convicted of her murder.'

'Why do you say that?' asked Mel.

'Because Lang was the dangerous one. He'd been arrested for

a violent rape in the '80s but was never convicted. Had a very good lawyer apparently and an alibi they couldn't disprove. Coreman was just dumb. I mean, clearly, he was there. And he had form, but, he was just a thug. Followed Lang around like a puppy. He was capable of violence but Lang was mean. Cunning.'

'So why would Coreman take the fall?'

'My guess is Lang convinced him to. As I said, Coreman wasn't the sharpest tool in the shed. Lang got time for being an accessory, but only three years. Reckons he helped clean up the mess, but likely it was the other way around.'

'Only three years?'

'Yep, gave evidence against Coreman, so got a lighter sentence.'

'Where's the justice?'

'There is none!'

'And Coreman. How many years?'

'Life, plus more. But rumour is, he kinda woke up to the reality of what that really meant once he was in the clink and was keen to tell some home truths but, mysteriously, that lump of metal from the gym found its way into his head and he was cactus. Been brain dead in some nursing home for years.'

'And they could never pin Lang with any of the murders?' said Mel.

'Nope.'

'I don't remember any mention of Lang or Coreman when Mum died.'

'As I said, they didn't get caught until the end of '93. I've got a mate who was part of those investigations He reckons they were questioned about unsolved murders, including your mum's, but neither gave anything away. Who knows how many others there are ...'

Dave's phone rang. He flipped it over, checked the number then turned it off without answering.

'Do you have any evidence it's Lang and not Coreman?' asked Mel.

Mel watched as Dave mindlessly drew abstract lines on the paper in front of him.

'Well, to be fair, when Kitty died and Coreman was convicted I did believe it was him. His DNA was on her. That's how he was caught.'

'So, not just an accessory then?'

'No. He was obviously involved. He raped her 'cause they found his semen, and for that, I confess, I was shamelessly glad when his head was smashed in. But now I don't believe he killed her. Or the others for that matter, because some years later, I learned of a similar death which started my investigation.'

Mel leaned in closer. Dave stopped doodling.

'After Kitty died, I just couldn't settle. Watching Mum and Dad wither away was too much so I went overseas for some years to work and escape. When I came back, I took a job with the Hunter Valley Chronicle and got to know the local cops. Turns out, one of them had a daughter who'd run away a few years before. She was like Kitty. Young, mixed with the wrong crowd, took drugs, you know the drill. Anyway, she turned up dead in Sydney with a profile like Kitty's, but not as violent. What I mean is, it was violent in the sense she had the beating, rape, and strangulation, but only an inch of hair was missing and part of her nipple. No one paid any attention to it. She had other cuts and torn skin so people just considered it part of the struggle. But it smacked of Lang and Coreman, because each woman they'd killed, had those same injuries and they always took a trophy of hair and some part of the female anatomy.'

Mel's hand flew to her mouth.

'I know, revolting. It got worse with each murder. Kitty had both breasts removed and a criss-cross pattern carved into her sternum.'

'Stop!'

Dave flapped both hands 'Sorry, sorry.'

Mel took a mouthful of coffee to buy some time but swallowed too much of it in one gulp. It burned and she coughed, bringing half back up into the cup. She grabbed a napkin and wiped her face.

'Ya right?'

She nodded madly, waving him away. She cleared her throat. 'Christ. Dave, that is just hideous.'

'I know. But it couldn't have been Coreman when the coppa's daughter died, because he was dribbling into his sheets. Could only be Lang. He'd been out of jail for ages by then. Over the years I've trawled reports for other women and found seven that fit the pattern, in different towns and cities along the East Coast. Interestingly, there are gaps when Lang was in prison, which was 2000 - 2006 for violent assault and 2015-2017 when he was out of the country.'

'Who did he assault?'

'Boss of another drug cartel,' said Dave.

'That would make prison pretty risky, wouldn't it?'

'Yep, but he was in a powerful cartel himself, so protected. Unfortunately, he gained power and a reputation in jail. Became something of a boss himself. Teflon fucking coated,' he said.

'Sounds like a real piece of work.'

'Yep.'

'Thinking back though,' said Mel, 'I don't remember any bits of Peggy's body being taken. Only some hair and that was just pulled out.'

'That's why we need to find out more. I can only get files from the initial investigation taken at the scene. Problem is, I don't have access to autopsy reports or all the old notebooks.'

'So how do we get them?'

'I'm applying to FOI for the reports on Peggy, so fingers crossed.'

'And what about the recent murders? There's been no mention of trophies other than their hair being cut.'

'Yes,' he said, rubbing the side of his nose. 'But again, that doesn't mean there aren't any.'

The waitress interrupted to take their cups and ask if they

wanted more. They both refused but Mel asked for a glass of water. If the waitress heard anything of the conversation, she kept a poker face.

'Thing is Dave, why would a man of his age keep doing this? And now, so obviously?'

'Because he can. He's gotten away with it for 30 and maybe more, years. He's cocky, invincible. Pumped up on smack. Protected by his cronies. Capable of anything.'

'Scary.'

'Bloody oath. And charming. He's mid-fifties but still a good-looking guy. Built. Dresses in smart suits and drives nice cars. Rich. Attractive to a lot of women.'

'And perhaps, back in the day, he was too, but my mum had a three-month-old baby. Why would she be mixed up with this guy?'

'An affair, drugs, debts?'

The glass of water Mel requested was gently placed in front of her. She smiled up at the young woman and suppressed an overwhelming urge to beg her not to go out at night.

'I don't know, Dave. Maybe? If it was any of those, she kept it very secret.'

'Everyone has secrets, Mel.'

She nodded. 'And truthfully, Peg and I weren't that close. I didn't know her really. I wish I had.'

'Maybe, in a weird way, you'll get to know her now,' he said.

Mel smiled. 'I hope I don't find too many skeletons. Oops, sorry. Bad pun!'

Dave tossed back his head and snorted out a laugh.

'So, what do you want me to do?' she asked.

'Write down everything you can remember about the night. About the weeks leading up to it. Anything about Peggy that seems relevant? What was happening at home, people she knew, old boyfriends, places she hung out, who she was fighting with, secrets she kept. Anything.'

'That could be tricky, but I'll ask around.'

'Thanks.'

'I have to get back.' Mel stood and thanked him for the coffee.

She turned to leave. As he called the waitress over, she turned back. 'Dave,'

'Yeah.'

'What's the chance it was someone much closer to her?'

'As good a chance as any.'

Chapter 13

'WHAT HAVE YOU GOT FOR US?' ASKED LOU AS MEL came through the door.

'Meeting with Dave has got me thinking.'

'That's a particularly dangerous thing to do, Mel.'

'Yep, around here it is, but not out there.'

'What did he say?' asked Sharin.

'He's got a theory about who the bloke is that Mum met on the night she died. And who is still around from those days. Could be one of two serial killers. Or Dan.'

'He said that?' asked Sharin, knitting her brows together.

'Well, he said Dan had an alibi and they discounted him, but you can tell he still thinks it's possible.' Mel glanced at Lou. 'If you say, 'I told you so', I'll ...'

'I'm not saying, "I told you so", just saying.'

'I'm confused,' said Sharin.

'Lou's always believed Dan killed Peggy.'

'Oh, Lou,' said Sharin.

'Well, it stands to reason. I tell 'ya when I worked at Corrections, ninety-five percent of all serious crime was committed by someone known to the person. Fact,' she said, thumping her palm on the table. 'But I don't believe he has anything to do with the girls who have died recently.'

'Well, that's a relief,' said Mel. 'So, we rule out Dan and focus on the other two.'

'Who are they?' asked Sharin.

'Robert Lang and John Coreman. But he thinks it's Lang because Coreman is a zombie.'

Sharins's eyes bulged.

'Not a real zombie, lovey.'

Sharin clutched her chest, 'Oh, thank goodness!'

Lou's eye twitched as she tried to control it.

'What happened to him?' asked Sharin.

Mel explained and Sharin looked sad. 'No one deserves that.'

'I think I remember reading about it,' said Lou. 'Pretty incredible a bike frame just comes apart and no one notices.'

'Isn't it though,' agreed Mel, 'and right at the time he was going to shed a little light on what he knew.'

'So, Dave thinks Lang is the most likely candidate?' said Lou.

'He does,' said Mel. 'Both for then and now.'

'Interesting,' nodded Lou.

'Yes, and that is where you two come into the picture,' said Mel, pointing from one to the other.

Sharin's eyes widened. Lou's narrowed.

'How?' they said in unison.

'You can help me do some investigating.'

'Don't be ridiculous!' said Lou.

'What's ridiculous about it?'

'I love the idea,' said Sharin, 'It'd be like CIA or CSU or whatever it's called.'

'You watch way too much trash TV,' said Lou.

'Do not.' Sharin pouted.

'And we're not cops,' continued Lou.

'No, but we're damn good at research. And detectives are just researchers with guns,' said Sharin.

Mel flicked a rubber band at Lou. 'You have to admit, she's got you there.'

'Yeah, fair point,' agreed Lou.

'I'm in!' said Sharin

'Can I have a gun?' asked Lou.

'If that's what it takes, sure.'

'Ok, then I'm in too,' she said, making her forefinger and thumb into a pistol and blowing into the tip.

Mel rolled her eyes. 'We're so fucked. I love you guys.'

For the next half hour, Mel relayed what she had learned from Dave as they cleared the spare desk of detritus and replaced it with a paper tray, string, and thumbtacks. Behind it, they placed a pin-up board and to one side, a whiteboard. They also moved the petition to the opposite side of the desk to shield it from the door. An incident desk might be hard to explain.

Mel stood back from the desk. Lou and Sharin stood behind her. The whiteboard was divided into three sections with blue marker pen. Each section was titled. One read, 'Murders 2019', the second said 'Peggy Hilliard, 1992', and the third, 'Prime suspects'. Lou drew a head with devil horns for effect.

'I feel all tingly,' said Sharin.

'That'll be the bloody air-conditioning,' moaned Lou, 'some moron's obviously played with it again. What is it they don't get? Hot for winter, cold for summer...'

'No, no. I mean, I feel quite excited,' said Sharin.

'Yes, I knew what you meant,' said Lou.

Sharin thumped her lightly. Lou drew her gun.

'We'll start tomorrow. I have some things at home I want to bring in,' said Mel.

'Cool. What can we do?' asked Sharin.

'Could you find everything about the recent murders and Lou can you find more about the guys Dave mentioned? And anyone else who seems suspect from 1992 but is still around today. Lang and Dan are Dave's idea of suspects but there must be others. Then and now.'

'Ooh I love a bit of bedtime reading,' she said clapping her hands together.

Mel covered her eyes. 'Lordy. Sometimes you scare me, Lou.'

Chapter 14

THE FOLLOWING MORNING MEL ARRIVED EARLY TO work with the few photos she found of Peggy. She'd hoped to find more than just photos but her search proved futile.

Mel had packed Peggy's belongings, excluding the photos, into a suitcase which she'd carried with her from one move to another. Time passed, life grew complicated, and the suitcase became buried under successively larger piles of discarded possessions.

The photos were thrown into an old biscuit tin and bundled with all her others, into a wooden trunk. It hadn't taken long to find them. The suitcase proved much harder to retrieve. After a great deal of swearing, messed-up cupboards and an unnecessarily late night, she gave up. She planned to try the garage on the weekend.

The photos provided a visual timeline of Peggy's short life. There was one of baby Peggy in the arms of Pop with 1957 penned on the back; another of her as a new mum with Mel and several of her as an older mum with Lexie. There were a few of Peggy and Gran and one of Peggy and Dan swinging a three-year-old Mel between them. Pop rarely appeared in photos. He was usually on the other side of the camera. There was a wedding photo of Dan and Peggy, taken when she was twenty, and a renewing of vows photo taken fourteen years later. The in-between years were highlighted by images of Peggy at parties mostly looking stoned. The only photo of Peg smiling straight into the camera was taken on the day she graduated with her enrolled nursing qualification. It was December 1987, she was thirty years old and as proud as she had ever looked. For the following three years, when she nursed in Ballarat, there were no photos, but from mid '91, when Peg and Dan rekindled their union and Lexie was born, there were several. If Peg was in them, she was always gazing at Lexie. Giggling, blowing bubbles on her tummy, nursing her or simply watching her sleep. If bliss can be captured in Kodachrome, then it was on show in technicolour brilliance. No photos existed after 1992.

Mel was pinning the last of the photos on the board when Sharin walked in. She dropped the printed pages she carried into a tray on the incident desk.

'That looks interesting.'

'Very interesting,' replied Sharin, tapping the pages with her car key.

'Anything you want to share?'

'Let's wait for Lou.'

It turned into a long wait.

Lou wandered in an hour or so into the morning. She was not an early riser. Work was inconveniently scheduled two hours before she was fully conscious. At fifty-five years of age, she was too old to start changing her habits. She arrived late and worked late. When she finally sauntered in, she stopped in the doorway, dipped her head low and ran a hand along the rim of the black hat she was wearing.

'Nice Trilby,' said Mel.

'Please don't tell me there's a gun in your pocket,' said Sharin.

'Nope. Just happy to see you,' quipped Lou.

'Oh dear,' said Mel.

Lou joined the others in front of the board. 'Nice pictures,' she said.

'She was really pretty, Mel,' said Sharin.

'Yes, she was.'

'You look like her,' added Lou, and Sharin agreed.

'Certainly can see the family resemblance in Annie too.'

'Tell me about it,' said Mel.

'So, where shall we start?' asked Lou.

Mel pointed to the papers Sharin had added to the tray under the board marked 'Murders 2019'. 'Sharin had a busy night,' she said.

'Do you want to fill us in? I have to confess I didn't get a chance last night. Grandkids dropped over,' said Lou.

Sharin bustled over her papers while Lou and Mel trundled their office chairs over to sit in front of her. Sharin rested against the edge of the desk.

'My mission, which I chose to accept,' she said pausing for effect, 'was to detail the information so far available on the current spate of murders rocking our fair city.'

'Just cut to the chase,' said Lou.

'Sorry,' she apologised with a reddening face. 'Right, well a lot of this is commentary. Police info is harder to find, so not sure how accurate it is but ...'

'It's a really good start,' said Lou. It was her way of making up.

It worked. Sharin looked up through perfectly mascaraed lashes and smiled.

'I'll start with Kristen. She left work, the café, at 5.30 p.m. on the 1st of February this year to catch the bus home. Her boyfriend said she was supposed to be home by 6 p.m. but she never arrived.'

'Boyfriend a suspect?'

'Mmm, he hasn't been arrested,' she said scouring the page.

'He couldn't have done the others though. Police would be watching him like a hawk,' said Mel.

'True.'

'Rule him out,' said Mel.

'What do they say about her?' Lou asked.

Sharin flipped the page. 'Quiet girl. She and her boyfriend went to the local church. They were planning their wedding ... really sweet photo of them,' Sharin held up a colour print of Kristen, leaning into her boyfriend as he held her hand up to the camera to show a small diamond ring on her left ring finger.

'Poor kids,' said Mel.

'Poor kids all right. Marriage. What were they thinking?' added Lou.

'That's not what I meant.'

'I know.'

Mel stood up. 'I'll pin that picture on the board.'

'What else?' said Lou.

'Well, I know we all know this but ...'

'Add it in Sharin, don't want to miss anything,' said Lou.

'Ok. Well, she was found in a lane at the back of the Rose St Art Markets on the 5th of March.'

'How far is that from the Café?' asked Lou.

'Not sure. We should put a map up and mark it,' said Sharin.

'Good idea. I'll print one later,' said Mel.

'What about Erin?' asked Lou.

Sharin separated more paper, dropping part of the pile into the tray. She held up another print of a teenager in school uniform.

'She was in her final year at Collingwood College. She walked to and from school every day, except Wednesday when she got a lift from her friend to go swimming. Her house was ten minutes from school in Otter St.'

'That is just streets away from Rosa's house. Makes me shudder,' said Mel.

'From what I've been reading, everything's happened around Collingwood, Carlton and Fitzroy. You and Rosa both live close. To be fair, it's not that far from any of us.'

Sharin shook her papers again. The whole business of murder spooked her. She took a deep breath, and went on.

'Erin left at 3.30 p.m. on Friday, April the 19th and that was the last time anyone saw her. Well not anyone,' she corrected herself. 'A few people from her school saw her walking along McCutcheon Way. But after that, nothing.'

'Anyone in the fray?' asked Mel.

Sharin consulted her notes. 'No one in particular,' she said.

'No boyfriends?' asked Lou.

'No,' said Sharin. 'It says here she was close to her family and well-liked by her classmates. Apart from swimming, she ran marathons and quilted. She worked one afternoon a week and Saturday mornings at a bakery and was a good student who hoped to go to university.'

'She quilted?'

'People do quilt, Lou.'

'No one quilts these days, Mel.'

'Lots of people quilt,' said Mel.

'Right,' said Lou.

'She was a runner,' said Sharin. 'That should have helped her.'

'Good thinking,' said Mel.

'Maybe she knew him?' said Lou.

'What makes you think it's a him?'

'It's always a him,' said Lou.

'We can't rule out any possibilities.'

'It's a him,' repeated Lou. 'They were all raped.'

'Yes,' agreed Mel, 'but there could have been more than one person involved.'

'That's a thought.'

'How about the third girl?' asked Mel.

'Lisa Harding disappeared on Friday, July 5th,' she paused. 'Have you noticed she and Erin disappeared on Friday?' she said.

'What about Kristen?' asked Mel.

Sharin sorted through the notes in the tray. 'Yep, Friday, Feb first.'

'That's important,' said Mel taking up the whiteboard marker and writing a note on the board.

'That *could* be important,' said Lou.

Mel paused, hand hovering over the board.

'But write it up anyway,' continued Lou.

'Is there a pattern to the days they were found?' asked Mel, writing notes under 'Murders 2019'.

Sharin checked her notes again.

'Kristen was found on Tuesday, Erin on Thursday and Lisa on Monday. Nope, no pattern.'

'None of them disappeared in the same suburb or turned up in the same place either,' said Mel.

'No, but all in close proximity,' said Lou.

'I need to get that map sorted,' said Mel heading to her computer.

'What else do we know about Lisa?' asked Lou.

'She'd finished her shift at the IGA supermarket on Victoria Pde at nine o'clock. She changed clothes at work and caught an uber into the city to a nightclub. She left her friends about midnight and caught an uber back to the IGA. She wasn't reported missing until the next day when her car was found near work in the same spot as the previous day. No forensic evidence was found on it.'

'What about surveillance cameras in the carpark of the supermarket?' asked Mel.

'The car was parked in a side street,' said Sharin scanning her notes.

'Why didn't she drive it to the nightclub?'

'One article I read said she'd planned a big night out but hadn't drunk much, so left early telling her friends she was OK to drive. I guess if she'd had the big night out, she'd still be alive.'

'So weird how this shit works,' said Mel.

'Fate can be an evil mistress,' agreed Lou.

'What else have you found, Shaz?'

Sharin referred back to the thin stack of paper in her hand.

'She was a college student, studying art and lived in a share flat with three other people.'

'Any boyfriends, lovers, jealous friends?'

'Could've been many,' said Sharin, flipping the page and reading further, 'seems she was a bit of a party girl. But no declared suspects.'

'Photo?'

Sharin held up the third printout.

Lisa Harding stood between two girls with pixelated faces. Their arms were linked together and she was laughing. Her slender figure was draped in a shimmery halter neck and her blonde hair was piled high in a bun. Joy radiated from her.

'Oh my God. That could have been me thirty years ago,' said Mel.

'Pin it up, Sharin,' said Lou.

Mel found a map of inner Melbourne and sent it to the photocopier. When she came back, she stuck it to the board and added pins to each of the key locations that Sharin had mentioned. She chose red pins for Kristen, blue for Erin and green for Lisa. The final one was black, for Peggy.

All three women stared at the board.

'And there's no connection between the three women?' asked Lou.

'Nope. Police even used the words 'no connection.'

'Something links them,' said Mel.

'And that something could be Peggy,' said Sharin.

'Through this Lang guy?'

'I don't know,' said Lou. 'I don't see how. He's clearly a crim and these girls don't seem the type to brush up against crims.'

'Maybe he chose them because of their looks, but at random. Sort of?' said Sharin.

'Possible,' said Mel, 'because Dave thinks there are at least seven other murders in the past 20 years, which are the same.'

They all contemplated the board and the endless possibilities.

'We don't want to be entirely fixated on Lang as the man who killed Mum,' said Mel. 'It could be someone else who did it. And who knows? That someone might be known to the girls?'

Lou shrugged. 'Dunno, but I'll write some ideas on the board.'

As Lou did so, Sharin ran a finger around the map Mel had pinned up.

'There's only a few kilometres between any of those pins, Mel.'

'Yep. Including Peggy's.'

Lou dropped the whiteboard marker into the tray and stood back. 'I think we need a break,' said Lou, slipping her feet behind the wheels of her chair and skating back to the desk. 'And, less importantly, I need to get this contract to the finance folk, before the home-time bell rings.'

Mel continued to study Lou's handiwork on the board a moment longer before joining the others at their desks. 'Thanks for humouring me with all this,' she said.

'We couldn't let you have all the fun,' said Lou.

'I hope we find something useful,' added Sharin.

'I have a feeling in my trilby we will,' said Lou, lightly touching the brim of her hat.

Chapter 15

THE JUNK IN THE GARAGE DISTRACTED MEL FROM finding the suitcase. She'd found an ab shaper, one ski, a bag of fabric, and her old sewing machine – all of which she moved into the study. Ricky wasn't happy.

Eventually, the suitcase was located under two others in a far corner of the shed. Apart from some water damage and an inch of dust, everything was in order.

She'd had the suitcase since she left home at eighteen to start University. She was on the second attempt at finding a course that interested her when Peggy died.

For a few months she moved home to help her stepfather look after Lexie, her three-month-old sister. Dan was catatonic with grief and alcohol and Lexie needed a mother. For a while, she managed, but the responsibility of being a carer to them both took its toll. By the time Lexie was six months old Mel was ready to leave. After a huge fight that ended with words they both regretted, Mel bundled Lexie up and left for Gran's. She threatened to take Dan to court for custody if he didn't pull himself together, and it worked.

He cleaned himself up, joined Alcoholics Anonymous, and took a year's leave from his job to become a full-time father. Three years later he met Sarah, married, packed up everything of value, except Lexie, and moved to Queensland. He'd found a care home for Lexie and in the early years spent considerable time and money visiting her. But as years passed and Dan settled into a busy life with Sarah, his visits became less frequent. He'd left Mel with the pieces of Peggy's life he couldn't bear to take with him. All of her belongings he left to Mel. Over the years Mel binned or donated most of her clothing, except her wedding gown, a green woollen coat with faux fur collar, a lace evening dress, and a striped turtle-neck jumper her mother wore around the house. It had a faint smell of Paris perfume, and Dan had kept it sealed in plastic so the scent wasn't lost.

Added to that was a leather handbag, a purse, some trinkets, jewellery, and a manicure set monogrammed with her initials which Gran gave her on her tenth birthday. There was also a diary.

Each year Peggy kept a diary. At the end of each year she burned it. The diary from 1992 only survived because of her death. It'd been trawled through for evidence but nothing was found. In it she wrote birthdates and notes about tasks that needed doing or upcoming events. From July 1992, it was blank.

On Monday morning Mel brought the diary to work with her. It joined the various papers in the tray on the incident desk. She checked her emails. One was from Dave.

'Hey. Found the waitress! In Tasmania (Thank you Facebook). She was great. Didn't hesitate to help. Memory like a steel trap. Described the detective who interviewed her as, and I quote 'a limp dick in a uniform who spent the entire time staring at my tits!' Brilliant!

She reckons the guy Peg met wore a brown jacket with a logo or brand name on the chest, but he kept his arms crossed and she couldn't make it out. She only thought about it later when she was going over it all in her head and recalled a corner of colour to one side of the zipper that was different from his jacket. It was orange. She also said that when he left he was a bit jumpy. Left by himself though. I'm going to start looking for any companies with orange logos operating in the 1990s. Dave.'

She forwarded the email to the others and left to make tea. She made three, knowing her workmates weren't far behind her. When she returned she found Sharin jotting notes on the board, her head bobbing up and down as she wrote.

'Hey Shaz. Great news about the waitress,' she said, putting the tea down on the closest desk.

Sharin stopped writing and turned around. 'Waitress?'

'Yeah. You didn't read the email I forwarded, from Dave?'

'No, sorry Mel, just wanted to get this up,' she said pointing to the board.

'What is it?' asked Mel, walking over to her.

'Tell me about Dave first?'

'It's all in the email, but essentially, she told him that the guy in the café was wearing a jacket with a logo. He's looking for logos now. Fingers crossed!' she said.

'Fantastic news!' said Sharin. 'We are all on the move!'

'Hopefully. Now tell me about this,' said Mel, waving at the board.

Sharin shimmied a little closer to it.

'I was thinking about this on the weekend and there are more similarities than we first thought. For starters, the girls worked at food stores and all the food stores are in this area on our map,' she said, tapping each location in turn. 'The IGA is here on Victoria Parade; the Café is on Rathdowne St and the bakery where Erin worked is right here on Smith St!'

'And the school is pretty much halfway between the bakery and the IGA,' said Mel.

'Yes, it is,' said Sharin. 'So, maybe the killer lives in this area and frequents those places.'

'Sharin Pentagast, you are a super sleuth!'

Mel held up a hand and high-fived Sharin. She finished it with an enthusiastic hip bump.

'You hip bump without me!' said Lou, coming into the room.

'You missed the moment, Ms Barnes.'

'So, tell me now.'

Sharin repeated her observations. Lou high-fived. 'Nice one, Shaz!'

'What about you, Lou, anything to report?'

'As it happens, yes,' she said reaching into her bumbag to pull out a tightly folded wad of paper.

'It was a deliciously evil evening of horror, reading this stuff,' she added, waving it in the air, 'and I put in a call to my buddy Nathan at Corrections. Left a message to phone back with any juicy gossip on Lang and Coreman.'

'Great.'

The phone rang as Lou was about to begin. 'Let it ring,' she said, 'it'll go to voice mail and this is far more important.' Lou handled most of her calls in a similar fashion. It was her way of vetting people she didn't want to speak to.

'It might be Nathan?' said Sharin.

'Nah,' said Lou, 'he doesn't work that fast. Bless him,' she added.

'Bless him, indeed,' said Mel. 'So, what have you been reading about?'

Lou lifted her papers and shook them free.

'To start with, not people you want to bring home to mother,' she said, straightening one of the pages. 'Serial killers are narcissistic, misogynous psychopaths who'd slice and dice their grandmother, if necessary,' she continued.

'Sounds like Eddy,' said Mel. 'Go on.'

'They're usually white men aged in their mid-twenties and thirties. A lot are highly intelligent but socially inept.'

'Except Ted Bundy. He was all charm,' said Mel.

'True, but not the norm. Many do badly at school because they don't fit in, but others do well. They usually have some form of obsession and frequently there is a sexual nature to their killings ... oh, and sadly, but significantly, most have suffered some form of abuse.'

'Well, that could be quite a segment of the population,' said Mel.

'Yep, but only a handful become sicko murderers,' said Lou, pausing to take a sip of tea.

Sharin sagged in her chair. 'I'm going to end up a spinster. I'll never be able to date a man again unless he's old, thick, and past it.'

'I'm safe then,' said Lou, 'that describes my husband.'

The phone rang again.

'You better answer it,' said Mel. 'It might actually be important.'

'We work in the Grants Department, Mel, nothing is that important.' But she answered it anyway. It was the Director of the Policy Unit.

Lou murmured several ah-ha's, mm's, and ok's before finally hanging up.

'Well, that was a turn-on. I think he was getting tough with me. I need a cold shower.'

'Really?' said Mel, 'what did he say?'

'He felt my briefing was a bit snarky. Said I need to tone it down. At least I know he reads them now.'

'I wonder if he put big red biro marks all over it,' said Mel.

'I can only dream of such pleasures,' said Lou, fanning herself.

'You need to get out more,'

'Yes, I do,' agreed Lou. 'Anyway, he can wait.'

'You have more?'

'I do. I looked up those fine gentlemen you mentioned and they really are pieces of garbage.'

'Is this going to be bad?' asked Sharin, gripping the edge of the table.

'Yup,' Lou nodded.

'Maybe I'll write notes on the board,' suggested Sharin.

Lou rattled off the list of atrocities exacted on women by these men but had little to add that Mel didn't already know.

Sharin wrote summarising notes. She couldn't bring herself to write words like gouged, blunt instrument, and mutilation, so she just wrote 'violent assaults' instead.

'Lang wasn't just a rogue thug. He was part of the 'Honoured Society,' which is a mafia group that's been in operation since the early '60s. Family affair. His father was a founding member. They were into everything you'd expect. Drugs, money, casinos, horse racing, restaurants, you name it. Apparently, Lang was very good at extortion. But heavy-handed. Got cut loose for a short while because he bashed a couple of blokes to death and the cops started to take an interest. He got away with it until he beat a significant member of another drug cartel into a state of apoplexy. Cops couldn't ignore that one. That's when he did jail time in the early 2000s.'

'Dave reckons he was up to his old tricks when he got out, but was never caught for them,' said Mel.

'Does he know it for a fact?' asked Sharin.

'Nope. But he's pretty confident,' said Mel.

'Well, I didn't find anything else about him. Clearly, not everyone sees what Dave does,' said Lou.

Mel nodded. 'I think Dave is a bit obsessed with Lang, but then, can you blame him?'

'No,' agreed Sharin, 'you'd go a bit crazy if that happened to someone you love. It's a life-long torture.'

Mel nodded. "It is."

"Oh, sorry Mel, of course. I didn't think."

"It's ok," said Mel.

'Speaking of torture,' said Lou, but hesitated as both Mel and Sharin winced. 'Don't worry, I'll spare you the details,' she continued, 'only to say that there was one other serial killer active at the time, but he was caught in NSW and died in prison shortly after. It wasn't known if he killed anyone in Victoria.'

'I think I might stay home on Saturday night,' whispered Sharin.

Lou took the pen from Sharin. 'We do need to add a bit more detail to this story. Sorry, Shaz.'

'Please don't.'

'I'll cover it with sticky notes.'

'Ok,' murmured Sharin looking away.

'I do wonder who Mum met that night she died. Either in the café or on the way home. It could be Lang or Coreman, or someone completely unrelated.'

'Or Dan,' said Lou.

'It's not Dan!' said Mel.

'This is so complicated,' said Sharin. 'I don't feel optimistic anymore.'

'You know, even if it's not Dan, he may know something about Lang and Coreman? It's a long shot but maybe he'll remember something the police or a journo said that could help,' said Lou.

Mel pulled at her top lip. 'Yeah, It's worth a try. I'll ask him,' she said. 'You know, let's rule out Coreman. He could have killed Mum, but he can't have killed Kristen, Erin, or Lisa,' she added.

'That's true,' said Sharin.

'Lang seems to be the most likely,' agreed Lou.

'But there are other possibilities. I don't think it's that simple Mel,' said Sharin.

Both Mel and Lou looked at her.

'It's someone who lives in this area,' she said pointing to the map, 'who's old enough to know about your mum and young enough to be capable of killing now. If it's the one person doing both, then he has to be older than forty-five years, but probably younger than sixty, which does fit for Lang, but if it's two different people, then whoever's killing these young women knows how your mum died and is copying it.'

'Miss Sharin. You are a dark horse,' said Lou.

'Mmm and most probably right.'

Chapter 16

MEL TRIED FOR TWO NIGHTS TO PHONE DAN. HE LIVED outside Rockhampton with his wife and two hundred head of cattle. His life had moved on and although he and Mel were close, time and distance meant they spoke less frequently. They caught up once a year when Dan came to visit Lexie. The visits were getting shorter.

On Wednesday night he answered.

'Hi Dan, it's Mel,' she said after he greeted her in his deep, throaty voice. She'd always loved the sound of it. He used to sing Barry White songs while he washed the dishes, rocking those low notes reserved for the precious few. It still made her happy when she heard it.

'Hey Mel, how's things?' he replied, sounding genuinely pleased to hear from her.

They chatted for a while about kids, partners, and the usual run of life, before Mel broached the subject of Peggy.

'I hope you don't mind but I wondered if we could talk about Peggy?' she said. 'It's just, some things have come up and I need to know more about the night she died.'

There was silence at the other end of the line. She couldn't even hear him breathing. She suspected, deep down, Dan knew this was coming. They'd avoided talking in detail about it for years. But with everything on the news and his recent text, he worried he'd stirred things up.

'I'm not sure what else there is to talk about,' he finally replied, 'You know as much as I do.'

'Can we go over it anyway?'

'Do you really want to dredge this up again?'

'Please Dan, it's important.'

'Why?'

'A journalist called me.'

Mel heard Dan groan. 'Me too. But I didn't speak to him.'

She suddenly felt like a traitor. Maybe she shouldn't have? 'Sorry, but I did.'

Again, he was silent.

'I had to. They found a body in a skip off Lygon St. It's so much like Peg's death. I had to.'

Still he hesitated. 'And what did he want to know?'

'Everything. And I hate myself for it, but I want to know to.'

Mel could hear Dan breathing hard now. She knew this hurt him, but she had to go on.

'What do you remember about the night she died?' she asked.

He didn't speak immediately. When he did, he sounded tired.

'Only what I was told. As you know I was away. The police phoned me at about 11 a.m. on the Wednesday. They asked for my address and a local coppa came to see me. I was still at the hotel. I thought I must have broken some Wangaratta law I was unaware of. They said Peggy was reported missing and a woman's body was found. They said she matched the description given by Joanna and asked me to travel back to Melbourne to identify her.' He drew in his breath. 'I didn't even know she was going out that night.'

His voice trailed off and Mel waited.

'All I know about that night was what the Police and Joanna told me. They said she left at about 7.30 p.m. saying she'd be back at around 10 p.m. When she didn't arrive home Joanna phoned her mum and she later phoned the police. I don't know who she met or why. We'll never know.'

Mel wanted to argue his last point but refrained. Instead, she asked, 'Was there anything odd about her in the days before she died?'

'Not that I remember. No ... nothing I can think of,' he said.

'Tell me about her in those few days,' she said.

He sighed loudly. It hinted at annoyance. 'I can't be sure, Mel. Everything was just like normal. We had a good weekend, as I recall, nothing out of the ordinary. Then on Monday I left to go to Wangaratta for the car show. I phoned Peggy that night and we just talked about the usual crap. You know, about the show, what Lexie was doing, not much.'

'How did she sound?'

'Normal, I guess. She said not to worry about phoning the next day as she knew I'd be busy and that she would see me Wednesday night.'

'Did that surprise you?'

'No. I *was* going to be busy. The motor show had a gala dinner on the Tuesday night and I was going to it. In the end, I didn't because I had a thumping headache, so I went to bed. That's why I was still at the hotel the next morning. I didn't have to go and mind the stand until lunchtime so I thought I'd sleep in. Lucky, I did.'

'Why lucky?' asked Mel.

'Well, I'd have missed the call about Peggy. I needed to get to her as soon as I could. Imagine if it was the whole day. A whole day for her in that place. Alone. No, I'm glad I was there.'

Mel could feel a lump rising in her throat. She tried so hard never to imagine her mother lying on a cold slab in a morgue waiting for someone to claim her. It was such a lonely, isolating thought and it haunted her to think it. She employed her usual strategy of shaking her head, taking deep breaths, and willing her mind free of the thought. She distracted herself with another question.

'Can you think of anyone she would have met that night?'

'No. I can speculate, but I don't know for sure,' his voice hardened.

'Do you think she was having an affair?' asked Mel. It was a question they both implied many times, but never openly asked.

'Yes. I do. Why else would she keep the meeting secret? Kathleen said she'd mentioned some 'ghost from the past' but even Kath didn't know who. I reckon she dropped that in, in case something happened to her and maybe Kath would be able to work out who it was. But clearly, she couldn't. Either way, she deliberately didn't tell me and she gave Joanna no information either. If the meeting was innocent, why be so secretive?' He was beginning to sound angry. Mel didn't want to hurt him but she needed to know more.

'Are there any other reasons you think she was having an affair?' asked Mel, hoping she hadn't pushed him too far.

'I don't know. You know your mother. Our history wasn't great, was it? It's not like it would've been a complete surprise. She had her share of men. I thought all that was over, but then this happens. I don't want to believe it, but what other explanation is there?'

Mel couldn't argue with that. Her mother loved men. A lot of men. She'd married Dan at twenty years of age but left him at twenty-four. She was a wild, untameable spirit, that couldn't settle. When they got back together a little less than ten years later, Dan hoped she would, but it appeared she couldn't. He asked nothing more of her than loyalty and she failed to give it. It was this, above everything else that disappointed him. He still loved her, but it was a tainted love. In the days and weeks that followed her death, he struggled to untangle grief from anger. It took many years and too much alcohol, to reconcile the two.

'I'm sorry. I don't know either. I wish there was some way we could find out.'

'Well, the cops couldn't. And it's been nearly thirty years without knowing. Let's just let it rest.'

'Can I ask one more thing?'

He sighed loudly. 'What?'

Mel cringed but pressed on. 'Did either of you know a man named Robert Lang or a John Coreman?'

'Why are you asking about them?' he snapped.

'The journalist. He reckons they might be involved in her death.'

He didn't speak immediately and Mel could sense him mentally filing through some information he may or may not share. 'I knew of them both. More by reputation than anything else. But Peggy didn't. Lang was into extortion and money laundering. Car dealerships were perfect fodder. I'd see him, and Coreman sometimes, at Lowbeck's Luxury Cars when I worked there. Coreman just hung about poking around the cars. But Lang – he was all business. Slimy prick.'

'So, you didn't work with them or get involved at all?'

This time Dan was angry. 'What are you implying, Mel?'

Mel flinched. There was so much she wanted to ask but it was obvious Dan had had enough.

'Sorry, I don't mean to push and pry. Just ...' her voice trailed off.

'I had nothing to do with them. I was just a mechanic. Contrary to what you may be thinking, I was not a crook!'

Mel crushed her face into the wall she was leaning against and wished she could take it all back. This whole sorry mess was tearing open wounds that were sealed but not healed.

'Sorry, I didn't mean that at all. I'm just ... confused.'

Dan's breath was audible but easing. When he spoke, he was the soft, caring man he'd always been.

'I get it. But please, can we just leave it now?'

Mel agreed and turned the conversation to other topics. One of them being Lexie.

'I haven't booked yet 'coz Sarah's mum's been having more heart problems and they're doing some tests, but what do you think about late next month? Should be ok by then. Maybe go away together somewhere?' he said, then quickly added 'Unless you don't think that's a good idea?'

'Dan, she'd love it. Perhaps the beach,' said Mel. 'She loves the beach.'

'Wonderful. Let me know how much you need. I can transfer the money.'

'And you'll book flights soon?' asked Mel.

'Yes, I'll do it this weekend.'

'Great.'

They finished with small talk and hung up. As with every phone call to Dan, there was a fleeting moment of sadness as the conversation ended. It always seemed so final.

Chapter 17

DAN'S HAND, WITH THE PHONE STILL IN IT, HUNG heavy over the side of his chair. He let the cool air wash over him, oblivious to the billions of stars that stretched ahead of him into the night. He lived thousands of kilometres and a lifetime away, but still the past found him.

He reached up to the small wooden table and swapped his phone for the half empty bottle of beer. The glass was firm and comforting in his hand. He rubbed a thumb along its neck and gave himself over to what he ached to forget. But it wasn't for the loss of a woman he'd loved with his whole being, it was for the only person who'd loved him without condition. The one little person who truly needed him. Who'd seen him as her everything. And he couldn't be that to her. He ached with the agony of sacrificing her, to save himself.

He drank and the beer was bitter. It stuck in his throat. It burned as he swallowed. And the pain came. And the memories poured over him until he felt he would drown.

He remembered his slide from loving father, to leaving Lexie. It started when Lexie was three months old. Peg died and he was alone. He'd drowned his pain in alcohol then too, until Mel forced him back to reality. He didn't want to come back, but he had no choice.

He took a year's leave from work, enrolled in parenting classes, and became both mother and father to Lexie. They were inseparable. She was a bright, happy child who rarely cried. She had her share of childhood illnesses, but she was born a month premature so that was to be expected. She seemed entirely content to share her whole existence with him. For Dan, life was as perfect as it could be.

Then one night, when Lexie was nearly three years old, Dan put her to bed with the usual routine. He read to her, tucked her in, kissed her goodnight, and turned out her light. He sat up watching television until midnight before heading to bed. On the way past Lexie's bedroom, he could hear whimpering. Soft throaty sounds that came in waves. He stood at her door for a moment trying to see in through the dim light of her room. The covers of her bed were writhing. He struggled to make sense of it, as he clamoured for the light switch. As light flooded her room, he was able to take in what was happening. It sickened him into paralysis. Lexie's legs were twitching and her arms were contorted under her chin. Her eyes rolled in her head so that the whites were visible and froth was bubbling from her mouth. Saliva trickled down her chin, staining the pillow that was already wet with sweat.

Dan yelled and ran to her, lifting her from the bed in one movement. Her body was hot and damp with fever. Her head lolled over his arm, and her body went limp.

The next few hours were a nightmare. An ambulance arrived to rush Lexie to hospital. For two hours the medical staff worked to save her. Dan sat, numb and sobbing in the foyer, faintly lit by fluorescent globes, with Mel holding his hand. Daylight brought little relief and the news that Lexie had permanent and significant brain damage. For the second time in his life, Dan spiralled into hell.

For a year and a half he tried to switch lanes again and become carer to a child who needed twenty-four-hour attention. He strug-gled daily with the loss of the child Lexie had been and the adjust-ment of who she had become. He didn't love her any less. If anything, he loved her more. But as time passed, his confidence and ability to provide what she needed ebbed away and by the time he met Sarah he was desperate for a lifeline. One he didn't hesitate to grab with both hands.

They'd met online. Just conversation and company to begin with, but it grew to be much more. For Sarah, whose family was close to grown, the responsibility of raising a small child was out of the question. She had a life in another State and no intention of moving, but she fell head over heels for Dan and they agreed to marry on the proviso he moved to be with her.

Within a year of their first communication, Dan had swapped cars for cattle and was living in Queensland, Lexie was in a care home in Melbourne, and Mel was giving whatever time she had in her busy life to Lexie to provide her the love she deserved.

For Dan, the chance to start again - to package the past and leave it where he found it - was intoxicating. But he'd paid for it with his soul.

He finished the beer and dropped it to the floor. He was cold to the core, but he didn't move. He stayed all night. In the dark and the memories, until dawn washed them away again.

Chapter 18

MEL PUSHED THE OFFENDING HAND FROM HER shoulder. She couldn't yet muster the power of speech so she growled.

'Come on Mel, wake up,' urged Ricky, shaking her harder.

She growled louder. 'Too tired,' she finally mumbled into the pillow.

'You're already late, come on!' he insisted.

'Too tired,' she moaned again, burying herself deeper in the bed.

It was a bad night. Her mind wouldn't let up. It took hours to fall asleep but that brought no relief. She'd woken endlessly. Now she was exhausted. Ricky gave up and left her to sleep.

By midday, she was on her feet. There were several messages on her phone. She ignored them all but sent a single text to Sharin and Lou to explain her whereabouts. She promised to be in by 1 p.m. to prepare for her meeting later in the day.

She made it by 2 p.m. The Wolseley had a bad night too. It took twenty minutes and a great deal of profanity to get her started. Mel arrived at work in a foul mood.

In the office, she threw her handbag into the filing drawer, clicked on the computer, and left to make coffee. It took three teaspoons and two sugars to make it palatable. She still had a headache so it would have to do. She swallowed a couple of aspirin and turned her attention to the folder on her desk. She had less than two hours to get her head around its contents. She wasn't feeling confident.

Both Lou and Sharin were out of the office which meant Mel had no distractions unless she wanted them. The only evidence they'd been there was a sticky note on her computer stating Dave had called and narrowed his company logo search to four that were around in the early 1990s. Mel read and re-read them. Fanta, Coles, Telecom and Mastercard.

'Gotta be one of you, I hope,' she said to herself.

She tried to focus, but emails kept popping up. She replied to them all, left to make another cup of coffee and read the meeting documents in-between. At five minutes to four, she gave up. There were twelve pages left to read, but it was too late. She'd have to wing it. She had just enough time to phone Annie before her meeting.

Annie was still at the school library when Mel called her. She was never certain whether Annie frequented the library for study or social reasons. Probably both.

'I wondered what time you were getting to Rosa's tonight,' said Mel. 'I thought we could shop for shoes afterwards.'

'I should be there by 5.30 p.m.'

'Excellent. I can be there by then.'

'Mum, you don't have to.'

'I know, but I want to.'

'I'll be fine Mum.'

'I won't. See you there.'

Annie rode to Rosa's in sixteen minutes. It was a personal best. Like her mother, she was into numbers. Mostly as a guide to improvement.

Mel arrived ten minutes later. The screen door was latched so she called through the heavy mesh. The pat, pat, pat of stockinged feet drumming a beat down the steps soon followed and Annie appeared to let her in.

Annie kissed her mother, then trotted back up the steps, leaving Mel to re-latch the door. She was pleased that Rosa finally made a habit of locking it. Unfortunately, her years in a suburban bungalow did not prepare her for life on a busy city street. Two break-ins and an unexpected guest who strayed into her living room one Monday afternoon convinced Rosa to lock the doors. Now she was militant about it.

Upstairs Mel found Rosa, Annie, and Marcus standing in a circle around a small glass jar. The tiny beads pinged and tinkled against the edge of the glass, as this one, then that, was plucked out and held up to the light for inspection.

'Ah, perfect timing,' said Rosa. 'Which of these do you like?'

The circle parted into a half-moon, as Mel made her way to take the two glass beads from Rosa's hand.

Annie bounced up and down on her toes, Rosa kept her hand dangling in mid-air and Marcus folded his in front of him. They all watched her closely.

'Mmmm, tough choice,' she said, holding each up separately and rolling them, first one way and then the other.

They were the size of a small pea, but one was clear and painted with a tiny sprig of pink cherry blossom, whilst the other was all swirls of opalescent green and silver. She knew Annie's taste and guessed that the decision was between the one Rosa loved and the one Annie had chosen.

She picked the opalescent bead. Annie sprung up and threw her arms around her mother.

Rosa tried hard not to look disappointed. Marcus said nothing but nodded approval.

'Very well,' said Rosa, stretching her hand toward Mel. 'Green it is.'

As compensation, Annie slid herself under Rosa's arm and

cuddled into her shoulder. 'I love it, Aunt Rosa.' The kiss on the top of her head said everything was forgiven.

Rosa didn't sew labels into her clothes. She thought it gauche. Instead, she secured a glass bead into the back seam of every garment she made. The beads were procured from artisans in the city, for which she paid a small fortune. But they were perfect. And they were uniquely hers.

'Right. Let's get this fitting underway, darrrling,' she said, leading Annie, still tucked under her wing, toward the bedroom. Mel began to follow. 'No, no,' said Rosa without turning, 'Not you, darrling. No seeing it until it's complete.'

Mel capitulated and pulled a chair from under the dining table to sit down. Marcus moved across from the sideboard to join her. He placed a bottle of Penfolds Bin 128 Shiraz with a red bow tied at the neck in front of her.

'What's this?' asked Mel looking up at him.

'The glass of wine you missed out on last time. Thought you could take this bottle home.'

'You didn't have to do that.'

He shrugged. 'I wanted to.'

'Shall I open it now?' she asked.

'No, no. Plenty more where that came from.'

Mel laughed 'Yes. A whole wine warehouse.'

'Not quite a whole warehouse, but good enough.'

Mel looked around to see Annie standing in the doorway with her hands on her hips. She was still in her uniform and stockings.

'Don't look at me like that Annie,' said Mel.

'Like what?'

'Like that!'

'You're not going to drink that are you? You have to drive,' said Annie.

'No. I am not going to drink it.'

'Good.'

'Honestly, you'd think I was a soak,' said Mel.

'You do drink too much.'

'Thank you, Annie, but I don't need your approval.'

'You don't approve of drinking?' asked Marcus.

'Nope,' said Annie.

'You might one day,' he said.

'No way. My body is a temple.'

Mel chuckled, 'I guess that makes mine a crack den!'

'What's a crack den?' asked Rosa coming back into the room.

'Me ... because of all the wine I drink.'

'Nothing wrong with wine, darrrling! It's in our blood.'

'Not this blood,' argued Annie.

'Darrling, you're half Italian. It's in your blood.'

'Aunt Rosa, apart from when Mum was pregnant with me, I can assure you there has never been wine in my blood.'

'Oi! I did not drink when I was pregnant!'

'Really! There is a photo of you with a wine glass resting on your big fat belly!' said Annie.

'Oh ... well, I might've had one drink.'

'Mmmm, huh.'

'Anyway, thank you, Marcus. This is very kind. But I will save it for later,' said Mel, flicking her head at Annie, who thumped her fists harder into her hips.

'Ok, find those shoes, Annie,' scolded Rosa.

Annie dug through her schoolbag and extracted the pair she'd borrowed from her friend Elena, before joining Rosa in the bedroom. Mel and Marcus sat opposite each other at the table.

The conversation ambled through the happenings of the day, landing at the place they now found themselves.

'So, no lurch tonight then?' said Mel.

'Lurch?' replied Marcus.

'Eddy.'

'You don't like him, do you?'

'It's complicated,' said Mel.

'He couldn't make it. He's doing a course. They have night tutorials sometimes.'

'What's he studying?'

Marcus shifted his weight, pushing a coaster across the table, then back again. 'I shouldn't say.'

'Now you have to!' said Mel.

'Promise you won't say anything?'

'Sure,' she agreed.

'Art classes. Painting nudes. But I reckon he's doing more than just painting them.'

'Nudes!' said Mel.

'Shhhh ... Rosa doesn't know.'

'How can she not know? He's not here.'

'He told her he was doing a business course,' said Marcus.

'How very Eddy.' Mel shook her head as she adjusted the sleeve of her jacket. 'He must really trust you, to tell you that.'

Marcus spun the coaster under his finger. 'Actually, I feel a bit bad about it, 'cause I'm not sure he would've.'

'What do you mean?' she said. 'And hang on, what do you mean you think he's doing more than painting them?'

Marcus leaned across the table and lowered his voice. 'Well, I was coming back from a delivery not long ago and saw him walking along Wellington St with a bag in his hand. It was dark, so I stopped to give him a lift. He tried to pretend he didn't know it was me. But, you know, how could he not? He knows my van. Anyway, he eventually got in but was really flustered. I teased him because he looked like he had lipstick on his lip and he got all weird.'

'Lipstick?'

'Yeah. But he claimed it was lip balm,' said Marcus. 'As if!'

'You don't think it was?' said Mel.

'No way. Lip balm might be tinted but this was full on colour. It was lipstick.'

Mel stared at Marcus. 'You think he's met someone?'

Marcus sat back. 'I'm sure he's met someone. But the cheeky bugger was keeping it close to his chest. Said nothing. It took a lot of prodding and most of the trip home before he'd even confess to doing art classes with nude models. He seemed pretty embarrassed actually. Made me swear not to tell Rosa any of it.'

'I think she'd be shocked,' said Mel.

'I don't know, I think she'd be happy for him.'

Mel was about to argue but Rosa and Annie came back into the room. Marcus whispered to her that they'd finish the conversation later.

'You two talking about me? You look like you've been naughty,' Rosa teased.

Marcus winked at Mel. 'Nope, just singing your praises, Rosa,' he said.

Rosa swatted his shoulder as she walked past but then came back and hugged him from behind. 'Naughty and cheeky,' she said over his head.

Chapter 19

ALL THREE GIRLS ARRIVED EARLY THE NEXT MORNING.
With redundancy looming, they wanted to tidy up all the documentation in their projects ready to hand over. By midafternoon,
Mel was finalising the last pages of a contract but struggling to
focus. She looked up over the monitor and saw Sharin twisted in
her chair, gaze fixed on the whiteboard above the incident desk.
'Clearly you've lost interest too,' she said. 'What's caught your
attention there?" she added.

Sharin continued to stare. 'I've been thinking,' she said.
'There's about six weeks between each girl being found and the
next one disappearing. That means it'll happen again mid to late
September. Do you think he stalks them first?'

'That's a point. It's possible,' said Mel.

'I mean, they just vanished. Would that happen if it was
random?'

'You'd think if it was random it would be more chaotic. More
chance of being seen or doing something careless,' said Lou.

'I agree,' said Sharin, 'and it's been nearly two weeks since Lisa
was found, so he's probably started looking again. What if he's
chosen someone already?' she said. 'What if it's Michel. Our date
is this Saturday!'

'I'm sure it's not, but just in case, take Mace,' said Mel.

'But how would I know?' said Sharin into her hands.

'Not sure. But we can sit at another table if you like?' suggested Lou, brightening at the idea, 'and follow you home.'

Mel pulled a face at Lou, who shrugged and mouthed, 'what?'

'I might take you up on that offer,' said Sharin. Lou jiggled in her seat.

'Maybe just have us on speed dial,' suggested Mel.

'You are such a killjoy, Mel,' said Lou.

'Could you please not use the word kill,' begged Sharin.

'Anyway, your man is only thirty-seven years old. Too young,' added Mel.

'What if he lied? What if he's forty-seven?'

'Shaz, it's going to be fine. The chance of Michel being an axe murderer is highly unlikely.'

'Possible,' said Lou, 'but unlikely.'

'Lou!'

'Ok, ok,' mumbled Lou.

'Anyway, if you get any vibes you don't trust, then don't go home with him. The restaurant should be safe enough,' said Mel.

'Even if it's not Michel ...' began Lou.

'And it's not,' said Mel.

'Either way, we need to add the likely date of the next abduction to the board,'

She said this as she stood and stretched. Her hip clicked and she winced. 'Getting too old,' she grumbled.

William, carrying a small parcel, silently materialised from behind the office door just as Lou was rounding the petition. She screeched and jumped sideways, ricocheting off the carpeted screen and into his outstretched arm.

'Jesus and Mary! You scared the crap out of me!' she gasped, clutching her chest.

'Louisiana! Sorry, I should have knocked,' he said, pulling her close and holding her steady.

Lou, who'd been named after the apparent location of her

conception, hated her name. It could have been worse –her mother spent her youth in a smoke-filled haze so Lou could have been conceived anywhere. She was eternally grateful it wasn't Fukatani. Nonetheless, there wasn't a soul alive who'd get away with calling her Louisiana. Except William. He was the department's senior administration officer and friend to everyone.

While Lou caught her breath, William tucked the parcel under his arm and reached out his free hand to straighten the petition. It gave him just enough time to take in the incident board.

'That looks interesting. Are you planning a new project?' he asked, placing the parcel in Lou's hands, before moving toward the desk.

Mel, Sharin, and Lou shot a look at one another from behind his back, but no one spoke.

'Richard Lang. John Coreman,' he read aloud. 'Those names sound familiar. Why do I know those names?'

'They were serial killers from the 1990s,' said Lou, finding her voice. 'Hideous excuses for human beings.'

'Yes, that's right. Coreman killed women then cut off their breasts, amongst other things, and Lang was an accessory.'

'NO!' moaned Sharin, slapping her hands over her ears, 'I don't want to know!'

'I'm so sorry Sharin, I didn't …?'

'It's ok Will, she's a bit fragile,' said Mel.

'I won't say another word,' he smiled stepping away from the board.

'Actually, I'm curious how you know of them?' said Mel.

'Yes, it's a bit morbid, isn't it? But my partner's father is, or at least was, a detective. He's retired now, but he was working up until about ten years ago. He's seen a lot of death in his day and he doesn't mind sharing it.'

Mel was immediately interested. 'So, was he working in Victoria then?'

'Yes, he's always worked here.'

'William, take a seat,' she said, pulling a chair up to the desk and gesturing toward it. 'We have much to discuss.'

For the next twenty-five minutes, he sat attentively, as Mel brought him up to speed on the case.

'Do you think your partner's father ... what was his name?'

'Mike.'

'Do you think Mike would have any information about Peggy's case?' Mel asked.

'I can ask,' said William.

'You are wonderful!' said Mel throwing her arms around him. He felt good. Lou coughed into her hand.

'Progress!' exclaimed Mel, releasing him. 'Thanks, William.'

'My pleasure,' he said, sliding forward on the chair. 'I'll talk to him this weekend.'

They were interrupted by a tap on the door.

'Think that might be my cue,' said William, moving to the door. He opened it, stood aside, and turned back to face Mel. 'I think mini-Mel just arrived,' he continued, ushering Annie into the room.

'I hope not,' said Annie, pulling a face and shaking her head. 'Hi, Lou and Sharin,' she added. Both women welcomed her in.

'Well, thanks!' said Mel, looking hurt.

'Only teasing,' said Annie, coming toward her mum with outstretched arms. 'Hug?'

'Oh Ok,' said Mel pulling her in.

'Soooo cute,' said William, turning back toward the door. 'Ciao!'

Annie let go of Mel and waved to William as he left. 'He's nice,' she said.

'He is,' agreed Mel. 'You're early.'

'Yeah, the last period of class was free time so thought I'd skip it. Can we leave soon. I really need to find those shoes today.'

'Didn't find any the other night?' asked Lou.

"No. If Mum would take me to Eddy's emporium I might have more luck," said Annie.

94

"Well, too bad. And sorry, but I have about a dozen emails to knock over before we go, so you'll have to entertain yourself.'

Annie nodded reluctantly and wandered over to Lou. 'Hey, Lou, any chance you could teach me a few more card games?'

'No!' said Mel, as Lou said 'Sure.'

Annie hooked her hand on her hip as she pivoted to face Mel. 'Why not?'

'Lou's busy.'

'No, I'm not.'

Mel pursed her lips.

'You don't need to know how to play card games,' said Mel.

'Why not, you do,' said Annie.

'She has you there,' said Lou.

Mel sighed and looked at Sharin, who just raised her eyebrows and shrugged.

Mel shook her head and sat at her computer. 'Whatever.'

'Great!' said Annie, pulling a chair up to Lou's desk. "Teach me everything. But can you start with card counting?'

Lou looked over the top of the glasses she rarely wore. 'I'll teach you tricks but that can wait,' she said.

Annie pouted. Mel smiled.

'Ok, I'll give you the brief version, but when you are of legal age, I'll skill you up properly,' said Lou looking at Mel.

Mel said nothing. She knew she'd lose that argument.

Lou cleared the keyboard from her desk and Annie slid in closer to watch.

'Let the show begin!' said Sharin.

Chapter 20

LOU OPENED HER DRAWER AND PULLED OUT ONE OF five decks of cards she had secreted away. She pushed her in-tray to one side and spread the cards out, folding them back and forth before shuffling them. She continued to chat about cards and tricks whilst she arranged and rearranged the pack in her hand.

Annie watched closely.

'Card counting is a game of numbers. Casinos have the advantage but you can get a system going that improves your chance of winning. It's played with Blackjack, where to win, you need a score of 21. You increase your odds of playing 21 by keeping track of the cards dealt by the croupier from the deck. If you keep an accurate count of those cards, then you can predict the cards left in the pack and the odds that the card you need to make 21, will be dealt to you. To do that, a score is assigned to each card and then you keep count of that score as the cards are played. Low numbered cards are +1, tens through to aces are -1 and all others have a score of 0. Casinos sometimes shuffle more than one deck together, so you are at a disadvantage, But a deck rich in tens and aces, is good for the player, a deck rich in small cards, is good for the dealer. If you know your odds are poor, then you bet less but if they are good, you bet more.'

'So how do you split the system up between the three of you?' Annie asked.

Lou splayed the cards in her hand into a circle on the desk, then scooped them up and kept shuffling.

'We take turns. But basically, one is the player and is keeping count, but the second one is also counting. They will signal to the first player the odds from their count, and hopefully this confirms their own count. They then bet accordingly. The third person is watching for security. Casino's hate card counters, although these days the advantage of playing the system is not as good as it used to be.'

'Is it worth it?' asked Annie.

'Oh yes, it's great fun,' said Lou

When she'd shuffled the pack into a neat bundle, Lou handed it to Annie. 'Right, deal the cards into four piles adding a new card to each pile as you go,' she said.

Annie started dealing. 'Like this?' she asked, as the four little piles began to build.

'Yep, like that.'

When she finished, Lou said, 'now take the top card off any pile, but don't show me,' she warned, as Annie slid the first card off the second pile.

'OK, turn it over to face you.'

Annie's smile was pure delight. 'Are you going to guess?'

'No guess, it's Ace of Clubs,' said Lou with a flourish.

Annie's jaw dropped open 'Oh, My God!' she said waving the card around the room. 'You are so good at this.'

'It's just numbers and patterns, Annie. Numbers and patterns.'

'And concentration,' added Sharin.

Lou pointed the card in her hand toward Sharin 'Exactly. Concentration is key.'

'And perhaps a bit of pre-planning?' suggested Mel.

Lou laughed, 'and that is the most important part!'

'How did you know?' asked Annie.

'Easy. I set the aces at the bottom of the pack before you began counting them out. They all ended up on the top. You can't fail.'

Annie threw the card down and flipped over the top card of each pile. Sure enough, every card was an ace.

'That is so tricky!!'

'I have lots of those,' said Lou.

'How can you remember them all?'

'Experience.'

'Do you have to practice a lot?' asked Annie.

'Not now. But in the early days I did. Which was easy because I worked at it every night so I had no choice but to become an expert at it.'

'And besides, the casino would have sacked you if you didn't deliver,' said Mel.

'Ain't that the truth,' agreed Lou.

'Was it fun working as a croupier? Did you meet anyone famous?' asked Annie.

'Sometimes it was so much fun. Other times it was just tedious. And yep, I met a few famous people, but more infamous than famous.'

Lou kept shuffling and dealing. Showing each card to Annie so she could understand how the counting worked.

'Tell me more about it,' said Annie, leaning on her wrist. 'Like who did you meet?'

Lou stopped dealing cards. Her hand rested on the desk with the pack in her palm.

Sharin stopped typing. Mel kept her eyes on her computer screen, but her ears were on Lou.

'Some Arab royals, a lot of Chinese millionaires, a few media barons, and plenty of cashed-up crooks, all rubbing shoulders with each other. The high rollers room was where the real action happened. The money being dropped on tables was insane. It's weird, but it becomes invisible after a while. You don't even think about the amount of it. Most of the clientele were men. Rich men. But not flashy. Just ridiculously rich. They played hard and for hours at a time, but it was sort of calm. Kinda mellow. Not like the gaming tables in the public areas. Jesus, they were nuts!'

Annie was mesmerised. 'Tell me everything about them.'

Lou looked over to Mel who peered over her screen. 'Go on,' she said 'I love your stories.'

Lou put the cards down on the desk. She settled more comfortably in her chair and removed her glasses. 'On most nights, the gaming tables were full of punters with too much booze and hopeless optimism. The money they lost was tragic. But it was fun. People just got carried away. Lots of noise and laughter. We'd work late and party after.'

'Isn't that where you met husband number one?' asked Sharin.

'Yes indeed. Bobby. Drove me crazy. Always at my table, throwing around cash he didn't have. But he was funny. And so freaking persistent!'

'Did he sweep you off your feet?' asked Annie.

'More like he fell over his feet!' said Lou flinging her arms in the air. She smiled at the memory of it. 'He was this big lanky goofball. I was twenty and he was twenty-eight. He should have been more mature but he wasn't. He loved a good time and I was all for it. We dated for a few months and then one day he came in at the end of my shift carrying a big white box with a pink ribbon around it and said, 'when you get off shift, put this on and meet me out the front. I'm taking you on a private jet.'

'No way!' said Annie.

'Yes, way! Except Bobby was a used car salesman and a few other dodgy things so there was no way he could afford a private jet.'

'What was in the box?' asked Sharin.

'A dress. Ah, it was so pretty. To be honest, it was more shoe-string than dress, but it was hot!'

'Did you meet him after your shift?' asked Annie.

'Yep. Right where he said to meet him. As I got to the bottom of the stairs, a limo pulled up, and a chauffeur,' she paused for effect, 'complete with cap and epaulets, stepped out and opened the door for me.'

Annie sighed.

'Well, I thought, yep, this is as private jet as I'll ever get and I loved it!'

'Was Bobby in there?' asked Annie.

'Sure was. Splayed out along the back seat in his white suit. Mr Cool.'

'Leather seats? Mirror ball?' asked Mel.

'Leather seats, no mirror ball. But a bucket with champagne and two fancy crystal glasses. Thought I was the ducks nuts climbing into that Limo!'

'Did he propose then?' asked Sharin.

'Yep. And got laid for his troubles!'

'Lou!!' said Mel.

'Oh, Mum!' said Annie.

'Yes, oh Mum!' said Lou.

'Oh, my God. You are corrupting my daughter,' said Mel.

'I think you've already done that,' teased Annie.

Mel shook her head.

'What happened to your marriage?' asked Annie.

'Well, that was all a bit sad. I guess we just grew apart. It was fun for a while, but he skidded too fine a line between the right and wrong side of the law and got caught up in all sorts of scams. He wasn't bad, just always chasing some way to make a buck. He'd make it good, then lose it all. I was working lots of hours at the casino but I didn't want to be there forever. We kinda drifted away from each other. One morning I woke up and decided that was it. I packed the few things that mattered to me and left. In Bobby's Mustang! God, I loved that car. Had to give it back eventually but it got me out of there for a while. It took me a few months and a lot of back and forth but in the end, I left for good. Ran off to India to "find myself".'

'And did you?' interrupted Mel.

'Well, found husband number two,' she laughed again, 'but

he didn't last long. He was my shortest marriage,' she said to Annie.

'How long were you there?'

'About two years. Came back, moved to Sydney, and got a real job. If you can call working in Corrections, a real job.'

'Did you see Bobby again?' asked Annie.

'No. We sent the odd postcard to each other, that sort of thing, but nothing more.'

'What happened to him?' asked Sharin.

Lou picked at the cards.

'He died.'

'Oh no!' said Sharin.

'Yeah, it stunned me too. Got a call about thirteen years ago from this random woman. I'd just come home from work and the phone was ringing. Picked it up and this woman with a Filipino accent said, 'Hello.' Well, of course being 6 p.m. I thought it was a telemarketer, so I started to give her the what for, but she yelled over the top of me –'Bobby's dead!'.

Lou shook her head at the memory of it. 'Could have blown me over with a fuckin' feather!'

'Was he in the Philippines?' asked Sharin.

'Nope, he married one. Angel. She said he'd had a heart attack. She'd gone out the back to tidy the storeroom and when she came back, he was slumped over the counter, dead.'

'Did they own a shop?' asked Annie.

'Sort of. A knock shop,' said Lou.

Annie scrunched her face 'What's that?'

Lou looked to Mel.

'Don't look at me, you're the one telling the story,' she said.

'It's a brothel,' said Lou.

'Ohhhh,' said Annie un-scrunching her face.

'Madame Angel,' continued Lou. 'Anyway, she said he'd left something for me and I had to come and get it. Couldn't believe it. The bastard left me his Mustang!'

'Wow! That is so sweet,' said Annie.

For a moment Lou looked sad. Her eyes glistened but she shook it away. 'It was. Angel said Bobby told her I loved that car and it was ours. Just his and mine. He wanted me to have it. Angel was good to keep his promise. I liked her. I like her. We stayed friends.'

'Does she still run a brothel?' asked Sharin.

'Nope. Gave it up when Bobby died. Became all respectable. Married a politician! Hilarious!'

'How have I never heard the story about the Mustang?' asked Mel.

'Dunno. You've heard the rest. Guess I didn't think much about it,' said Lou.

'You've had an interesting life, Lou,' said Annie as she ran her hands along the length of the desk.

'Yeah, I have. So, let's teach you a few more tricks and you can have one too,' she said, scooping up the cards and handing them to Annie.

Chapter 21

THAT EVENING ON THE WAY HOME FROM SHOPPING Annie asked Mel more about Lou, Angel, and Bobby.

'Do you think Lou was into the same stuff as them?'

'What do you mean?' Mel asked.

'You know, drugs and brothels.'

Mel thought about the stories Lou had told her over the years.

'I think she dabbled early on but, as she said, it wasn't where she wanted to go. She told me once that Angel saved Bobby and she knew she never could have. She loved him but it wasn't working. Bobby got into all sorts of tin pot scams and ran at the edge of a bad crowd. He was dealing cocaine and selling dodgy cars at overinflated prices. He was headed for a major fall. When he met Angel, she put a stop to all that. She is one savvy businesswoman according to Lou. Her mum had a brothel in the Philippines and she grew up watching the worst of it. She figured out how to keep it a clean show and still make money. When her mum married some fat old Australian, they moved here and she set up again, but Angel took it over. Pretty sure Angel would have the dirt on a lot of men in this city.'

'Have you met her?'

'Nope. Would love to though. I think she is part of Lou's past that belongs there and not here, now with us. That's ok. We all have things we keep for ourselves.'

Annie leaned her head back into the headrest and stared ahead. 'I've got so much to learn,' she said.

'Just stick to card tricks and books,' said Mel, smiling sideways at her.

'Mmmm,' said Annie.

'And not so much on the card tricks!'

Annie turned to look at her 'Did Lou teach you and Sharin?'

Mel returned her look. 'Yep. She'd play cards at lunchtime or when she was stressed. She told us about the casino and the tricks they employed to beat the punters. She hatched the idea that we do it as a team.'

'You're all good with numbers, but was it hard to learn?'

Mel tilted her head from side to side. 'Mmmm, yes and no. The counting got easier with practice, but the ability to not look obvious took some doing. Particularly Sharin! She wears every thought on her face. But in the end, we all got good at it.'

Annie was silent for a while. 'Mum,' she said, 'how often do you play the casinos?'

Mel paused, unsure she should share all her secrets. 'Occasionally,' she said.

'When Dad plays golf?'

Mel smiled. 'You know too much.'

'He really hates it, doesn't he,' said Annie.

'Yep. He reckons it's cheating, but it's not.'

Annie reached over and touched Mel's arm. 'I think it's cool. I won't tell.'

Mel touched Annie's hand in return. 'Thanks.'

'But can you teach me more sometime?'

Mel sighed. 'Is that blackmail?'

Annie giggled, 'No. But good thought!'

'Annie Melloncelli. You are an imp!'

'Is that a yes?'

Mel sighed again. 'Yes.'

Chapter 22

MEL WOKE TO RAIN HAMMERING ON THE WINDOW – perfect weather for being indoors on the computer. She climbed out of bed before sunrise which was not her usual style. Ricky was concerned.

'You ok?' he murmured.

'Yep, sorry, I didn't mean to wake you.'

'You didn't,' he said, opening one eye. 'What are you doing?'

'I want to find Kathleen. It's been years since I saw her but I'm sure it won't be too hard.'

'It's Saturday, can't it wait?'

'No. I really need to do this.'

Ricky rolled onto his side and pulled back the sheets. He was naked from the waist up. 'Are you sure it won't wait?' he asked, sliding his hand into the band of his Bonds hipsters.

Mel threw herself on the bed and kissed him. He wrapped both arms around her, pulling her close.

'You are so irresistible,' she said, 'but today I am resisting!'

He kissed her cheek, ran his hand down her back and held her tight. 'You don't want to do that,' he whispered.

'I promise I will make it up to you,' she said, wriggling backwards. He didn't let go. This wasn't going to end well. 'Ricky, please, I really need to do this.'

Ricky released her with a huff and flopped onto his back. 'Fine. Go and play with your computer.'

She felt bad, but she would have been pretending if she'd stayed. It wasn't how she did things.

The study was cold, so Mel ran upstairs to get another jumper while the computer fired into life. By the time she returned, it was ready for her.

She sat with her fingers poised over the keyboard. It was more than twenty years since Mel had spoken to Kath. They had kept in touch for a few months after the funeral, but Peggy was the only thing they had in common. After she died, there was no reason to keep in touch. Mel sent Christmas cards for a few years, but nothing since. At the time, Kathleen was living in Ballarat with her family. There was a chance she was still there, so Mel typed 'Kathleen Teale' into the search engine. A few 'Kathleen Teals' attached to Facebook pages popped up. She clicked through them. There were some with photos, but none looked like Kath. The others without photos provided so little information, it was impossible to tell.

Instead, she tried the White Pages. She couldn't remember Kath's husband's name, so just typed in 'Teale' and 'Ballarat'. Three listings appeared. One with the initials B & K. Bingo.

Mel wrote the number and address on a piece of paper and walked into the kitchen where she'd left her phone on charge. As she reached for it, her heart began to race. She was excited and nervous. This call could open a can of worms and she wasn't sure how Kath would feel. She dialed the number and waited. The phone rang several times. Each time it did, Mel's heart skipped another beat. Finally, it answered. But it was only a recorded message. The woman's voice was soft and mellow. It sounded like the Kathleen she knew. The message confirmed it.

'Hi there, sorry we can't get to the phone, but if you'd like to

leave a message for Brian, Kath, Toby or Jake, we'd love to hear it. Please wait for the beep. Bye.'

Mel waited for the beep and plunged in. 'Hi, this is Melinda Cooke. I hope I've contacted the right Kath Teale; if I have, would you please call me back on 0443 967 210? I would love to talk to you about Peggy. Ok. See you.' And she hung up.

She'd blurted out the message without really thinking it through. She wished she hadn't. It could have been so much better. She hoped Kath would call.

The weekend came and went. Mel fluctuated between grumpy and fuming as time went by without a phone call. Her mood worsened every time the phone rang and the unfortunate caller wasn't Kath. Mercifully, there were only three calls, but the last one was a man from a market research company. He wore much of her wrath.

Annie and Ricky gave her a wide berth. On Sunday afternoon they needed a break.

'I'm going to see Lexie,' said Annie.

'I'll drive you,' said Ricky.

They left but nothing had changed when they returned that evening. They came in to find her crashing dishes into the dishwasher. She stopped long enough to ask how Lexie was, but part way through Ricky's explanation her phone beeped, and she immediately grabbed it. Ricky stopped mid-sentence and waited. Mel checked the phone then slapped it back onto the kitchen counter and swore. Ricky turned and walked away.

"If you're not listening, then I'm not talking,' he snapped as he made his way into the lounge room.

"I AM listening," she said, even though she'd picked up her phone again. She followed him into the room as Annie poured herself a glass of water.

'Don't leave that glass on the bench, when you're done,

Annie. Put it in the dishwasher. I'm sick of cleaning up after you lot.'

Annie started to say something but stopped. Instead, she gulped her drink and did as her mother told her.

Ricky settled into his recliner and flicked his shoes onto the lounge room floor. Mel lost it, snatching up the shoes and flinging them, along with a barrage of profanity, across the room. Ricky threw them back.

'Enough!' he roared. Annie took flight to her bedroom.

Words, spittle and wild gesturing followed. It ended in tears with Mel on the couch. Ricky stood beside it. The air and the heat went out of the room.

'If it's going to be like this, Mel, then stop now. I can't stand it.'

Mel sobbed. 'I just want to know. I just want to know what happened to her. I need Kath to call me.'

Ricky softened. No one could make his ire rise like Mel, but her tears never failed to quell it. She cried so rarely. He leaned over the couch, took her by the hands and lifted her to him. 'If she calls, she calls. You just have to be patient.'

'You know how hard that is? I have no patience.'

'Well, you are going to have to learn it.'

Mel sobbed some more. Ricky held her. Annie came back into the room. 'I'll get you some wine,' she said. How well she knew her mother.

Chapter 23

On Monday, Mel dragged herself out of bed. She was hungover - exhausted from drinking wine and crying. She felt like shit.

She dressed in black, skipped breakfast, packed a muesli bar for lunch and went to work. To think about the day ahead was insufferable.

The Wolseley sat in the garage looking glum. 'What are you staring at,' growled Mel as she approached. The Wolseley answered her by not starting. For the second time in two days, Mel cried. The Wolseley started. It was 7.45 a.m.. Mel just managed to get to work with one minute to spare. But she needed coffee.

Twenty minutes later she was walking into the office with three coffees. She knew Lou would microwave hers when she arrived, but it would still taste reasonable. Sharin was at her desk.

'Hello you!' she sang.

'Hi yourself,' Mel responded, in a tone flatter than a pancake on Shrove Tuesday.

'Oooh! You don't sound happy.'

'Life's a bitch.'

'Did something happen?'

'No. Something did NOT happen. That's the problem.'

Sharin worked through a range of facial expressions as she listened to Mel recount the weekend. She hugged her once she'd finished and offered words of consolation. Sharin made everything all right.

'Maybe Kath was away for the weekend and she'll call tonight?'

'Yes, that's probably true. I just wish she'd hurry up.'

'All good things come to those who wait. Apparently?' said Sharin.

'Waiting is not my fortè. So how was your weekend?' asked Mel, before remembering. 'The date!' she yelled.

'Yes,' Sharin grinned.

'Tell me all. Did all good things come to you?' said Mel.

'Mmm, sort of. Shall we wait for Lou to get here? I know she will want to hear it too.'

'Of course. Good idea. I'll phone to see when she'll be in.'

Mel dialed Lou's number. The phone rang. It sounded loud. It got louder.

Lou walked through the door, carrying it in her hand. She smiled at Mel as she checked the number ringing on it. 'Hello,' she said into it.

Mel hung up. 'You are too funny.'

'Yes, I am! What can I do for you?'

'Sharin was just about to tell us about her date!' she said.

'Brilliant. Just give me a minute to offload these bags and make a coffee.'

'Coffee is on your desk. It's probably still warm enough but you might need to zap it.'

'I don't mind lukewarm. Thanks for buying it. What do I owe you?'

'Don't be ridiculous. Just get your arse in that chair so we can enjoy the peep show.'

'You're not getting that much detail,' said Sharin.

'Like hell,' said Lou, 'don't you spare us a thing!'

'I'd hate to disappoint you!'

'I need to get my jollies somehow. I am extremely deprived you know.' She poked her bottom lip out as she finished the sentence.

'If only that were true,' said Mel. It was Lou who did the depriving. Her poor husband was routinely deprived. It was a method she used to keep men exactly where she wanted them.

'Go ahead, Sharin,' said Lou.

Sharin told them she'd arrived at Agostino's café at 8 p.m. on the dot. There was standing room only, with patrons lining the bar in hope of a table. She squeezed past a party of six in the foyer, before joining the queue. The line moved fast. More people lined the bar. Sharin told the waitress she had a reservation and was taken to a dimly lit corner on the far side of the restaurant. She scanned the tables for her date. She hoped his profile was genuine. She'd had one date whose only resemblance to his photo was a tattoo on his forearm.

The waitress stopped at table thirteen. Fortunately, fate was favourable, as a tall, handsome man stood to greet her. He was perfect.

He thanked the waitress and then greeted Sharin with a kiss on both cheeks. How very French, she thought. She had the presence of mind not to giggle like a schoolgirl. She sat. He sat. The wine arrived and the evening took off. He was everything her fairy-tale heart desired.

'What did you find out about him?' asked Mel.

'Bugger that,' chipped in Lou, 'did you bed him?'

'Not much and no,' she replied to each of them.

'What do you mean 'no'!' exclaimed Lou.

'Well, we talked for hours, but mostly about me. He just seemed so interested. I got a bit carried away.'

'A man who is interested would carry a girl away,' said Lou.

'Did you learn anything?' asked Mel.

'He lives alone but has an eight-year-old son which is why he is living in Australia. He didn't say much about it, just that he'd met an Australian girl in France and followed her here. They'd been together a year when she fell pregnant, so they got married but it didn't work out. His son lives with his ex, but they see each other every week. He showed me a photo. He's very cute.'

'Did he show you a picture of his puppy too?' asked Lou.

'How did you know he has a puppy?'

'Lucky guess.'

'How crazy! His dog is called Boo. He is sooooo adorable.'

'Of course, he is.'

'And what does he do?' asked Mel.

'Boo?'

'No, love ... Michel.'

'Oh. Ha! Something to do with security or or ... I don't know. It was a bit confusing. He has to travel though. He goes to Canberra and Sydney quite often.'

'A spy?' said Mel.

'No, I don't think that was it?'

'Did he keep talking into his collar?' asked Lou, straight-faced.

'No. That would've been weird.'

'Then he isn't a spy.'

Mel shook her head. 'Tell us more.'

Sharin thought about it. She wound the tiny strand of hair which had escaped its clip around her fingers. 'He talked about sport, and opera and sailing. He loves sailing. I don't know, he was just really attentive, funny, gorgeous.'

'But you didn't bed him?'

'No! I desperately wanted to, but he was such a gentleman. He said he would drive me home, which he did. He walked me to the door, and he kissed me goodnight.'

'Thank heavens you got a kiss.'

'Only on the cheek.'

'You're not serious?'

'Yep.'

'Do I dare ask, are you seeing him again?'

'As it happens, I am.'

'Honestly!' said Mel.

'Yes. He phoned me on Sunday, said what a great night he'd had and invited me to a movie this Thursday. I can't wait!'

'Where? What movie?' asked Lou.

'Not telling. You are not coming.'

'You are a callous woman.'

Mel's phone rang.

'Hello, Mel Cooke speaking,' she said, turning in her chair.

'Hi Mel, it's Kath.'

'Shit.'

Kath laughed.

'Sorry, Kath. I just wasn't expecting it to be you. I mean I was, but not now. Sorry, I'm raving. How are you?'

'I'm well. How are you? I must say, I was surprised when I heard your message.'

'Yes, it must have seemed odd. I'm fine. I just really need to ask you some things about Mum.'

'What would you like to know?' asked Kath.

'Well, actually, I wondered if I could come and see you. I have so many questions and I don't want to rush you.'

'Sure. Where are you living now?'

'In Melbourne. I could drive up this weekend if you have some free time?'

'Ok,' she hesitated, obviously thinking through her weekend. 'What about Saturday? You could come for lunch.'

'Lunch would be great, but I don't want to put you out.'

'You're not. It will be nice to see you again.'

'Thanks, Kath.'

They made arrangements and hung up. Mel didn't turn around immediately although she knew Lou and Sharin were waiting. She needed to take a moment for herself. When she finally did, she simply said, 'That was Kath.'

Chapter 24

Tuesday morning started with a phone call from Lou. She was taking sick leave. Her son had wrapped his motorbike around a tree the night before. Fortunately, he had the presence of mind to throw himself off before it did, but he slid several metres on his back before a ditch caught him. He broke two bones and tore the skin from his hands, but otherwise he was intact. Lou was relieved he survived but livid the bike hadn't. She'd lent several thousand dollars for its purchase and it was not six weeks old. She was not happy.

'At least he wasn't hurt more badly,' said Mel, when she'd heard the story.

'Thanks to his leathers. He'd have been mincemeat without them.'

'Yes. They're expensive but worth the money. What price can you put on a life?' asked Mel.

'Well, several thousand, in my case. Won't be seeing that again.'

'At least he's all right.'

'Yep, I know,' she said before hanging up.

Mel was sliding the phone into her pocket as she passed reception, when it rang again. It was Lou.

'Hey. Everything ok?' asked Mel.

'Yep. Just forgot to tell you I spoke with Angel,' said Lou. 'I've been thinking about Lang and Coreman. In her line of work there had to be something she knew.'

'And did she?'

'Yep. She said Bobby had done a few jobs for Lang but that was early on when they first met. About 1990. She made him end it 'coz she knew Lang from the brothel. A real piece of work. Knifed one of her girls. Used a blade instead of his manhood. Mean mother fucker.'

'Christ! That is horrendous,' said Mel.

'Isn't it though. Angel employed really good security after that. Made men strip and dress in a robe before they went into the rooms. Didn't happen again but she was really careful around him.'

'And Coreman, did she know him?' asked Mel.

'Knew of him. He'd been in a few times. Liked it rough. But nothing like Lang. He had a bit of a reputation as a lap dog. Always at Lang's beck and call. Said she never understood why. He came from money. Family had a construction business. He had a job with them. Didn't need Lang.'

'Bet Lang needed him though.'

'Yep. Probably made him feel superior. And construction is a great way to clean money,' said Lou.

'Didn't pay off for Coreman. No loyalty among thieves if Dave's intel is correct,' said Mel.

'Total narcissist.'

Mel shuddered. 'Well, if it's him on the loose, then heaven help us.'

'Mmm. Keep that Annie confined to barracks, Ms Cooke.'

'Will do Ms Barnes.'

'Righto. Gotta go. See ya,' she said and hung up.

Mel switched off the phone and walked absent-mindedly through the final corridor to her office, where Sharin was at her computer, absorbed in a typing frenzy.

'Hey girl,' said Mel, 'Just heard ...'

'Sorry Mel, can't chat,' replied Sharin, not looking up. 'Got a meeting at nine o'clock but have to finish this service agreement first. They can't sign it if it isn't written.'

'Ok, I won't disturb you,' said Mel, throwing her bag under her desk before turning on her computer.

'Ta,' murmured Sharin.

Mel left for the tea room with her thoughts still on the information Lou gave her. Shortly after, William strolled into the tiny alcove of a kitchen.

'I had some luck with Mike,' he said.

Mel stopped reaching for her cup and spun around. 'Do tell!'

'He said he remembered the case but he didn't work on it. He said a guy called Terence Bailey did. Mike described him as 'one weird nutter', and not much of a detective, but it was his case. He'd be the one to talk to.'

'That is brilliant, Will, thank you. Did he happen to keep in touch with him? I assume he isn't working anymore?'

'No, he's not, he retired just before Mike, but they don't keep in touch. However, he said he was the kind of guy who wouldn't have moved because he was too lazy to get out of his own way. He looked him up and he is still living in Melton. I have a phone number for you,' he said, pulling a piece of paper from his pocket and handing it to her.

She leaped around like a lunatic. She hugged William. It was becoming a habit.

'This is so fantastic. Thanks, Will!'

She made a drink then raced back to the office. Sharin hadn't moved.

'I'm sorry, I said I wouldn't interrupt,' she blurted out, slamming the door, 'but Will just gave me the phone number for the detective who worked on Mum's case. Isn't that brilliant?'

The sound of plastic on plastic stopped. 'That's great news!' she said 'When are you going to call him?'

'I don't know. I should do it soon. I need to think about it.'

Sharin returned to her typing while Mel sat at her desk staring at the phone. She wasn't expecting this. She had to prepare.

It took forty minutes and several pages of dot points, most of which ended up in the bin, to make a plan and decision. Mel picked up the phone and dialed the number. Sharin had left, so she was alone in the office.

The phone almost rang out when a frail female voice answered. 'Hello' is all it said.

Mel tried to calm her voice. 'Hello, my name is Mel Cooke and I am trying to contact Terence Baily. I wonder if I have the right number.'

'Yes,' said the woman. Her voice was shaky and hesitant. She sounded tired. 'I'll just get him for you.'

Mel straightened up and unconsciously smoothed her skirt as she waited.

'This is Terence,' said a voice so loud and gruff that it startled Mel. For a split second, she wondered if this was a good idea.

She cleared her throat. 'Good morning, Mr Bailey, my name is Melinda Cooke, and I was hoping to talk to you about a case you worked on some years ago. I hope you don't mind me calling?'

'Are you a reporter?' he yelled. Mel held the phone away from her ear.

'No, I'm the daughter of a woman who was murdered in 1992. Her name was Peggy Hilliard.'

'Hilliard. Hilliard. Peggy Hilliard,' he muttered off into the distance. There was such a long silence, Mel wondered if he'd left the room. She sat down.

'Do you have any recollection of her?' asked Mel. She held the phone away in readiness for his reply.

'Yes, I do actually. Pretty woman, blonde, dah, dah, dah.'

'Yes, that's her!' Mel felt excitement rising.

'What about her?' Then fading.

'Well, I was hoping I could meet you to discuss her case. I am trying to find out what happened to her.'

'What for? Won't bring her back!'

Mel was beginning to think Terence Bailey was a wanker, but unfortunately, he was a wanker she needed.

'No, but I just need to know. It's very important.'

'For closure or some bullshit, dah dah dah dah dah,' he said.

Crazy and a wanker. Mel pushed on.

'Would you be happy to meet sometime?' Mel asked again.

'Do you look like your mother?' he asked.

'A bit,' she said, wondering what that had to do with anything.

'Except not dead,' he laughed.

A creepy crazy wanker. She was taking Lou to this meeting.

'Yes, I'll meet you,' he continued. 'Break up my boring day, dah dah dah. You'll have to come here. I look after the wife. She's on a disability pension you know. Had diabetes for years, a heart attack two years ago, and arthritis in her legs, dah, dah, dah. Useless old cow. Can't leave the house because of her. You'll have to come here.'

Mel thumped her head on the desk. *Why me? Why him? Why am I a shit magnet?* she thought.

'You still there!' he yelled.

'Yes, sorry,' she mumbled, summoning the strength to go on, 'that would be great if I could meet you at your house. When would suit you?'

The arrangements took more than five minutes to make. Mel decided that if the phone call was indicative of his style of investigation, then she had no hope of learning anything. Thursday at ten o'clock was looking bleak. She texted Lou with the details and prayed she could make it. She wasn't at all sure what to do if she couldn't. Going alone would be akin to Ishmael feeding himself to Moby Dick.

Chapter 25

THURSDAY DAWNED GREY AND STORMY. IT WAS AN omen Mel shouldn't have ignored.

The Wolseley refused to start. It sat in the garage like a teenager at his grandmother's birthday party. Sullen and difficult. Mel tried for thirty minutes before calling a cab. She didn't have time to wait for the RACV. It would've taken the better part of a morning and that was time she could ill afford.

She met Lou at the office and they drove, in her car, to meet Terence Bailey. Mel warned her what a weirdo he was so Lou came dressed in loose black clothing that covered her from neck to toenail. She also packed 'Aerogard'. A great defence against unwanted pests.

Lou owned a sporty black Mazda MX-5. It was so low to the ground you practically had to slither on your stomach to get inside it. Once in though, the front was roomy, but the back was a tight squeeze. Lou liked that feature. It limited the number of passengers she could carry. She'd bought the car after her fourth divorce, as a gift to remind herself life was short. She drove it as she lived her life. Fast.

Terence Bailey lived fifty minutes' drive down the highway in a suburb described by many as one of the worst in Melbourne.

They found the street easily enough but it was a little harder to find the house. An overgrown hedge, metre-high grass, and some insidious vine reclaimed the land. A narrow break in the undergrowth conveyed an opening, so they took it. Lou kept her purse, and Aerogard, close.

The house stood several metres inside the perimeter. They pushed through the weeds that grew between the bricks that once formed a pathway to the door.

'Just stay on the path,' whispered Lou. 'You know what happens if you stray from the path.'

'I'm not sure we need to get off the path to meet a horrible fate,' Mel whispered back, but she stuck close to Lou anyway.

By the time they reached the door, they were damp to the skin. The water from the weeds and the softly falling rain saw to that.

A heavy wooden door, buckled from water damage, and peeling paint like a leper shedding its skin, stood closed behind a rusty screen door.

Mel looked at Lou, drew in a deep breath, and knocked loudly on the door jamb. From behind it, she heard a dog bark. Then the heavy fall of paws as the dog came running, closely followed by more barking.

'I hope it's not a fighting dog,' said Lou, reaching for her Aerogard.

'I hope it's eaten today,' replied Mel.

They braced as they heard heavier footsteps approaching.

'SHUT UP ya mongrel!' a male voice yelled. 'Get out the bloody way you useless lump of dogmeat.'

Mel gripped Lou by the arm. There was still time to retreat. A few steps back and they wouldn't be visible.

But the wooden door flew open before they had a chance to move. A great hulk of a dog was pushing through the unclad legs of his owner. Mel wasn't sure which was the more frightful sight.

Terence Bailey stood behind the screen door wearing nothing but a pair of white, polyester short shorts, and a heavy gold medallion, which sat askew amongst a nest of greying chest hair.

Lou audibly gasped. She later described him as a Les Patterson impersonation of Bob Hawke.

'Ya, made it then?' he said. 'Which one of ya is the dead girl's kid? Wasn't expectin' two of ya.'

'I'm Mel,' she said pointing to herself, 'and this is my friend, Lou. My car broke down so Lou gave me a lift. I hope you don't mind?'

'Na, she's right. Come in,' he finished, as he pushed the screen door open and stood aside. He held the head of the dog between his knees.

Lou pushed past with her back against the door jam. It wasn't the dog she was avoiding. Mel followed.

Lou was hardly inside when she retched. Fortunately, Terence didn't notice. He was busy hauling the dog outside.

The place stank of damp flooring and stale urine. There was a well-used kitty litter tray in one corner and piles of newspapers in another. They were standing in a lounge room that was dark from poor lighting and grey weather. The loosely snarled threads on the floor constituted a rug, offset by a faded plaid couch with armrests stained deep brown from grime and smoke. 'Come through, come through,' said Terence waving at them. He led the way into a small kitchen that opened out to a covered patio. Despite the rain and cold, Mel prayed they would sit on the patio.

'Take a seat at the table,' he said. 'I'm making tea. Do you want some?'

Both Mel and Lou replied. 'No' a little too quickly, then covered it up with excuses about having just finished breakfast. Terence made some quip about them being public servants if they could eat breakfast so late, but they let it slide. He was helping Mel after all.

Mel moved some papers off a chair and sat down facing the patio. Lou took a seat to her right. The table sat adjacent to a wall on the right-hand side of the kitchen. A bench, sink, and array of appliances sat to the left. Between the bench and table was a narrow walkway covered in black and white linoleum that curled up at the edges. It was sticky and gritty. The room was lit by a single round bulb in the middle of the room. The stark white light just made the bleakness of the room all the more evident.

Mel and Lou sat silently as Terence made a cup of tea. He was mumbling something about 'crap kettle' and 'bloody expensive electricity', as he did. Now and then he chuckled to himself.

Mel took the opportunity to take out a pen and paper. Lou surveyed the room for weapons and exits. A faint sound of groaning could be heard coming from somewhere in the house. Lou hoped it wasn't the last person to visit.

'So ya want to know about ya mother's death, huh?' said Terence taking a seat opposite Mel. He balanced the cup on a stack of magazines and rested his head on his hand.

'Yes, I do. There is a lot I don't know and I was hoping you could help.'

'Well, it was a long time ago, and my brain ain't what it used to be,' he said, grinding a finger into the side of his head. 'I had to leave all me notes when I retired but I got some recollections.'

'Can you tell me what was known of the person she met that night?' asked Mel getting straight to the point.

'Yeah, well, you know. We couldn't find much. Took a bit of time to find the café they met in. Waitress there said Pat had a cuppa with some guy.'

'You mean Peg?'

'Yeah, yeah, Peg. She had a drink with this guy, but the waitress couldn't really describe him. Cute little thing she was. Tight white shirt. Could see her nipples through it. Yeah, she was worth stopping for, dah dah dah.' Then he laughed to himself.

Lou kicked Mel under the table.

'So, what could she tell you about the man?' asked Mel.

'Not much. It was cold and he wore a beanie, pulled down low. He was wearing a jacket, which he left on while they were in the café. Apparently, your mum got up after she finished her drink and didn't come back. The guy stayed for a while and then left.'

'Yes, the waitress said they left separately.'

'You know the waitress?' said Terence.

'A journalist we know spoke with her,' said Lou.

Terence flicked his head. 'Bloody scum those journalists. Don't trust any of 'em'.

'She said there was a patch of orange on his jacket. Maybe a logo or brand or something?' said Mel.

'Wouldn't know about that. Probably nothin' dah dah dah.'

This time Mel kicked Lou under the table.

'The waitress said Mum left before the man but she didn't see her go. She said he left about 10 p.m. or 10.30 p.m.,' said Mel.

'Yeah, that's right. But if you know all this, why you talkin' to me?'

Mel asked herself the same question.

'Well, you were the detective on the case. I'm sure you know more,' she said.

'Huh,' said Terence, 'clearly. Can't trust waitresses either. Schemers, all of 'em, dah dah dah.'

'So,' said Lou as Mel's fist turned white under the table, 'They said Mel's mum was killed around midnight. That makes it possible this guy did it, right?'

'Could have. Who knows? Couldn't ID the guy to find him. No camera surveillance back then. Not like now. Cameras everywhere. Can't fart without someone knowing, dah dah dah.'

Mel tried to keep him on track.

'Were there any other suspects apart from him?' asked Mel. She wanted to know if Dan was a serious suspect.

'Yeah, her husband. Your dad,' he said, nodding at Mel.

'Oh, he's, my stepfather.'

'Right. Dah dah dah. Well, he could'a done it. No one saw him the night before so he could'a come back to Melbourne then back to the 'wang. I interviewed him and he put on a good act. But my money's on him.'

Mel looked sideways to where Lou sat. She looked smug. Mel bristled.

'How can you be so sure it's Dan?' she asked.

'Come on, Love. She sneaks out for a quickie with some guy. He's been suspicious for a while. Pretends he's at a car show. Follows her, catches her out. Gives her one and kills her. Oldest crime in the book. Dah dah dah.'

'Any proof of that?' asked Mel through gritted teeth.

'Wasn't much proof of any sort,' he replied.

'What about forensic evidence?' asked Lou.

Terence pulled at this bottom lip. It revealed a set of teeth stained yellow from nicotine and caffeine. A sliver of gold glinted in the light.

'Yeah ... bit of a botch up. Not much to collect.'

'What do you mean?' asked Mel.

'The body was dumped behind a skip between some bags of garbage. It rained real heavy during the night and the ground was wet and muddy. A lot of ground and garbage got trampled. They took samples from her but couldn't get anything conclusive.'

'What about semen? She was raped,' said Mel.

'Raped. Yep. But no semen. There was a faint trace of some bodily fluid on her thigh but the rain washed most of it away. And the boot that cracked the bone contaminated that anyway. Couldn't get anything conclusive.'

Mel winced.

'Surely there'd be some DNA?' said Lou.

'Nah. Rain cleaned up the mess.'

Mel's nails dug into her clenched fists.

'She put up a fight though? What about skin under her nails or something?' she said.

'You been watching too many crime shows, girlie,' he said with a smirk. It creeped Mel out.

'She put up a fight all right. Chunks of hair pulled out, cuts and bruises everywhere, a couple of broken fingers. I had a broken finger once. Bloody painful. Didn't do her much good though, did it? Still dead.' He chuckled. He was really amusing himself.

'For heaven's sake,' thought Mel, but instead asked, 'were any trophies taken from her body?'

'What, like jewelry or something?'

'No,' she drew a long slow breath, 'like parts of her body. Apart from her hair.'

Terence studied the space across from him. He stared without blinking for a full minute.

'Nah. Nothin' that I recall. She was pretty cut up though, so who knows?'

Lou leaned over her arms and eyeballed Terence. In the manner of speaking to a very small child, she said 'So what DID you find?'

Terence's glazed expression remained unchanged. Somewhere in the house the groans were getting louder.

'Oh, shut up, you whinging old bag,' he yelled at the wall. 'Jesus, she goes on,' he continued, still staring at the wall. 'It's the wife,' he said, by way of explanation.

'Is she ok?' asked Mel.

'She's never ok, bloody barnacle, dah dah dah. Can't do nothing' for herself. Expects to be waited on hand and foot. Bloody chain around my neck, dah dah dah.'

'Do you need to check on her?' asked Lou.

'Nah. She'll find her way out here eventually. Only gets up to eat and shit. Burden, that's all she is. I could be having a life if it weren't for her. Best years bein' wasted.'

The groaning turned to whimpering.

'Shut up!' he yelled. For a moment there was silence. Then it started up again.

'Ah, ignore her!' he said. 'Now, what did you ask?'

Lou had to think for a moment. She was worried about his wife.

'I asked what evidence did you find.'

'Nothing definite except she died around midnight and she'd

been raped and strangled. That's about it. No one saw her after she left the café and that was somewhere between 9.30 p.m. and 10.30 p.m.. There was nothin' where she was found to indicate who did it.'

'What I don't get,' said Mel, 'is if Peggy was having an affair with this guy, then why didn't they leave together? And why would she meet him at a café if they were 'nicking out for a quickie' as you put it?'

'Maybe it hadn't gone to plan. Waitress said they looked like they were havin' a bit of an argument. No yellin' or nothing but he was causin' her agitation. Waitress said she didn't look happy. They were all right when they walked in, but not after.'

'So, they came in together?' asked Mel.

'No, he came in first and she came in a bit later.'

'What time was that?'

"Bout 8 p.m.'

'Did they kiss or sit together?' asked Mel.

He hesitated for so long, Mel worried he was having a stroke. The sound of groaning filtered through the room.

'Well surely if they were having an affair, they would kiss, or hold hands or cuddle together?' Mel added trying to prompt him.

'Wait! They were sitting opposite each other!' he said unexpectedly. 'Man, crazy to remember that!'

Mel wanted to say, 'You're a detective, you moron. You're supposed to remember facts.' But she didn't.

'They were sitting opposite each other. The waitress said they were in a booth. He was in the booth already when your mother came in. He ordered a coffee before she arrived and she ordered a chamomile tea later.'

Mel was caught off guard. She wasn't expecting that detail. It made the conversation so much more personal. Her mother drank chamomile tea, long before it was trendy to do so. She never slept well, so someone told her it would help her relax. She said it calmed her. Mel felt sad and drained. This meeting was going nowhere and Terence's lack of respect for anything other than himself was starting to grate.

'Did the waitress catch anything they talked about?' she asked.

'Not really. She said they went quiet whenever she came over, but he was definitely annoying her.'

'Did any other witnesses from the café come forward?'

'Weren't many there. One woman said she saw Pam go to the toilet. That was about 9.30 or 9.45 p.m. She probably left after that.'

'Her name was *Peggy*. Did anyone see her after she left? She would have been heading to a bus stop,' asked Mel.

'Nah, didn't have any luck there either. And, like I said, none of them fancy surveillance cameras back then. Not like now. Police work's all IT and tech these days. Don't need those problem solving skills we used to have. Nah, policing 'aint what it used to be,' he said.

Lou's face contorted in several different directions but Terence didn't seem to notice.

'Exactly how long were you on the case?' asked Mel.

Terence thought about it. 'A few weeks. I went on leave after the wife was diagnosed with diabetes. You know, the insulin one. Bloody inconvenient. I was supposed to go fish'n up North that weekend. She fucked that up. The next three damn months were fucked up. Been going from bad to worse ever since, dah dah dah.'

He took out a cigarette and lit it. Smoke curled around his eyes, making him squint. He sucked hard on the filter, holding the smoke in before slowly releasing it through his nose and mouth, all over Mel and Lou.

'So did you interview any suspects at all?' asked Lou, turning her head away from the smoke. It wasn't the fear of inhaling that made her do it, but the fear it would start her smoking again.

'What? Oh yeah. Dan for one. He was bloody cool though. Had an excuse for everything. Tears didn't fool me. Could see right through that crap. Unfortunately, nobody else could.'

'Did he have any marks or injuries that would suggest he'd been in a fight?' said Mel.

Terence slurped his tea. 'No injuries. A small bruise on his cheek and a few scratches on his hand but he said that was from working in the shed on the weekend. Lame excuse.'

'Wouldn't there be more damage if he'd been the one to kill Peggy? I mean, she put up a hell of a fight apparently.'

'You haven't seen much in your day, have your missy?' he said. 'These guys dish it out, they don't take it. She'd be fighting him but he'd have the upper hand. She might land a punch or gouge, but he'd be the one doing the real hurtin'.'

Mel didn't want to believe any of it. Dan loved Peggy. She'd been the one he waited for all his life. He finally got her back after ten years, so why would he kill her? But a seed of doubt crept in. Maybe he preferred that, to losing her all over again. She pushed the thought away.

'Anyone else?' she asked.

'We did a line-up with some known sex offenders, but the waitress didn't pick any as the guy from the cafe. Did interview a few of the slimy little scrotes though. Nothin'.'

'So, who took over after you went on leave?'

'No one in particular. Case got shared around. Leads went cold. Unsolved case, dah dah dah.'

Mel put her pen down. Terence took another drag on the cigarette and Lou leaned back in her chair. The groaning became a low moan. It was sorrowful.

'Maybe she's in pain?' said Mel turning her head toward the sound.

'She's a pain in the arse,' he muttered, taking a final drag of the cigarette. When he'd sucked it dry, he crushed it into the ashtray. Mel knew how it felt.

'I better go and see what the hell she wants,' he sighed getting to his feet.

'We better go too,' said Mel, taking the opportunity to escape. She didn't think she could endure much more.

'No need. You can stay. I won't be long.'

'No really, we need to get back,' said Lou, scraping her chair along the floor as she stood.

'Thanks very much for your time,' added Mel, as she reluctantly extended her hand.

Terence shrugged his shoulders and reached forward to take it. 'No problem. Nice to have good company,' he said, gazing down her cleavage, as his hand curled around hers. His palm was sweaty and the long dirty fingernails dug into her flesh. Mel worked hard not to pull herself away. And then the unthinkable happened. He lifted her hand to his mouth and slobbered on it. Mel shuddered. She'd be soaking that hand in Dettol for days.

Lou didn't wait for her turn. She grabbed her bag and headed for the door. Mel wrenched her hand away and grimaced. 'Right, then, see ya.'

He escorted them to the door. Lou was already halfway through it. Mel folded her hands together, keeping the contaminated one in front. Terence managed to position himself between Mel and the exit so she had to press past him to leave.

Once outside she didn't hesitate. Lou was already at the gap in the undergrowth. A metre more and she'd be free. Mel wasn't so lucky. She made it halfway when the sound of something heavy and panting closed in behind her. She prayed it wasn't Terence. Lou heard it too and spun around. Her eyes said it all. 'Mel,' she shouted, 'look out!' but it was too late. She was down. Four great paws in the middle of her back, and fifty kilos of wildebeest behind it. She didn't stand a chance. The dog dripped saliva onto the back of her head. Mel screamed. Terence stood at the door laughing hysterically. Lou scrambled for her can of Aerogard, wrenched off the lid, and ran for the dog. She emptied half a can into its face before she released the trigger. Mel was gasping from the fumes and adrenaline, as Lou helped her to her feet. Terence didn't move.

'That was fantastic,' he called from behind the screen. 'Funniest thing I've seen this year!'

Mel felt Lou's grip loosen. She was re-positioning the can in her hand. Her index finger was on the nozzle when Mel realised what she was doing and pressed her hand over it. 'No, don't do it. He's not worth it,' Mel whispered.

'I just want to smother that twisted little arsehole ...' she whispered back.

'Me too, but I may need to talk to him again.' Lou had a wild look in her eyes. She was close to snapping. 'Please, Lou,' Mel begged.

Lou lowered the can but tightened her grip on Mel. They didn't look back. Lou held Mel by the waist all the way to the car. She found a towel in the boot and gave it to Mel, who used it to wipe the stickiness from her hair and hands.

'I need to drown myself in antiseptic,' said Mel. She looked a fright.

Lou collapsed into the driver's seat. 'I need scotch.'

Chapter 26

THEY DROVE BACK TO THE OFFICE VIA MEL'S HOME SO she could shower and change. Lou drank a thimble full of scotch while she waited. Mel would happily have stayed home but Campbell had arranged to meet with the three of them that afternoon, so a sickie was out of the question.

Mel reappeared washed, disinfected, and deodorised. She'd finally stopped retching. Lou was comfortable in the recliner with her feet up and a magazine in hand. 'No need to rush back,' she said as she flipped the page.

'Lou, it's nearly one. We need to go.'

Lou put the magazine down and reclined for a moment longer, before dropping the footrest to the floor and climbing out of the chair. 'If Ricky ever decides to sell that, you have to let me know,' she said.

'I promise, you'll be the first. But you may be in your 90s by the time he does. He loves that chair.'

In the car, they reflected on the frustratingly little they'd learned from Terence. They were still no closer to finding out who the mystery date was. Mel hoped Kathleen would be more helpful.

Sharin was deep in conversation with William when Lou and Mel came into the office.

'How'd you go?' they both asked in unison.

'It was like going ten rounds with Mike Tyson,' said Mel.

'And then he bites your ear off,' added Lou.

'Oooo!' Sharin winced.

They spared no detail in their recollection of the morning. William just shook his head when they finished. 'He sounds like an animal. He's the kind of guy who gives the police a bad name.'

'Yep, not a good look,' agreed Lou.

'I'll talk to Mike again if you like?' said William, 'he may be able to find something else out.'

'Thanks, that would be great,' said Mel.

William left, Mel checked her emails and Lou opened a document she was working on. Sharin was preparing a form for a funding submission that needed to be sent to organisations by the end of the week, so they were all conscientiously working when Campbell made his appearance.

He sauntered in with one hand in the pocket of his freshly pressed designer jeans and the other holding a leather-bound folder. His purple check shirt was perfectly complemented by a velvet jacket of a slightly darker shade and faux reptile skin shoes. He was a tall man, with a tanned complexion and shaved head. Lou once unkindly suggested the tan came from a bottle, but it was always consistent so no one was sure.

'Afternoon folks,' he crooned. 'How is everything going?'

'Just cut to the chase, Campbell. What's our last day, and how do you want these projects packaged?' said Lou over her computer.

Campbell shifted his weight from one foot to the other and tried not to look intimidated.

'I'll shut the door then unless you want to go to a meeting room?'

'Shutting the door will be fine. We're at the arsehole end of the building anyway, so no one will hear the screams.'

Sharin pulled a look that said 'Don't swear', but Lou just shrugged. Sharin could feel the tension rising and it scared her.

Campbell positioned himself on the edge of Mel's desk facing the partition. The whiteboard poked out above it. Mel froze.

'I think we should go to a meeting room,' she said jumping up. 'I think that would be more appropriate.'

Lou was about to argue, but Mel's head was tilting back and forth in a frenzy at the incident board, so she stopped. 'Oh, all right,' she huffed, 'if we must.'

Mel's shoulders fell forward with relief. She hurried toward the door, hoping Campbell would follow. He did.

All four of them walked the length of the corridor to the meeting room. Halfway there, Campbell excused himself and ducked into reception.

'That was close,' she said to the others.

They waited in the meeting room until Campbell finally arrived with a handful of biscuits he'd scabbed from one of the reception staff. For the next thirty minutes, in between munching shortbread, he conveyed the final arrangements that would end their careers as grants administrators.

That night Mel drank a whole bottle of wine. She figured she might as well enjoy a good one while she still could. She was supposed to call the RACV for the Wolseley, but after the first glass, she couldn't be bothered. Ricky and Annie came home to a half empty bottle and a mopey Mel.

Annie took refuge in her room with her iPad and headphones and waited for dinner. Ricky ordered home-delivered pizza, poured himself a beer, and dragged Mel to the couch. He noticed the magazine on the arm of his recliner. 'There is a magazine on my chair,' he said.

'Yes,' said Mel with her head resting back over his arm and her eyes closed. 'Lou was here.'

'In my chair?'

'Yes, your chair. She loved it. Said she wanted to buy it if you ever sell it.'

Ricky nodded approvingly. 'She has excellent taste.'

Mel peered through one eye at him. 'That recliner does not represent good taste.'

'This, from a woman who chose a leopard print sofa.'

'Now, that is taste.'

Ricky took a swig of his beer and pulled Mel into his chest. He felt warm and safe.

'Why was Lou here?' he asked.

'We went to see Terence Bailey. Oh my God, what a day!'

She re-told the day's events, without moving or opening her eyes. She finally felt ok.

Ricky was amused by the visit to Terence but concerned by the work discussion.

'Doesn't give you much time to look for another job,' he said.

'I know but the redundancy will buy me time.'

'Not that much time,' he said gently.

Mel sat up. 'Are you doubting I can get another job?'

'No, but it does take time looking, applying, interviewing,' he said.

Mel laid back against his chest and closed her eyes again. Her wine glass was close to empty. She knew Ricky would worry. He was on a contract that paid better than the average, but it was time limited. As an IT consultant, he worked hard to attract contracts and even harder to extend them. He was currently halfway through a project but with only nine months to go, anything could happen.

'I promise, as soon as we get this case sorted, I will start looking.'

Ricky didn't reply. Mel opened her eyes and sat up again. 'What's wrong?' she asked.

'Just thinking about the mortgage, Annie's school fees, replacing the shed ...'

'And I will get a job!'

'I know. But this case? It's important, I get it, but more important than looking for a job?' he asked.

Mel pulled away. 'Ricky. Seriously? The next girl to go missing could be your daughter! Yes, it's important.'

Ricky shook his head but said nothing. Mel felt his body tense and knew she'd pushed him too hard. They sat in silence. Mel drained the last drops in her glass. The rest of the evening, along with the pizza they'd ordered, turned cold.

Chapter 27

THE MAN FROM THE RACV PRONOUNCED THE Wolseley DOA. It was going nowhere. Mel rang Ricky and called a cab. There was no way she was taking the bus if she could avoid it.

When she arrived at work, she found Sharin working steadily on her application proforma in an attempt to meet the 1 p.m. deadline she'd set herself. She wanted all the groups who would apply to have a copy before the weekend. She had her email list ready to go, but two more pages to add, before proofreading it and sending it.

'Hi, Shaz.'

'Hi, Mel. Sorry, can't stop.'

'No probs.'

'Is Lou in today?' Mel asked as she passed her empty desk.

'No, she's taking her son home from hospital. She'll be back on Monday.'

'Ok. I'll stop asking questions now,' she said smiling. Sharin just nodded silently.

Mel let her be and by 12.30 p.m. Sharin was finishing her form and hitting 'send' on the email. Mel completed a spreadsheet of programs and costings and both were ready for lunch.

It being Friday, and Mel having left home without any lunch, they decided to eat at the 'hole in the wall' downstairs. Some enterprising twenty-year-old had turned a cupboard space into a servery selling vegetarian fare and before long there was a queue down the street.

'Had another date last night,' said Sharin unexpectedly while they waited in line.

'Of course! How was it?'

'Nice. Very nice.'

'Very nice?'

'Not as nice as that, but still very nice.'

'Past first base yet?' asked Mel.

'No, not really ... you know a kiss, but ...'

'That's something.'

Sharin shrugged, 'after two dates?'

'Well ... slow,' agreed Mel, 'but moving in the right direction.'

'I guess.'

'So? Fill me in. How was the movie?' asked Mel.

'We went bowling instead. Nothing at the cinema we could agree on,' said Sharin.

'Is that a concern?' said Mel.

'Bowling?'

'No. The fact you couldn't agree on a movie?' said Mel.

Sharin laughed. 'No. Bowling was fun, and we talked a lot. Couldn't do that at the movies.'

'Did you learn any more about him?'

'Not really. That's the thing I find a bit odd. He sort of gives general answers and then changes the subject back to me. It's nice to have someone interested but I'd like to know him better. I'm not sure I know him at all.'

'Are you seeing him again?' asked Mel.

Sharin bit into her felafel and chewed.

'Yeah ...' she said when she'd finished, 'Dinner at mine.'

Mel nudged her, 'That should do it.'

Sharin took another bite and ate staring at the ground. 'Do you think it's bad if I make a move on him?' she asked.

Mel laughed, 'Sharin Pentagast! This is 2019. It's expected you'll make a move!'

Sharin flushed. 'Maybe that's what I'm doing wrong.'

Mel lowered her kebab into the serviette on her lap and turned to face Sharin.

'There is nothing you're doing wrong. Maybe he's been rejected before and he's shy. Who knows? You are too gorgeous to be ignored. There will be some reason and it won't be you!' Sharin tried to smile without felafel falling out of her mouth.

'Ok. Thanks.'

Mel swayed into Sharin's arm and nudged her again. 'Go get 'em, tiger!'

Sharin snorted and this time little bits of felafel flew out her mouth. They laughed all the way back to the office.

———

Later that afternoon, Mel caught a cab to Rosa's. The dress was ready for collection so she and Annie were meeting there for one final fitting. Annie was riding her bike from school. Normally Mel would have hung it off the bike rack on her car and driven it home, but today she didn't have the Wolseley. Annie would have to ride home.

In the cab, she took a call.

'Hi, Dave.'

'Hey, Mel. I've got some news.'

Mel straightened up. 'Yep.'

'Got a few words out of the forensics assistant. Turns out Kristy, Erin and Lisa all had broken thighs. But broken after they were dead. Reckons they were stomped on,' said Dave.

'Jesus!'

Mel looked up to see the cab driver's eyes reflected in the rear-view mirror. She smiled reassuringly and lowered her voice.

'That fits for Peg as well, but what about Kitty?' she continued.

'No, but she had other broken bones.'

Mel glanced up to the rear vision mirror again but the cab driver wasn't looking back.

'So, did forensics get any clues, like boot prints or that sort of thing?'

Dave laughed. 'Becoming quite the detective!'

Mel's face burned.

'No. Unfortunately, it gave them nothing. He's well practised at cleaning up.'

'Thanks for letting me know, Dave. Wish it wasn't still more of the same as Peg's. I doubt it's a coincidence.'

'No such thing as coincidence, Mel.'

The cab pulled up to the curb in front of Rosa's house.

'Sorry, Dave, have to go.'

'No probs. Catch you soon.'

'See ya.'

She handed the driver the fare and climbed out of the car. She felt his stare at her back as she walked the short distance to Rosa's door.

Chapter 28

Annie was already there when she arrived.

Rosa, Marcus, Annie, and Rosa's sister Maria, were sitting at the table eating afternoon tea. Maria had brought her famous fruitcake. The cake won so many ribbons at the Melbourne show they asked her to stop entering. Of course, she didn't. She liked to win.

A place was laid for Mel. A delicate tea set of fine bone china painted with purple violets sat on a white lace tablecloth. In each saucer was a silver teaspoon and under it a white linen napkin. Rosa poured tea into her cup as she sat down and Maria offered her cake. She felt loved and wanted. It was a familiar ritual and one she'd been doing all her life. When she was little, Peg was absent a lot, so she would live between her grandmother's house and Mrs Rebello's. There was always a warm welcome, something to eat, and a loving embrace. It was where she learned the gifts of hospitality and generosity.

Although Mel created a break in conversation, she didn't distract it. Discussion flowed as if she was there from the beginning. Annie was the centre of attention and the semiformal the topic.

By way of update, Maria informed Mel that Annie had a date

for the occasion. Although it was Rosa's house, Maria took charge. She was the eldest in her family, and everyone deferred to her.

'Let me guess,' said Mel. 'Lucas.'

'How'd you know!' exclaimed Annie.

'Mothers intuition,' she said smiling at Rosa and Maria. 'And the fact he has been hanging around you for weeks with stars in his eyes!'

'MUM!'

'Well, he has. He definitely has a crush on you!'

Annie rolled her eyes. 'Now I'll feel funny with him.'

'It's better to have someone who likes you taking you to the formal than someone who's really not that interested. You'll have the photos for a long time and you don't want to cringe every time you look at them,' said Marcus.

'Hear, hear,' agreed Mel.

'Did you go to a formal, Marcus?' asked Annie.

He was sitting opposite her, between Rosa and Maria. Mel noticed how blue his eyes were and wondered if he wore contact lenses. He was cutting his cake into small pieces but put his knife down as he spoke. 'Yes, I did. What an unfortunate experience that was.'

'Can you tell us?' asked Annie leaning forward.

'Only if you want to,' interjected Mel. But she was just as curious.

He pushed the knife to one side and rearranged the napkin. 'I asked this girl called Charlotte to be my date. She was gorgeous. Every boy in our year wanted to go out with her. I thought I'd won the jackpot when she said yes. I don't think I have ever been more nervous in my life.'

He fidgeted with the teacup and Rosa refilled it.

'Anyway,' he continued, 'I took her along thinking my night was going to be the highlight of my school life, but she was only using me to make Jake Hoffman jealous. Charlotte was all over me for the first half hour but never took her eyes off Jake. It worked. He dumped the poor girl he was with, and the two of them made out all night in the corner of the room. Turned out to be the greatest humiliation of my school life!' He'd been looking at his plate the whole time he spoke. He looked up and grinned. 'I burned the photos.'

'What a bitch!' said Annie.

'Annie!' exclaimed Mel, and Rosa together.

'Well, she was, wasn't she?' said Maria.

They all agreed.

'Did they end up together?' asked Annie.

'Not for long. He learned a few truths about her and gave her the flick. I felt some satisfaction with that.' He took a bite of cake.

'And the moral is,' said Mel, 'that Lucas is a good date for you.'

'Yeah, he is,' agreed Annie.

'Now, let's see this dress,' said Maria.

Annie and Rosa left the table, leaving the others to chat about the weekend.

'I was hoping to visit my friend Kathleen in Ballarat,' Mel was saying, 'but the Wolseley's in for repair and Ricky's got a golf tournament.'

'I might hire a car,' she said as an afterthought.

'When were you thinking of going?' asked Marcus.

'I'm supposed to be meeting her for lunch tomorrow.'

'I could give you a lift,' he said.

'Really? But you usually leave tonight.'

'I can delay it. If Rosa doesn't mind. I'll need to check?'

'She won't,' said Maria on Rosa's behalf.

Mel smiled behind her napkin. 'If you don't mind, that would be great,' she said.

'Only problem is getting you home. I'm not back 'til next week,' said Marcus.

'Oh, that's no problem, I can catch the train. That works for me.'

'Ok then, it's a date!'

'Terrific! Thanks, Marcus. What time shall I meet you here?'

'I can pick you up if you like. Save a cab fare,' he said.

They agreed to meet at 9.30 a.m. and Mel made a mental note to check the train timetable when she got home.

'Annie! You look exquisite!' gushed Maria getting to her feet. She was not easy to impress, so Annie knew she looked good.

Mel turned and caught her breath. Annie was radiant as she moved silently across the carpet. Light became shade and shade became light as the fabric glided back and forth across her body. A cascade of translucent silk flowed from hip to floor, but the bodice clung to her, defining her youthful figure.

'You look incredible,' said Marcus. 'That Lucas is one lucky young man!'

Annie blushed crimson, but her smile beamed pure joy.

'Turn around, turn around,' said Maria spinning her hand in front of her.

Annie obeyed, twirling slowly like a ballerina in a jewel box.

'Truly breathtaking,' she concluded. 'You have done a brilliant job, Rosa!' This time it was Rosa who beamed. Praise from Maria was hard won.

'Mum?'

'You look so grown up ... so, so beautiful.' Mel's voice caught in her throat. Maria leaned into her. 'Just like her mother.'

With the dress packed in a suit-bag, shoes in their box, and money exchanged, Mel headed home in a cab, called for her by Marcus. Annie left on her bike, determined to beat her mother home. She had a small head start and a tailwind. Chances were in her favour.

In the cab, Mel considered how lucky her life was. Time with the women she loved always did that for her.

Chapter 29

TRUE TO HIS WORD, MARCUS ARRIVED AT 9.30 A.M.. Mel rushed around trying to find her sunglasses, so Ricky met him at the door.

'She won't be long,' he said, as he held the door open for Marcus to enter. They stood in the hallway making small talk until Mel barreled through with her handbag, glasses, and keys in one hand; water bottle and shopping bag in the other. She was puffing from fluster rather than exertion.

'Right, ready,' she smiled at them both.

'Have a good day,' said Ricky, kissing her. 'And thanks for driving her,' he said to Marcus.

'No problem.'

Marcus drove a white Prado. With heated leather seats. Mel was impressed. 'Nice car,' she said approvingly.

'Thanks, I like it. Too big for the city but perfect for Avoca,' Marcus replied.

They began the ride with general chit-chat about the traffic, weather, upcoming horse racing events and Eddy.

'I'm starting to wonder about Eddy's girlfriend,' he was saying.

'You know for sure he has a girlfriend?' said Mel, surprised.

'Not for sure, but I suspected.'

'Not anymore?'

'Don't know. If he does, she's a wild one. He has some interesting stuff on his Instagram feed.'

Mel turned to look at him, 'What do you mean?'

Marcus diverted his eyes from the road for a moment. 'The other day, he'd gone to his room for something and left his phone on the coffee table. It was still open when I came back from the loo, and there was a picture of someone in a leather harness and another one wielding a whip.'

Mel gasped. 'Oh!'

'I'm no prude, but I tell you what, 'still waters run deep'. I wouldn't have picked him for being into that,' said Marcus.

Mel thought for a bit. 'Mmm. Me neither. Hope Rosa never sees it. She'll think he's a pervert.'

'Yes. She's very Catholic, isn't she.'

'Mmm. And very old school!' said Mel.

'Maybe Eddy's breaking free from all that control,' said Marcus.

'I'm not sure it was 'control' in a bad way. Just a way to manage the unmanageable after Gino died.'

'Fair call. Must've been hard for her, raising kids and building a business on her own.'

'I think it was. But she never showed it. If anyone could succeed, it was Rosa,' said Mel.

'And you've known her all your life?' asked Marcus.

'Yep. Rosa was a second Grandmother to me. I think part of my attraction to Ricky was his Italian heritage. It was so familiar.'

The conversation explored Mel's youth and made its way to the eventual discussion of Peggy's death and the reason for her visit to Ballarat. They rehashed what Mel knew and what she might find out.

'I'm hoping Kathleen can shed some light on the man Mum met at the café the night she died, or at least some of the people she might have been seeing around that time,' she said. 'I know it's like trying to find a needle in a haystack, but I need to do it.'

'Yeah, I can imagine,' said Marcus. 'And if you find the man, then what?'

Mel thought for a moment. 'I guess I'll do a bit of investigation on him. He may not be the one who murdered Mum, but he could well fill in a whole lot of gaps. And if he is the one, then he's a dead man.'

'Sounds like you have it all worked out.'

'No, not really. It will probably take a lifetime to find the truth, but I have that, so why not?'

'Absolutely,' agreed Marcus.

They were silent for a while before Marcus spoke. 'You know I could have a look through old records or newspapers, for any news about your mum at the Ballarat library if you like. There might be something from when she lived there. I'd have time and it could be interesting.' He paused and looked at Mel. 'Add a bit of spice to my quiet country life!'

'Wow! That would be great. Thank you,' said Mel. 'If you're sure,' she added quickly.

'Of course. Give me a week or two and I'll see what I can find.'

'Do you get to Ballarat much?' asked Mel, worried she was putting him out.

'Most weekends. My fiancée lives there. We have one night at hers and two at mine. I need to help out at the farm so we are in Avoca most of the weekend, but escape for the bright lights of Ballarat on Saturday nights.'

Mel shook her head. 'Not bright enough for me, I'm afraid. I'm too much of a city girl. I think I'd go mad!' she said, then quickly added, "Oh sorry, that sounds so rude!'

'Not at all. It *can* do that to a person,' replied Marcus.

'Have you lived there all your life?' asked Mel.

'Yep. Except for three years when I did Agricultural Science at Uni, and now, of course, going to Melbourne during the week. Mum and Dad have always had the farm so its home for me. I do

like the breaks away but coming back is nice and Dad needs the help now, so it works for all of us.'

'I imagine that a vineyard's a lot of work,' said Mel.

'Yeah, it is. And Dad isn't getting any younger.'

'No brothers or sisters to help?'

'No, just me.'

'And your fiancée – did she grow up here too?' Mel was watching him, but Marcus kept his eyes on the road. She hoped she wasn't prying too much.

'No, she's a Daylesford girl but she moved to Ballarat when she finished Uni. That's where we met. Didn't get together then but reconnected when she moved up here.'

'I bet she's lovely.'

'Yes, she is,' he said smiling.

'Not Charlotte then!'

'God no!'

'I guess your parents will notice the difference when you marry and move on.'

'Oh, we'll live with them,' he said, then laughed. 'Not with them exactly. I have the smaller house on the property.'

'That's convenient.'

'Very. We both have our privacy, but I could never leave them alone. Farming is more a lifestyle than a job.'

'Of course,' said Mel, 'It's the city girl mentality again. Sorry.'

'No offence taken,' he said.

But it turned out to be a conversation killer.

'And you just have Annie. Happy with one?' asked Marcus, changing the subject.

'Yep. We broke the mould so she's the one and only!'

'She's certainly a terrific kid,' he said.

'Thanks. She's a good fit for us. Not so much like us that we clash constantly, but not so different that we don't understand each other. She's a good kid.'

'And, what does she want to do when she finishes school?' asked Marcus.

'Not entirely sure. She's one determined girl and thankfully has her dad's brains, so she should be fine.'

'And her mother's looks, which can't hurt.'

'You're too kind! Actually, she looks a lot like Peggy. As she's getting older, she looks more and more like her. It's strange to think Annie is the age Peggy was, when she had me.'

'She was very young, wasn't she?'

'Young and wild. In that way she and Annie are complete opposites,' said Mel.

'Annie's not a risk taker then?'

'No, she's quite conservative. I don't think she'll be running off too early.'

'Not even with Lucas?' said Marcus.

'No! No. She is super keen on a career. She likes school, likes studying ... Not me, I hated it. And thankfully she goes to a good school.'

'Which one is that?' asked Marcus.

'St Cristobels in ...'

'Ah. A fine catholic institution!'

'Yes, that's the Italian Catholics' influence,' said Mel.

Marcus nodded.

'It's what Ricky wanted. He's a devout but non-practising catholic who insisted his daughter be raised in the faith. I couldn't have cared less. Besides, they do guilt so well! I'd never have managed that as successfully!'

'I guess it can be useful.'

'It'll keep her on the straight and narrow for a while anyway,' said Mel.

'My parents made me play sport to keep me on the straight and narrow.'

'Well, she does that too.'

'What does she play?' he asked.

'In winter she plays hockey and in summer, soccer.'

Marcus raised his eyebrows. 'Soccer?'

'Yep. Another of her father's influences. Ricky gave her a

soccer ball the moment she could stand up. It's fabulous 'coz they play together.'

'Sporty, clever, and beautiful. She has the world at her feet.' Then he added, 'Sounds like my fiancée.'

'How wonderful. And what does she do?'

'She's a teacher. Trained as a primary school teacher. Loved it,' he said.

'Where does she teach?'

'At the moment she's not. She's taken some time off to travel.'

Mel looked surprised. 'Without you?'

'Yep. I encouraged her. She always wanted to backpack in Asia, so I said she should just go. Get it out of her system. I have no interest in backpacking or Asia, so she might as well.'

'That's very mature of you!' said Mel.

'Not sure she would agree with the mature bit!'

'Has she gone for long?'

'Just the term,' he said.

'That'll go quick.'

'Hope so,' he said. 'I miss her.'

'I bet,' said Mel.

Marcus nodded and returned his attention to the road. The conversation lulled and Mel took the opportunity to open her water bottle and take a sip. Marcus commented that he wished he was so organised and asked if she would mind if he pulled into a servo to buy himself one, which he did at the next opportunity.

Mel watched as he climbed down from the cab and weaved his way between a car and the bowser. He was a catch for anyone. Tall, football shoulders, strong thighs.

'God, stop it,' she said out loud to herself. She stretched her legs. Her toes touched the wall of the footwell. She stretched still further and tapped the wall. She surveyed the cavity beneath her. It was immaculately clean. She'd never managed a clean car. It drove Ricky crazy.

Her gaze followed the line of the glove box across the dashboard and down into the cavity behind the gear stick. It was as tidy as the rest of the car, except for a nail file and sparkly silver clip tucked at the back of it, and two gold lolly wrappers in the front. At least he had one vice.

She looked up and around. He was still inside the kiosk, waiting his turn in line. Mel ran her finger across the thumbnail she'd snapped in her rush that morning and reached for the nail file. She kept watching Marcus in the queue as she ran the file back and forth until it was smooth. She brushed the nail filings off her lap into her handbag and slid the file back into place.

Marcus returned carrying water and a packet of Werther's caramels. He climbed into his seat, dropped the water bottle into the cup holder, and opened the packet.

'Want one?'

'Thanks,' replied Mel as she reached in and took one.

'I can't travel without them,' he said.

'My Gran always kept Pascal's fruit bonbons in the glove box. Remember them?'

Marcus shook his head. 'Nope, sorry.'

'Too young!'

'Were they good?'

'Delicious. Fruity. Tooth breakingly hard!'

Marcus dropped a Werther's into his mouth. 'These just pull your fillings out.'

Mel laughed. 'Yes, they do!'

Marcus started the car and pulled out into the fast-moving traffic.

'Are you sure you're happy to go to the library in Ballarat if your fiancée's not there? I don't want to put you out,' said Mel.

Marcus opened his drink and swallowed a mouthful. 'It's not a problem at all. I told her I'd check on her apartment when I could, so it's no imposition.'

'Well, thanks a lot, I appreciate it.'

Marcus nodded. 'All good,' he said.

Half an hour later they were on the outskirts of Ballarat, with Mel fumbling in her handbag for the piece of paper on which she'd jotted Kathleen's address. Marcus didn't know the street so pulled over to check his street directory.

'You need a GPS,' said Mel.

'I'm avoiding one as long as possible,' he replied. 'I don't want to lose my navigating skills.'

Mel confessed, that she had long ago lost hers. In fact, she wasn't sure she'd ever had them.

Marcus found the address, noting the streets that led to it. As it turned out, they were only a few minutes away.

The Prado pulled into the driveway of a neat, double brick home, with freshly cut lawns and evenly spaced beds of white and purple agapanthus. It was 90s suburbia. Mel felt instantly nostalgic and nervous. She hoped Kath was ok with this visit.

She prayed it would go well. Marcus sensed her anxiety and touched her arm. 'Good luck,' he said, 'hope you find what you're looking for.'

'Thanks,' said Mel, pulling her lips into a half smile. 'I've got my fingers crossed,' and she held up two interlaced fingers, before reaching down to collect her bags. She thanked him for a final time and climbed down from the cabin.

Chapter 30

KATH WAS STANDING IN THE DRIVEWAY. SHE WAS JUST as Mel remembered. A little greyer, with creases around her eyes, but still with that same Kath smile.

They hugged, chatted about the trip, and fell into step as if no time had passed. Kath was the warm easy-going one of the Kath and Peg duo.

Whether by coincidence or convenience, it was only the two of them for lunch. Her men were at football. Mel waited until they were halfway through their ham salad before asking the questions that would take an afternoon, or perhaps a lifetime, to answer.

She started with the evening Peg disappeared and the call a few nights before, but Kath had nothing new to add. She was also unaware of anyone called Robert Lang or John Coreman.

'I'm sorry I can't give you more Mel, I just don't know anything else.'

'I've always wondered who the 'ghost from the past' was or if she was just being sentimental.'

'There were plenty of ghosts, Mel.'

'Tell me about them.'

Kath gently laid her knife and fork on the plate. 'How long have you got?' she smiled.

'All day?'

Kath poured some water into her glass and refilled Mel's. 'The thing I loved about your mum,' she said after she took a sip, 'was her passion for life. The good and the bad. Ah, I learned a few things from her!'

Mel raised both eyebrows.

'And no, I am not sharing,' said Kath.

Mel pouted, then nodded. 'Fair enough.'

'The point is,' continued Kath, 'all those investigators assumed Peg's ghosts were bad. But they weren't. Not all of them. You know, when she worked at the nursing home here, she was adored. Her way with the people she nursed was beautiful. She just *got* old people...and babies. It was everyone in between she struggled with. She had this patience you didn't see anywhere else in her life. She was like two people.'

'I never saw that in her,' said Mel.

Kath cocked her head and studied Mel's face. 'When you were a baby, she sat for hours by your cot watching you sleep, and when you cried, she rocked you for however long it took to calm you. If there were shards of glass in her feet, she would still have kept rocking until you were settled.'

Mel felt the sting of heat behind her eyes. 'So why did she leave me?'

'She didn't. You left her.'

Mel opened her mouth but Kath raised her hand. 'Not deliberately. I mean, she gave you to others to care for because she thought, or was more likely convinced, it was best. You must remember Mel, it was 1972, she was fifteen, and society considered her a juvenile delinquent. An unfit mother. She was none of those, but she didn't know better. Everyone made it clear, that's what she was. So that's what she became.'

Mel choked back a sob and Kath covered her hand with her

own. 'For Peg, giving you up to Gran was both the best and worst thing she could do.'

'I never knew that, Kath,' Mel said when she trusted herself to speak.

'I know. She wanted you to belong, so she didn't interfere. But she was always there, Mel. In her crazy Peggy way!'

'Why did she stay away so much then?'

'I think it was her way of coping. You had a nice life with Gran and Pop. It was stable. She knew you were ok. She didn't want to mess it up for you. She felt she'd screwed it up when she left Dan. And it hurt to be close to you but not close – do you know what I mean?'

Mel burned with the pain of loss all over again. She hadn't expected this and she wasn't sure she was ready. A tear escaped and she rushed to brush it away.

Somewhere in the house a clock chimed. The Westminster gong heralded a quarter past the hour. The air in the room smelled faintly sweet and the cool breeze flowing from one open window to another cooled the heat in her face.

Kath stood up. 'I've got some of Peg's things for you to take,' she said moving to the hallway.

The carpet muffled the sound from her rubber soles as she moved lithely along the hall. Her slender hips dipped slightly to the right but her shoulders were square. She'd been a practising yoga teacher since her retirement and it kept the sagginess of age at bay.

She came back with a cardboard box and placed it on the table beside Mel.

'Peg left these with me when she moved back to Melbourne. She said she'd come back for them, but she didn't. They've been in my spare room cupboard for years.'

Mel lifted one thing after another out of the box. There wasn't a lot – two handbags, one a black and silver evening bag, the other a cheap denim holdall; a black and silver fascinator that matched the evening bag; two framed photos – one of Mel and one of Gran and Pop; a wooden elephant, two glass swans, a teddy bear holding a red heart, a cushion with orange sequins in circular patterns, a set of sheets and doona, a small Turkish lamp, a crocheted purple knee rug, eight doilies, and a dolly Vardan toilet roll cover.

Mel held up the last three items and winced 'Truly, these are hideous.'

'I think they were gifts from the nursing home,' smiled Kath.

'And this fascinator,' Mel grinned 'I could never imagine Mum wearing it!'

'Yeah, not her thing at all, but the nursing home held an annual ball, and the year she wore that, it was a 1920s Cabaret. She looked sensational.'

'I can imagine,' agreed Mel, reaching for the evening bag. 'I assume this went with it?'

'Yep. She bought it especially. And it all went together with a black beaded rah-rah dress that shook and shimmered when she moved. I did her makeup and hair. Even managed one of those little kiss curls at the front. I am sure there's a photo somewhere and if I find it, it's yours.'

'I'd love that,' said Mel opening the evening bag. It held a comb and hanky. 'She'd have broken a few hearts that night, I bet!'

'As it happens, I think she won one,' said Kath.

Mel put the bag down. 'Do tell.'

'Not much to tell really. She met someone. I remember because she was staying with us that night but didn't come home till morning. She didn't say too much. All the families with relatives in the nursing home were invited to the cabaret so he was among them I imagine.'

'Any juicy details?'

Kath laughed. 'No. Like I said, she really didn't talk about him. Probably had the one night and that was it. It was only a few months before she went to Melbourne. I'm sure she didn't make a relationship of it. Maybe she dated him a few times but she never spoke of him.'

'Wonder who he was?' said Mel.

'No one, I'm sure.'

'Mmm...' Mel mused as she fiddled with the strap on the denim holdall. 'She had a few one night stands in her life.'

'That's an understatement!' said Kath. 'But, no judgement from me. She was a beautiful woman and she knew what she liked.'

'Lucky girl,' agreed Mel, opening the holdall and reaching inside. It was empty apart from a hardcover book that she pulled from it.

It was a pink Hollie Hobbie hardcover with 'address book' embossed in neat cursive gold print. Mel flipped it open and through page after page of pencil-written names, phone numbers, and sometimes addresses. Crossings out, updated digits, and a note here and there were dotted throughout the book.

'Have you seen this?' asked Mel.

Kath caught her lip between her teeth. 'Yep. I feel wrong for looking but I did.'

'Anything?'

'Honestly I don't know. A lot of those people are way in the past. I knew some of them, not others. Pretty sure she hadn't updated it in a long time.'

'Do the police know about this?' asked Mel.

'Yep. They interviewed me a couple of times and I showed it to them. They didn't seem that interested. Pretty sure they took a copy though. No one asked me more about it.'

Mel studied the pages. The handwriting was small and neat. She recognised a few names but the addresses had long ago changed. Many she'd never heard of.

'She left this stuff with you the year before she died?'

'Yes. She and Dan got together at a wedding and within a week she moved to Melbourne. Packed a suitcase, chucked the rest in the box, dropped it to me, and drove to Melbourne. That was it.'

'Why didn't she take the box?' asked Mel.

'I reckon because it made the move permanent. And I'm not sure she thought it would be.'

'Really?' said Mel.

'Yep. She loved Dan, but I don't know... maybe she just didn't trust things could ever work out for her. Anyway, she said she'd come back for the box when she was sure.'

'But she didn't.'

'Nope.'

'She didn't have much did she?' said Mel.

'Didn't need it. Rented a room from a friend of one of the nurses she worked with.'

'Did you see much of her when she lived there?' asked Mel.

'Not lots. I had the kids. It was busy. But we were always close, you know?'

'Yeah.'

'She'd drop in. Sometimes we'd have a night out together. Not often ... but ...'

'Do you know the nurse she rented from?' asked Mel.

'Not really. Her name was ummmm ... Tanya. Tanya ... I don't know, Crompton or Crowley or something like that. I met her a couple of times, but I didn't know her.'

'I'd love to talk to her,' said Mel.

'Not sure how you'd find her. Could be anywhere.'

'Guess I could start with the hospital.'

'Yeah. Or I can ask around if you like?' said Kath.

'Would you?'

'Of course. Ballarat's not that big. Everyone knows someone. If she's here I reckon we can find her.'

'That'd be great,' said Mel.

'What are you going to ask her when you find her?'

'I don't know yet,' said Mel.

Chapter 31

MEL RE-EXAMINED THE ADDRESS BOOK ON THE TRAIN journey home. Kath packed Peg's things into a suitcase which sat awkwardly at her feet. They'd parted with a promise to speak soon.

Nothing in the pages provided a clue. There were names. Men and women. Local addresses, overseas addresses. Phone numbers without prefixes long since added. There were no John Coreman or Robert Langs amongst them.

Mel phoned Dave to update him. 'I'll photocopy the book tomorrow and email you,' she said.

'Excellent. Glad you had some luck. I can't say the same.'

'Nothing new from your forensics mole?' asked Mel.

'Nope. Waiting on some toxicology reports.'

'That'll be interesting.'

'Will be. Also, there's a re-enactment being filmed for Tuesday night's news. Only for Kristen. In a few weeks there's one for Erin and then Lisa.'

'Fingers crossed it leads somewhere. Time for the next poor girl is running out.'

When they hung up, she leaned back into the seat and stared at a blur of green and blue whizzing past her window. She thought of the things Kath had told her about her mother. Of truths she had not known. Of fabrications she'd told herself to fill in the gaps she hadn't understood. It was as if something large and unmovable was pushed aside and she could see the view. A view she didn't know existed. But somewhere in the very fabric of her, it felt right. Knowing her mother had loved her enough to sacrifice her own needs for Mel's, had shifted the sense of loss and replaced it with a deep feeling of joy that served to close that tiny space in her heart that had been open for so long. She let her eyelids softly close and for nearly two hours lost herself in the past and what could have been.

The suitcase with Peg's belongings sat open on the lounge room floor with Annie inspecting each one carefully. She claimed the Dolly Vardan toilet roll holder for her own.

She stood the partly faded photo of Mel, on the coffee table. 'You were so cute!'

Ricky broke into song. 'You must have been a beautiful baby, coz baby look at you nowwwww'

Mel hit him with the orange cushion.

'It's a cool pic of Gran and Pop too,' said Annie.

'Yeah, it's beautiful. Wonder who took it?'

'Clearly not Pop!' said Annie.

'Peg?' suggested Ricky.

'Maybe.'

'There are some pretty retro things in that suitcase,' he said.

'Yeah, might be worth a fortune,' suggested Mel.

'You surely wouldn't sell any of it?' said Annie.

'Nah.'

'What will we do with it?' asked Ricky.

'Do we have to do anything?' said Mel.

'No, I guess not.'

Mel knew Ricky was mentally adding another pile of junk to the shelf in the shed.

Annie lifted out the evening bag from the bottom of the suitcase. Kath had wrapped some tissue around it, but it slipped out from the folds of loose paper.

'Oh Mum, this is lovely,' she said running a hand along the smooth satin 'And ... it would match my dress!'

Mel nodded 'It would.'

'May I?'

'I think that would be terrific.'

'Yay! Thank you.' She jumped up. 'Just going to see how it looks.'

'Well, something positive came from that trip,' said Ricky, watching Annie leap up the stairs two at a time.

'Lots did. So much I didn't know about Peggy. So much I have to tell you. I assumed, when I shouldn't have. Never gave her a chance really. It's weird, isn't it? You have this idea of someone, but then something changes and it's a whole new idea. Life's a veneer, Ricky. Nothing is as it appears.'

Ricky slid a finger under her chin and moved her gently toward him.

'This isn't a veneer, Mel. This is very real,' and he kissed her – gently, longingly. And she believed him.

Chapter 32

MEL RELINQUISHED AND CAUGHT THE BUS ON MONDAY morning. She'd armed herself with sunglasses, a big bag and a game of solitaire on her phone. It was still in her hand as she stepped down from the bus. It rang and she answered to a very upbeat Ricky.

'Guess what?' he said.

'What?'

'Annie's found something that could be useful.'

Mel's footsteps slowed.

'That purse, the one she wants for the formal,' said Ricky.

'Yep.'

'She was snooping ...'

'Dad!' Annie yelled in the background.

'Ok, investigating ... and found a piece of paper, well a torn corner really, stuck under the frame. It has four digits and part of a fifth written on it and the letters n..o.. like abbreviated for number.'

Mel stopped. The guy walking too close behind her smacked her shoulder. They both swore, then apologised. Mel moved to a wall and pressed herself against it.

'It might be nothing but ...'

'But it might be something. Can you send me a picture? I'll check the address book for numbers.'

'I will, as soon as I get to work.'

'Thanks honey, that would be great,' said Mel.

'And I'll have a chat with Liew. He's the contractor doing the ATM and phone programming for our project. If those numbers are part of a phone or credit card number, he'll find it.'

Mel smiled at the phone. 'Did I ever tell you I love you?' she said.

The first photo Ricky emailed, showed four digits in black pen 3758, a gap and then a fifth number that was hard to determine. The girls considered it could be a part of a letter or a number, so discounted it as something to follow up.

Mel scoured each page of the address book looking for a match with the numbers they had. Sharin and Lou stood over her, scrutinising every number in case she missed one. The only one with matching numbers was a postcode. Wandong in country Victoria. The address was for White St and the name against it was Susie Preston. A phone number was penciled in, rubbed out, and written over.

Mel punched the air. 'This could finally be something!'

'Or nothing,' warned Lou.

'Please Lou, just for once go with me on this.'

'Just sayin'.'

Mel's shoulders slumped 'Please.'

'Ok, I just don't want you getting your hopes up. This thing's years old. We're joining dots in the milky way here.'

'Give her a call,' urged Sharin.

Lou looked sideways at Sharin, who turned to face her full-on. 'She should phone her,' repeated Sharin.

Lou picked up the office phone and handed it to Mel. 'At least it will be a private number so she can't phone you back if she's a nutter.'

The phone rang until it rang out. Mel phoned again.

On the second ring, it answered. The voice sounded breathless. 'Hello, sorry I had to run from outside. Did you call just now? Missed it by a whisker.'

'Yes, I did, my name's Mel Cooke and I hope you don't mind me phoning but I'm looking for some information about my mother.'

'Right.'

The voice was efficient, pragmatic.

'Umm, my Mum was Peggy Hilliard and she has an address book with a Susie Preston in it with this number. Does she live there?'

'Not anymore. Lives in Perth. Only get to see her about once a year if that. She's my daughter.'

'Uh right. Did you know Peggy?'

'Name doesn't ring a bell. Has something happened?'

'Not recently. Mum was murdered in 1992 and I'm trying to find out more about it. I hoped Susie could help.'

'Dear me. So sorry. Come to think of it, I do remember Susie mentioning a girl she did nursing with died in that way. I'd forgotten. It was so long ago.' She paused. 'I'm so sorry, that was insensitive.'

'No, it's fine. It *was* a long time ago,' said Mel, but a tightness in her chest was forming.

'Look, I can give you Susie's number. Not sure how she can help, but if there is something, then maybe?'

Mel took the number. It was another hour before she called. Perth was two hours behind and she didn't want to catch Susie at breakfast. When she phoned, the voicemail answered. Two hours later Susie called back.

They spoke for only a few minutes and ended where they began. With nothing. Susie had studied nursing with Peggy but then she'd met a West Australian Miner and moved to Perth and

CLAIRE HARRISON

they lost touch. She'd been shocked by the news of Peggy's death when it happened, but she knew nothing of her life at the time.

Mel tried, and failed, to keep the disappointment out of her voice. Susie apologised too many times for something she didn't need to apologise for. Mel hung up and excused herself. The girls let her go. She sat in a toilet cubicle and stared at the back of the door. She wondered if the answer might be there because she sure as hell couldn't find it anywhere else. When she'd finished tearing several sheets of toilet paper to shreds, she came back to the office.

Sharin and Lou were fixed on their screens. Lou held up a few sheets of paper and waved them at her. 'Yours is on your desk. Time to work,' she said.

For the second time in as many hours the spike of agitation she was feeling for Lou snared her.

'I get it, Lou, just had a few things on my mind.'

Lou looked up. Her hand fluttered with the papers slowly to the desk.

'Melinda Jane Cooke. I might be a pain in your arse, but I am not always an arse. These papers ...' she said, waving them again 'are copies of your address book. We're working through the list of names again, checkin' every detail and running them through Google. We'll make phone calls later. Your pile is on your desk.'

All the muscles in Mel's face softened. 'I ...'

'Don't ... just get your toosh into that chair,' said Lou.

Mel sat down, picked up the list, and started working her way from R to Z.

At the end of the day, she gathered all the pages and emailed them to Dave with the notes they'd made. Progress was slow. Life had split like light in a prism in the years since the address book was used, and travelled in all directions.

Dave phoned. 'Got the info thanks.'

'Not sure what's worth following up? You're the journo, I need some help.'

'Leave it with me and I'll have a look.'

'Thanks. The girls and I can do some calls tomorrow. Just let me know where to start.'

'No probs,' said Dave.

'You found anything to make my day?' asked Mel.

'Nah. Still waiting on the toxicology report. Might give my new forensics friend a call now.'

'Ok, speak to you tomorrow.'

The phone went dead. Lou and Sharin were gone. The gloom of early evening settled itself on the walls and ceiling. The light in the hall buzzed but otherwise it was quiet.

Mel stood in front of the incident desk. It was days since they'd updated it. The last thing added was the map and a web of string that crisscrossed the page, tying death together. She threw the cover over it, turned out the lights and left with only the hope that tomorrow would be better.

Chapter 33

Sitting in front of the TV in a dark room watching the re-enactment of twenty-two-year-old Kristen relive her final hours was a peachy way to end a day. Mel had come home grumpy. Dave had phoned late in the day with little to add to their search of the address book, and all the calls they'd made proved fruitless.

Ricky was working from home. When she stomped through the front door that Tuesday evening, he sat her in a chair, poured wine, put a plate of cashews on her lap, and went into the kitchen to make dinner.

They ate it in front of the TV, watching misery unfold for half an hour. Neither spoke.

At 7.30 p.m., Mel's mobile rang. She glanced at the number. Didn't recognise it at first, then leaped up knocking her plate to the floor.

'Shit,' she said, as the phone stopped ringing and the call connected.

'You seem to answer with 'Shit' a lot,' laughed Kath.

'Sorry, Kath, not having a good night.'

'Well, hopefully, I can improve it. I found Tanya!'

'No way! Brilliant. How'd you do it?'

'Turns out she still lives here and she's a senior administrator at the Hospital.'

'Kath, that's fantastic.'

'Brian plays cricket with a guy who's been the finance manager at Ballarat Base for years. Knows everyone. Tanya Crossley... I got the Cro bit right ... works with him. Never married. Never changed her name. Damn good luck.'

'Damn good work, Kathleen Teale!' said Mel.

'Got her number at the hospital. I'll text it to you.'

'You are the best, thank you.'

'No problem. How's it going?' asked Kath.

Mel told her about the piece of paper Annie found. She mentioned the numbers on it but Kath didn't recognise them. They discussed more of the last few days and by the time she rang off, Mel was in a better frame of mind.

Ricky had dozed off to sleep in his recliner chair. She woke him and dropped onto his lap.

'Am I dreaming?' he smiled at her. His arms slid around her waist. She wrapped hers around his neck.

'No. All real. Kath had news.'

'Good, I take it?'

'She found Tanya.'

He pulled back from her. 'That's great news. You'll contact her tomorrow?'

'I will.'

'She must know things about Peg that will help. I wonder if Dan knew her?' he said.

'Never thought of that. I should ask him. Actually, I should send him the address book. Might be entries in there that mean something to him.'

'Good idea.'

'I'll do that now,' she said, and she climbed off his lap. He reluctantly let her go.

The few days that followed, dragged. It turned out Dan didn't know Tanya and he only recognised a few names in the address book. None of them were significant.

Mel phoned Tanya but she proved to be an ice queen, delaying Mel's conversation until 'a more suitable time. Perhaps Friday at 7 p.m..' Mel quietly crushed a ball of paper on her desk but agreed with a lightness in her voice she didn't feel. Turns out, anything other than a work conversation between the hours of 7 a.m. and 6 p.m. was 'impossible.'

By Thursday, Mel was grumpy again. She sat at the kitchen table waiting for dinner to arrive, dealing herself hands of black-jack, until she heard the key in the door, and replaced them with a game of solitaire. Ricky swaggered in, with a bag of takeaway and a smirk that was all self-congratulation. Her tension eased.

'Riccardo Melloncelli,' said Mel, laying down the cards, 'you are looking entirely too smug for a man who has done little more than bring home the bacon.'

He let go of the bag and lay across the table, bringing his face up to hers. 'I bring you the bacon AND the beast!'

Laughter started low in her gut then burst out all over the room. She leaned into him, took his face in both hands and pulled his lips to hers.

Annie walked in just as they were draining the last of their reserves.

'Oh, My God! Why do I have to have those parents who like each other? You two are disgusting. That, that, ewwwwww is for the bedroom!'

Lips peeled apart and both parents looked up. 'This could be you and Lucas at the formal,' said Mel.

'Bullshit!' said Ricky.

'Bullshit is right! Ewwwwww, Mum!'

Ricky slid back onto his feet and Mel rolled off the chair. Annie found a cloth and wiped the table. They'd just started dinner when Ricky stood up, walked over to his jacket laying over a chair, and took out a folded piece of paper from the pocket.

'I have one more treat,' he said, grinning at Mel.

'No, please, Dad. Is this going to get ugly?' said Annie.

'Your ugly is our beautiful,' he laughed.

Annie shook her head. 'I can't take much more.'

'Tell me!' begged Mel.

'Check theez out,' he said handing her the paper.

Mel unfolded it and read. Then she read it again. 'Is this for real?' she said, looking up at Ricky.

'As real as I'm standing here.'

'I can't believe it. Telecom.' She said.

Mel stared at Ricky as if that would pull the jigsaw pieces together. The number on the edge of paper in Peg's bag matched a raft of phone numbers, but one stood out. It was the number for a Telecom office in Exhibition St in the city. As Dave would say 'no coincidence.'

Although Telecom had long since become Telstra, the office still existed. Extra digits had been added as prefixes to the phone number over the years, but the last four numbers remained unchanged.

'That Liew is a genius!!' she said.

'I'll tell him that.'

Again, the smirk returned.

'Ricky this is fantastic!'

'I know.'

'Ricky,' said Mel starting to lean toward him.

'NO! no, no, we are eating!' squealed Annie.

Mel straightened up and took another mouthful of food, shooting Ricky a smile that told him what he could expect when dinner was over.

Chapter 34

THE GIRLS CONVENED TO PONDER OVER THE NEWS Ricky had shared the night before. They phoned Dave and put him on speaker.

'The bloody wonders of digital,' he was saying as Mel pinned Ricky's printout on the incident board. 'Imagine what AI will do,' he continued. 'We'll all be redundant. Oh, sorry, you already are.'

'Thanks for the reminder, Dave,' said Lou.

Sharin pouted.

'Anyway,' said Mel, ''I was thinking ...'

'Yes, we could see the wheels spinning,' said Lou.

Mel pulled a face. 'I was thinking that it's likely the person Mum hooked up with at the cabaret gave her a phone number to contact him. And that is part of the number we have, and it matches, among other numbers, one for Telecom. The guy she met in the café had a jacket with an emblem that could have been Telecom. So maybe it's the same guy?'

'Or,' began Lou.

'No, don't shut this one down, Lou. Please.' Mel pleaded.

'We have to consider all possibilities, Mel. She met that guy well over a year before she met up with someone in the café. She may have taken the number just to get her phone fixed. We don't even know it came from her date at the cabaret.'

'And we don't know he was from Melbourne. He could have lived in Ballarat,' said Sharin.

'Thank you, Miss Sharin. Good point,' agreed Lou.

'Dave, please, help me out here,' said Mel.

'Well, Lou has a point,' he began, 'but we have nothing else to go on, so let's say it was him. If it was, that means he was working for Telecom in 1991 and 1992, so maybe we can start looking at men working there at that time.'

'Dave, seriously!' said Lou, 'that will be hundreds of people.'

'Well, we can start with the office in Exhibition St. We have the number, so maybe he worked there?'

Mel gripped the desk with both hands and hung her head low. When she lifted it again, she looked defeated. 'Or maybe that was the general phone number for all of Telecom in Victoria and he could have worked anywhere. Lou's right. That's like finding a needle in a haystack. It's simply impossible.'

'I agree it's a long shot, but let's not exclude it yet,' begged Dave. 'Mel, do we have any way of finding out who the cabaret guy was? Anything else about him? Could you try Kath again?'

'I could but she really didn't know much at all. I guess there's a chance Tanya might know something. If she ever bloody calls,' said Mel.

'Tonight, isn't it?' said Dave. 'Grill her then.'

'Will do. We can reconvene after that,' said Mel, 'although, to be fair, I am not feeling optimistic.'

'Glass half full,' said Dave, 'speak with you soon.'

They hung up together.

'Sorry, Mel,' said Sharin, 'I wish this made more sense.'

'It's ok. Honestly, I wonder where all this is going. I'm starting to consider we leave it to Dave and concentrate on finding new careers.'

Lou shrugged.

'Don't give up,' said Sharin. 'We're not out on the street yet.

We can still do both for a bit longer.' She tried to smile but didn't quite make it.

Two hours later a team of departmental boffins rolled in to measure their office for its transformation into a compactus and storeroom.

'You might have spoken too soon, Shaz. We're not even dead and they're measuring up the coffin. Screw this place, we're going out to lunch to get drunk!' said Lou loudly, as she snatched up her handbag, and waved at Mel and Sharin to do the same.

They lingered over lunch for longer than necessary, but once over, staggered back to the office. That afternoon the government received little return on its investment in the Grants and Funding Department. They all agreed motivation was hard to find knowing their days were numbered. Instead, they set three chairs at Lou's desk and pulled out the cards. Lou dealt, Mel counted and Sharin played. It was a well-rehearsed routine, but one they never tired of perfecting. Casinos had all the tricks. They just needed to be trickier.

That night Mel caught a cab home. On the way through the gate, she noticed a pile of paper and plastic sticking out at all angles from the letter box. She wrestled the bulkier items out of the slot and opened the box to find 4 envelopes on its floor. All four– two Real Estate letters, one local MP newsletter, and a happy-clappy church flyer went in the bin. The rest of it she crushed into her bag. The lack of any meaningful correspondence saddened her. The mail arriving used to be a source of excitement and mystery. Now it was as predictable as death and taxes. She checked the letter box less and less these days.

Inside, the living area was strewn with shoes and bags; a straw boater lay abandoned on the kitchen table; the cutlery draw was open, an empty glass and half-full milk container sat on the bench and the sound of some screechy female band doof, doof, doofing echoed down the stairs. Annie was nothing, if not obvious.

Mel threw frozen spaghetti bolognaise into the microwave to defrost and set about relaxing into the evening. But for Mel, it was relaxation with an edge. They'd all finished dinner in front of the TV when Mel's mobile rang. It was 7 p.m. on the dot. The number was new but familiar. Her edginess sharpened. She carried the phone with her to the study and answered as she folded herself crossed-legged into the bean bag in the corner.

'Hello, Tanya,' she said.

Chapter 35

Tanya's voice was clipped and efficient. She was all business. For a nurse, she lacked a bedside manner. Perhaps that's why she worked in hospital administration.

'Not sure how I can help,' she said, 'it's been a long time and Peg only lived with me for a few months.'

'I need anything you can tell me about her,' said Mel.

'You'd know more, she was your mother.'

'She was my mother but she had a private life. I'm sure you don't know everything about your mum.'

There was a silence that Tanya didn't fill, so Mel did.

'Can you tell me about friends or places she might have visited regularly?' continued Mel.

'No idea. We didn't do anything together. She rented a room, kept to herself and went to work every day.'

'So, you never saw her with anyone?'

'Occasionally one of her friends dropped in and there was a guy who came around a few times. But then she left for Melbourne. That was sudden. Least she paid her rent up for the month.'

Mel sat up straighter and unfolded her legs.

'The guy she was seeing. Did she meet him at the Nursing Home? Do you know his name?'

'No idea. Can't remember. Only saw him a couple of times. Average sort of guy; tall, glasses, beakish nose, balding. Bit nerdy looking.'

So not Dan, thought Mel.

'Do you happen to know where he worked or what he did for work?' asked Mel.

'Umm, not sure. Maybe a tech or tradie of some sort? Maybe a farmer? Drove a ute.'

'Any markings on the ute? Names, logos. Telecom perhaps?'

'Honestly, I don't know. Maybe?'

Mel suppressed a frustrated sigh.

'Ever speak to him?' asked Mel.

'Only briefly. He came back twice after she left. Wanted her address, but she didn't leave one. No idea where she'd gone. Only knew it was Melbourne. Actually, he was a bit agitated the second time he came. I was heading out, so didn't stop. There was an older lady in the car with him. She looked kind of apologetic. He seemed pissed off I couldn't give him any details. Not my problem.'

'Peg never said anything about him?'

'We didn't have that kind of friendship. She just rented. I do remember one night she came in, really drunk. Had a bruise on her neck. Said he liked it rough and laughed. I really didn't want to know. Tell ya, it's the quiet ones you gotta watch.'

Mel stood up. 'Was she scared?' she asked.

'Didn't look like it.'

'Mmmm, wonder who he was?' said Mel.

'I don't think he was that important to her. She clearly never told him she was moving.'

'Yeah, true. Did you know any of her other friends?'

'Only one I remember was a Kath. Didn't know her well but she dropped in enough times I knew her name. Seemed nice.'

'She's how I found you.'

'Right.'

'Anything else you can remember?' said Mel.

'Like I said, we didn't do anything together. Different shifts, different routines. She was at the Nursing Home and I was at the Hospital. We pretty much kept out of each other's way. That's about it.'

'No worries. Thanks anyway. I appreciate you calling me back. If you think of anything, would you be happy to let me know?' asked Mel.

'Yeah, sure. And sorry about what happened to Peg. That was bad. The worst.'

'It was. Thanks.'

There was a pause. Neither seemed sure how to end the call. Then Tanya spoke. 'I did phone the police you know, when it happened. Said we'd lived together for a few months and if there was anything I could help with. They weren't interested. To be fair, it had been over a year since I'd seen her, but you know, I thought, maybe?'

Mel folded herself back into the chair. 'I appreciate that, Tanya. Mum would have too. Thanks for trying.'

'No worries,' she said softly.

They hung up. Mel stared at the rectangle of light poking in under the door. Was this guy someone to Peg? Or just another in a long line of forgotten lovers?

Chapter 36

Two weekends came and went without incident, but on Monday morning events took a turn. Mel was shutting the gate on her way out as a gust of wind dragged it back toward the fence post. As she leapt to grab it, a flickering sheet of white caught her eye. The empty letterbox was empty no more. Mail was rarely delivered more than twice a week and never on a weekend so she assumed the envelope waving in the breeze was junk. Nevertheless, in this wind it would end up junk in the garden so she snatched it out of the box. She turned it over. In neat black pen was her name. No address, just Mel Cooke.

She slipped it into her bag. She'd open it on the bus. She had less than five minutes and she didn't want to miss it. Thankfully it was the last one she'd have to take. Tonight, she was picking up the Wolseley. Getting parts had taken forever, but finally it was ready.

She found a seat by the middle door and crawled over to the window. With her bag tucked into her lap, she pulled out the envelope and slid her nail along the sealed flap. It opened easily.

Inside was a note and a photocopy of a photo taken many years before. The note read:

Hey Mel, how's this? Ballarat Bugle, March 1991. Picture of Peg at the nursing home. Unfortunately, only photo I could find. But maybe people there would have more information? Cheers, M.

Mel slid the note behind the photocopy and stared at the photo she could hardly believe existed. She ran a thumb over the faces and stared at the names. She'd never believed in God, but now she was beginning to have doubts.

The heading read 'Enid celebrates 100 years!' and the colour photo showed Enid smiling at the camera, seated behind a large oval cake decorated with cherries and cream. On one side of her was a woman, younger than Enid but not young, smiling with the same smile, and on her other, a man, younger again, his head angled toward Enid. Behind Enid, and slightly to her left, was a beautiful young woman beaming down at her in her chair. Her hand sat lightly, tenderly, on Enid's shoulder. It was Peg. The caption underneath read 'Enid Cowell celebrating her 100th birthday with daughter and grandson, Margaret and Peter Schneider. Enrolled nurse Peggy Cooke, Enid's favourite nurse, looks on.'

A young girl with headphones dropped into the seat next to Mel. She thumped Mel in the arm with her bag but didn't bother to apologise. Normally, Mel would have taken umbrage but today she hardly noticed. She stared at the faces. At her mother. So young, so happy. At the man who sat before her, his profile emphasising a beakish nose, glasses perched on top. He was tall, even as he sat, and his head was shining, bar for the ring of neatly trimmed brown hair. He was well built, evidenced by the polo shirt that strained at his biceps.

The bus trip disappeared before it started. Her mind took her to a place where time stood still. He looked like the man Tanya described. Could this Peter Schneider be the man her mother was seeing? Could he tell her things about her mother she didn't know? Things to put the pieces of her life together.

She realised, almost too late she'd reached her bus stop and had to rush for the closing door. Her handbag hit the teenager with the headphones in the head as she leapt out of her seat and into the aisle. She squeezed through the door and onto the street, pushing the sheets of paper deep into her bag as she did.

On the way through the hall to her office, she spotted Jill grilling a contractor about signing in. Mel was reminded of the interagency meeting they were attending later that day.

Sharin and Lou were wordlessly typing on their computers when she arrived. Her hurtle through the doorway lifted the heads of both girls.

'Guess what!' Mel panted as she rushed in.

'You won the lotto and you plan to split it three ways with us?' said Lou.

'Damn, no. Sorry.'

'Then it can't be good news.'

'It could be,' Sharin chipped in.

'It is really good news. I have a link to Mum's past that might help.'

Lou folded her hands behind her chair. 'Go on.'

Mel sat on the edge of Lou's desk and told them what she knew.

They took turns studying the photocopy of the article Marcus found for her. Nothing in the article itself was useful but the photo was gold.

'You think this guy Peter was her boyfriend?' asked Sharin.

'Not sure if he counted as a boyfriend, but Tanya said she'd seen him enough to sleep with him. Well, I guess 'him liking it rough' meant that?'

'Mmmm, maybe that was the attraction. It sure wasn't his looks,' said Lou.

'Looks aren't everything,' said Sharin.

'No, but they help. And she was a good-looking woman.'

'He's got a good bod,' said Mel.

'And maybe he was nice to her?' said Sharin.

'Are muscles and nice enough?' said Lou. 'Still, pin it up on the board Mel,' she added.

Mel pinned the photocopy to the board in the section marked 'Peg.' It now contained the piece of paper Annie found, the photos Mel brought from home, Ricky's printout from Liew and two plastic sleeves holding the address book and diary.

'I might give Kath a call. Maybe she remembers Peter. If Mum mentioned him to anyone it would be Kath.'

The girls left her to it. The phone rang only twice before Kath answered. 'I'm enjoying these regular chats with you,' said Kath after their greetings.

'Me too,' agreed Mel, 'and I'm sorry to cut straight to the chase, but did you know a guy called Peter Schneider?'

'Umm, Peter Schneider. Let me think ...' she said.

Mel waited.

'No, can't say I know the name at all. Who is he?'

'Not sure. But a friend found a photo of Mum with Peter, his mum and his gran, taken at the nursing home in July 1991. He fits a description that Tanya gave me, of a man Mum was sort of seeing at the time. I wondered if it was the person she met at the cabaret.'

'I truly don't know. I never saw him,' said Kath.

'Damn. I just wish I could find out who he is. I really need to know if he was from Melbourne or not, and if he worked for Telecom.'

'Interesting,' said Kath.

Mel filled her in on what they knew.

'He may well be from Melbourne. The cabaret was here but families came from everywhere,' said Kath.

'But he was seeing her while she was living in Ballarat,' said Mel.

'Have car, will travel,' said Kath.

'Good point!' agreed Mel, 'Tanya said he came around only a few times.'

'So maybe he visited his Gran and then Peg. All pretty casual,' said Kath.

'You need to join our investigative team,' said Mel.

'That would be fun!' agreed Kath.

'Casual fits. Except he must have been keen, or at least, more keen than Mum,' said Mel, 'because Tanya said he came looking for her after she left Ballarat.'

'Did Tanya tell him where she was?' asked Kath.

'No. She didn't have an address. But he was persistent and came back a couple of times. Tanya said he was a bit aggravated the last time she saw him.'

'Maybe she had something of his, or she owed him. Or like you say, he was just really keen to see more of her,' agreed Kath.

'I am so curious to find out,' said Mel.

'You haven't changed, my sweet.'

'Leopards don't change their spots,' said Mel.

'Your spots are precious, Mel, and I'm sorry I can't be more help.'

'You are a great help, Kath. Thank you for that. I have to go, but I'll call again soon.'

'Do that, I'd love it.'

They hung up in unison.

'It's weird. I feel like I know my mother better now than when she was alive. We take so much for granted, don't we?' Both girls nodded. Sharin stood up and joined her. 'I have no idea what she was doing during the years she was in Ballarat. I was too busy being a teenager, I guess. I wonder if Annie thinks about what I do?' she added.

'Doubt it. Kids live in a bubble,' said Lou.

'I wonder if my Julia lives in a bubble?' said Sharin.

'Julia's a dog. I'm not sure she's a thinker,' said Lou.

'Oh no, she's very thoughtful,' said Sharin.

'Ah ha. So ... this Marcus, did he find out anything else?' said Lou.

'Don't know yet, have to phone him. But this is more than I'd hoped for,' said Mel.

'He sounds like a nice person ... Marcus,' said Sharin.

'He is. It was good of him to look that up for me.'

'Single?' asked Sharin.

'No, fiancée,' said Mel.

'Bummer.'

'Why?' asked Mel.

'In case Michel doesn't work out.'

'You having doubts?' asked Lou.

'I don't know. Just being prepared.'

'It'll work out,' said Lou.

'Now how can you know that?' said Sharin.

'I feel it in my waters.'

'And your waters are rarely wrong,' said Mel.

Sharin shook her head. 'I hope you're right.'

Lou slapped the desk. 'Hey, if I can meet a half-decent man, you will.'

'Are you calling Trevor half decent?! Lou, that's the greatest compliment you've ever paid the man.'

'I'm feeling generous today.'

'Did someone have a little fun last night?' said Mel.

'Stop it. Little fun indeed,' and she slapped the desk again. 'It was a 'swing me from the chandelier', don't take ya boots off, bonk from the rafters! Thank you, Viagra!'

Sharin hooted. Mel whistled. Jill appeared at the door.

'Oops, look like you're working,' whispered Lou.

'Sorry to wreck the joy, but we have an interagency meeting today, Mel.'

'Yes. I need to contact Fleet about a car.'

'I'm taking one, we can go together. See you in the car park at 1.15 p.m.,' said Jill.

Mel nodded. 'Guess I better put some notes together,' she said.

'Break the bad news to them,' said Lou.

'What do you mean?' said Mel.

'Redundancy. They'll be running the project on their own now.'

'Yep. Maybe they'll offer me a job,' said Mel.

'Can you round up two more if they do?' asked Sharin.

'Goes without saying,' said Mel.

Chapter 37

MEL WAS THREE PAGES INTO HER NOTES, WHEN THE phone on her desk rang. It was Dave and he sounded happy.

'I have news,' he said.

'Me too, but you go first.'

'Righto. So, the toxicology and some forensics, came in. They found a few black polyester fibres on two of the girls and a filament of wood fibre on Kristen,' said Dave.

'That's positive, isn't it?' asked Mel.

'Would be if they were uncommon but the polyester could be from a million different items of clothing and the wood was treated pine.'

'No DNA or hairs or something?' asked Mel.

'Nope. Says the bodies were washed and they found sulphur on their skin. Report suggests it might have been a sulphur wash to clear away bacteria or residues. Bastard was meticulous.'

'Creepy. Didn't find anything else?'

'Only a trace of sedatives, but no other drugs. Which means he didn't use them or only before they died,' said Dave.

'Those poor girls,' said Mel.

'I don't get it. He must've kept them somewhere. They were missing for a month. Bodies were only dead for a short time when they were found. How could he keep them quiet for so long without drugs?'

'What about that guy in New York? He had a bunker he kept women in. No one could hear them,' said Mel.

'A bunker would make sense. Or a secluded building or, I don't know, a bloody soundproof cupboard! Who knows how these people think?' said Dave.

'It's just awful. But different to your sister and my mum. They weren't held anywhere before they died. It's very different.'

'Yeah, that bit, but not the rest.'

Mel could hear Dave tapping paper with a pen. She shifted the phone to her other ear.

'On that, I found out about a man Mum was seeing before she left Ballarat. Don't know much about him yet, but he was looking for her after she left. Hoping I can track him down.'

'Terrific. If I can help, let me know.'

'I have a name – Peter Schneider. It might be a wild goose chase, but he seems to fit the picture. If you come across it anywhere, look into it.'

'Doesn't sound familiar. But I'll keep an eye out,' said Dave.

'I'll send the photo I have. Not a great one, but something to go on.'

'Roger. Back to work then,' said Dave.

Mel hung up and relayed the update. Lou slid out from behind her desk and all three women walked over to stand in front of the incident board.

'You know it's the week a girl will go missing if he keeps to the pattern,' said Shaz.

Mel shivered. 'I've got Annie covered. If she isn't in school or at dancing, she's with us or friends. She's pissed at me because I won't let her ride this week.'

'Better safe than sorry,' said Lou.

They all stared at the board hoping something would leap out and give them an answer. It didn't.

'Damn, I wish we could work this out,' said Mel.

CLAIRE HARRISON

Sharin drew a line under the list.' Let's not give up yet. The three girls we've lost recently and the one who could be next, deserve everything we can give this,' she said.

'Just hope it's enough,' said Mel.

Sharin nodded. 'So, Peg died the night she went missing and was found in the morning in Lygon St. The rain washed her clean. The three other girls disappeared within a 5 km radius of each other in suburbs around Lygon St, and all turned up in locations close to it. Their murders are like Peg's, especially the last one, and their bodies had also been washed clean. Albeit with sulphur. Apart from the fact they were kidnapped and held for a month, it all seems the same,' she continued.

'There has to be a link,' said Mel. 'Even the broken thigh. That wasn't public knowledge.'

Above them a fluro light flickered. The room dimmed as a cloud floated across a weak sun outside their window.

'And we have only a few days to work it out,' said Lou.

They all stared at the words and pictures that delivered more questions than answers. It suddenly seemed amateurish.

Mel gestured at the board. 'Do we honestly have anything? Enough to work this out? And more importantly, the time to find out something that could make a difference?'

A muscle in Lou's lip twitched. 'It does seem impossible. There's really no time at all.'

Sharin turned from the board and pointed her marker at Lou. 'It isn't much time but it's not nothing. We can't give up now.'

Lou looked to Mel 'Your call.'

Mel stared at the board, reading and re-reading what was written. 'Ok,' she said. 'Let's plough on.'

'Great,' said Sharin, wagging the marker at Lou again. 'You dig up absolutely everything you can about Lang since his release from jail.'

'You,' she said aiming the marker at Mel, 'get to work on Peter Schneider. And, sorry, but Dan too.'

Mel opened her mouth to protest. Then closed it.

186

And I,' she said, turning the marker on herself, 'will update the map with everything we know. There has to be something we're missing. And maybe sulphur is used in some place there?'

Lou jumped to attention and saluted, 'Yes Ma'am.' Sharin threw the marker at her. It missed.

'You did good Miss Sharin. You'll be a detective yet,' she added.

'Might be the only job I can get when I lose this one.'

Chapter 38

THE DAY WHIZZED BY UNTIL 1.15 P.M. WHEN MEL MET Jill in the carpark. She'd been absorbed in her notes when she glanced at the clock at 1.10 p.m.. At 1.10 p.m. and 30 seconds, she shrieked, grabbed a pen and notebook, tore her jacket from the back of the chair, her bag from under the desk, and bolted for the door.

Thankfully, given her bus-catching routine, she'd worn ballet flats. She took the stairs two at a time, slipping gracelessly on the bottom one. She caught the rail with one hand as her foot slid from under her, spinning her in a half arc back onto her feet. The security boys manning the camera had a laugh at her expense.

The trip was twenty minutes across town. Traffic was building so Jill allowed thirty, plus time to park and find the meeting room. Mel settled in for a chat and a chance to get to know Jill better. They'd barely begun working together when all of it was ending, but it didn't hurt to make alliances. She needed references going forward.

Jill was sharing a few anecdotes from her previous workplace when Mel's phone rang. The name of Lexie's home appeared on the screen. Mel considered not answering it. She didn't want to interrupt Jill, but a call from the home was a cause for concern, so she answered.

She kept the conversation to a minimum, using 'ah ha' and 'mmm' frequently. But as she hung up, she knew she'd have to share it with Jill. Lexie was ill and Mel needed to see her as she'd been asking for her. She didn't want to wait until tonight. She had to pick up her car and collect Annie from dance. It would be late by the time she could visit.

'Look, I need to stop at my sister's home on the way back, if that is possible?' asked Mel.

'Is something wrong?'

'She's not well and my car's at the mechanic so I won't be able to see her until tonight and that will be too late.' Mel hesitated deciding how much information was necessary. 'Lexie has disabilities and she is prone to pneumonia. She's had a few close calls in the past and I need to check on her.'

Mel fidgeted with her seatbelt, stretching it back and forth. Jill watched from the corner of her eye.

'Normally we can't take a fleet car for personal reasons, but on this occasion, we can,' she smiled, still looking forward at the road.

Mel let go of the seat belt and the breath she was holding. 'Really appreciate it, Jill.'

'No problem.'

They chatted about the meeting until they arrived and headed inside. The time dragged. Mel provided her update, and worked hard to concentrate on the other presentations. An hour and a half later, she and Jill were back in the car, snaking through school pick-up traffic to Lexie's.

The place was new, and Lexie had been there for two years. It was a four-bedroom group home she shared with three other women and two carers who changed shifts every twenty-four hours. Mel arrived as the shift was ready to change.

Jill turned off the engine.

'Won't be too long,'

'I'll be here,' said Jill. 'It's fine, Mel.'

'Thanks so much. Truly appreciate it,' she replied.

Inside, Mel found Lexie propped up in bed with a flannel on her forehead. She was flushed and coughing. Her eyes were dull but a spark flickered when she saw Mel. She lifted her arm from the bed and held her hand out. Mel came to her and hugged her tight. The carer joined them, and they spoke for a short while about Lexie's condition. Mel and Lexie held hands throughout the conversation and Mel was reluctant to let them go when it ended.

Elspeth, the carer, walked Mel to the front door.

'If anything worsens, just get her to hospital,' said Mel. 'Last time she was like this it worsened quickly and she nearly died. We can't go through that again.'

The carer promised to keep on top of things. As she opened the door to let Mel out, another carer walked in.

'Hi ladies,' she said. 'Hey, guess who I just saw out the front?'

'Who?'

'Jill Hayes!'

'No way. Haven't seen her in ages,' said Elspeth.

Mel looked from one to the other 'You know Jill?'

'Yeah. Used to look after her son at Oakleigh,' said Elspeth.

'A son? Like Lexie?' asked Mel.

'Yeah. We used to help care for him about three years ago. Nice family.'

'I should pop out and see her,' said Elspeth.

'Nah, she said she has to head off,' said the carer.

'Shit, she's giving me a lift. Better go,' said Mel.

The woman stepped back a few paces to let her pass.

'Keep me posted,' said Mel.

'Will do.'

Both women went inside and closed the door.

Mel looked through the wire fence to the road where the fleet car sat. She could just make out Jill through the tinted windscreen and a large magnolia that blocked the passenger side window.

The footpath was smooth and wide. It was a dozen steps to

the gate but she took them slowly. Jill had a son like Lexie. And fate had brought them together, right when she needed it.

———————

Jill smiled at her as she climbed back into the car.

'You spoke to Deidre then?' she said.

'Yes. I had no idea.'

'I didn't want to say anything. You clearly had enough to think about.'

'You have a son. At Oakleigh?' said Mel, even though she knew it already.

'Yes, Damian. He's been there most of his life.'

'How old is he?'

'He's twenty-five years old,' said Jill.

'Lexie is twenty-seven.'

'She been here long?' said Jill, pointing at the house.

'Two years. She seems to like it better than the last place she lived,' said Mel.

'Your parents not alive?' Jill asked softly.

'It's a long and complicated story. Mum died years ago, and Lexie's dad couldn't cope. Lexie is my half-sister, but I hate that term.'

'Fair enough,' said Jill. 'Damian is mine but he needs continual care and I just didn't have capacity. I was posted overseas, in the army, when I fell pregnant. I came home, managed as long as I could, but I wasn't good at it.' She stared straight ahead. 'I stopped apologising for my failings long ago. I would be rocking in a corner if I didn't.'

Mel slid a hand across to touch Jill's shoulder. 'I totally get it, Jill.'

'I was on my own. I had a good career, and I'd never been one to be cooped up. I couldn't stay home day in and day out to give Damian what he needed. So, I found the best support home I could afford and between me and my brother we've looked after him that way ever since. It's not that much different to working all day and coming home to a family.'

Mel nodded. 'We do something similar. Between my husband and daughter, we see Lexie at least three times a week. Ricky often pops in on his way home from work. I think he's Lexie's husband as much as mine!'

For a few minutes they didn't speak. Just watched as tail lights spread ahead and behind. Peak hour traffic crawled and gave them space to think.

'How is Lexie?'

'Not well,' said Mel. 'But how unwell, I don't know. That's what makes me anxious. She can go from not bad to dire in a short time. She is so placid and gentle. She just doesn't complain.'

'Does she speak?'

'No, not really. A few words. Names mainly. But I know her. She's not herself.'

Mel pulled on the seat belt again. 'I should have been paying more attention,' she added. 'I really should. I've been so distracted lately and I'm missing things.'

Jill looked over to her. 'Don't beat yourself up. Facing redundancy will do that,' she said.

Mel snuck a look sideways at Jill but remained silent. She couldn't tell Jill the truth. Sure, the redundancy, the formal and even her car being out of action, seemed reasonable excuses. But the fact she was investigating murders. It sounded foolish. Such a ridiculous pursuit by a woman who, if she had to be honest, knew nothing about what she was doing. Some grandiose idea that now seemed insane. If she had niggling doubts before, they were screaming at her now. She'd let Lexie down by being absent and she vowed to change that.

Chapter 39

IT WAS AFTER 6 P.M.. THE GARAGE LEFT HER KEYS IN A safe box outside the entrance and the Wolseley under a light pole in the street. She sat in her beloved car and hugged the wheel. Finally, something that was solid and real.

That night she collected Annie from dance and picked up dinner from the Taj Mahal Indian. She didn't bother with wine. Instead, she bought Lassi.

At home she insisted Ricky curl up on the couch with her. She fretted about Lexie. She told him about Jill. They talked about the 'investigation' and how Sharin had ordered them into action, but Mel felt so unsure about any of it now. They seemed to be clutching at straws. And then Ricky ventured into discussions about Mel finding a new job. He tried to keep concern from his voice but failed. Suddenly Mel felt every fibre in her body. She was taut and tense.

On the TV, they watched the re-enactment of Erin's disappearance. The model, dressed in Erin's school uniform, her hair in a ponytail and bag over her shoulder, walked out of the school and onto the street. She waved to 'friends' before heading in the direction of McCutcheon Way under a canopy of leafy Plane trees. The camera panned out, then cut to a reporter standing at the intersection of the two roads that bordered the school, his words and actions documenting the final hour before Erin's disappearance. The camera panned in again, on the young girl bouncing carefree along a busy suburban road. All Mel could see was an image of Annie and the fear made her heart contract. For the third time in as many weeks, Mel cried in Ricky's arms. Her world was spinning off its axis. Ricky rocked her and smoothed her hair.

'Mel, theez hunt you're on. Eets no good for you.'

She didn't lift her head but mumbled into his chest, 'I'm so confused Ricky. And I'm scared.'

He rubbed her head and stroked her neck until her sobs subsided.

She pulled back against his hand and sat up.

'We'll never work this out. It's stupid, isn't it? It's too big, too … I don't know! I can't do anything, can't help anyone!' she thumped her thigh as she said it. Ricky grabbed her fist and held it firm.

'Then stop. Leave it to the police. Tell them what you have. They can follow it up.'

Mel fell back against him. Warm and safe. Her head rested on its side against his shoulder and she stretched up to kiss him under his chin. He held her and she wiggled in closer. She closed her eyes, heavy with exhaustion and gratitude for this man who loved her. She didn't want to think anymore. She wanted only to be in this moment.

By morning she'd decided to end it. She would call Dave, call the police and put this stupidity to bed. She needed only to look after Annie and Lexie. The police could do the rest.

Ricky was at the table checking emails. It was a rare day he was working from home. His laptop was open beside a bowl of muesli he was spooning into his mouth. He stopped chewing mid-mouthful as Mel came into the room.

'You ok?' he asked.

'Yes, I'll talk to the girls and Dave today. Promise. Just want us to get it all straight first so I don't sound like a lunatic when we hand this over.'

After she'd phoned Lexie's home to see how she was, Mel called Dave on her way out the door, but he didn't answer. She left a voicemail to call her back. She drove with her mind on all they knew. Tried to put some order to it. Perhaps Dave should pass it onto the police. He had more credibility.

She thought about Peter Schneider and the phone number in Peg's evening bag. *Had* he given it to her? And did he work for Telecom? Tanya said he might be a technician, so it was more than possible he did. And he'd come looking for Peg when she left Ballarat. Maybe a year later, in Melbourne, he found her. Perhaps Dave's hunch was right after all.

When Dave phoned back, she put it to him. She didn't want to tell him straight up that she was giving up the investigation. She knew he'd be upset. She decided to ease into telling him. 'I'm thinking you might have been right about Peter, after all,' she said.

'Is that humble pie I hear you choking on?' he said.

Mel laughed. 'Maybe,' she said. 'But don't think I'm apologising.'

'God forbid!' said Dave.

'Anyway, I thought we could contact Telstra and ask if he worked there when it was still Telecom. We also have a photo now, so that could help.'

'I like it,' said Dave. 'When can you get there?'

'Actually, I wondered if you could. You're better at asking the right questions.'

Dave hesitated a moment. 'I would Mel, but I'm on my way to Canberra. Not back till Thursday I'm afraid.'

'Oh, I didn't realise,' said Mel.

'It's Mum. I always visit her on the anniversary of Kitty's death. She struggles a lot around this time.'

Mel gave her condolences and said she'd see if she could get to the Telstra office instead, but really she planned to leave it for him when he was back. She didn't tell him she was giving up the case. The timing was all wrong. At work, Mel told the girls about her conversation with Dave. She held back on the rest of her news.

'It's still possible the piece of paper and Peter have nothing to do with each other,' said Lou. 'Did Tanya actually *say* he was a technician?'

'Well, no,' Mel conceded, 'she said he could be. She also said he could be a farmer or a tradie.'

'I rest my case,' said Lou.

'But if Peter *was* a technician,' said Sharin, 'then Telecom was a utility company with technicians.'

'Electricity and gas are also utility companies,' said Lou.

Mel flopped against the wall.

Lou continued 'All we have is four numbers that form part of the phone number of a Telephone company. But it's also the four digits of a bunch of other numbers. And sure, there is a possibility that Peter was a tech for that company, and he gave the piece of paper to Peg, and he is the one she met all that time later. But there are a thousand other possibilities.'

Mel slid a little further down the wall.

'I only want this one possibility,' she said. 'I want so much for it to be him.'

'I know you do, but I'm just trying to be realistic,' said Lou.

Mel nodded. 'Life sucks,' she said.

'It does,' agreed Lou.

'Actually, worse,' said Mel, 'it sucks the life out of you. And, on that, I've made a decision.'

Lou's eyes narrowed, 'What decision?'

Sharin, who'd been rolling an eraser between her palms, stopped rolling.

'I'm going to ask Dave if he'll take all we've found to the police, and end what we are doing.'

'No! Why?' asked Sharin.

'Because, honestly, we don't stand a chance of working this

out. At least not in time for the next girl who is about to go missing. And, really, probably not at all. Lou's right. We need to be realistic.'

'Oh, Mel. Are you sure?' asked Sharin.

'No, but yes.'

'When?' said Sharin.

Someone wearing hard-soled shoes stepped into the corridor and walked the distance to the tea room. A drill whined somewhere outside the building. Mel pushed back against the wall and gazed from Sharin to Lou. 'Today?' she said.

For a long minute no one said anything. Finally, Lou spoke. 'Give it another day. I know I've been the sceptic here, but let's finish what Sharin set us yesterday. At least we'll have a neat package to hand over.'

'And I've nearly finished the map. It's a narrow corridor. I'm sure the police have done it too, but hey, it can't hurt to have another version,' said Sharin.

'One more day, Mel,' said Lou.

Mel tapped the wall with both hands and tilted her head back over the prison grey paint. The ceiling was prison white. Bleak and miserable. It looked how she felt.

What was another day? Would anything they find make a difference anyway? She hadn't told Dave yet. Give it till Thursday. He was back then. Wrap it up in a bow for him to pass on. He'd be disappointed. She'd feel bad. But it would be behind her and the proper authorities could deal with it.

'Ok,' she said.

'Right then,' said Sharin lifting herself from her chair, 'let's go visit the Telstra office and see what we can find.'

Chapter 40

LOU INSISTED ON TAKING HER CAR. SHE HATED everyone's driving except her own. Sharin, being the smallest, was squeezed into the tiny rear seat. She sat sideways across it with her feet up on the seat.

Lou entered the address into her GPS and a woman speaking German relayed instructions.

'Why is your GPS speaking German?' asked Mel.

'Came that way,' said Lou.

'I'm sure you can change it,' said Sharin.

'Probably, but I'm used to it now.'

'I guess you're learning German at the same time,' said Mel.

'Yep. Bad luck if I need food or a loo, but I know left and right.'

At that moment, her GPS ordered her to '*in hundert Metern biegen Sie links ab*' and in 100m she spun the car 90 degrees at 55 km an hour around the corner. Sharin slid along the seat and back again.

'Hold onto your wig, Shaz, we're in for the ride of our lives!' shouted Mel into the back seat, as Lou wound down the window and cranked up the music. She might move slowly on two legs, but not on four wheels.

Less than seven minutes later they cruised past the building where Telecom used to be, and Telstra now stood. Lou found a park a street away and, after they'd extricated Sharin from the backseat, the three made their way into it.

The building was old, but the refurbished reception area glinted like a gold filling in a decaying mouth. The counter stretched the breadth of the room with only glass panels every metre to break it up. Behind three of the panels were fresh faced twenty somethings engaged in conversation with customers in various stages of agitation. The fourth panel housed an older man, grey around the edges, efficiently avoiding eye contact with everyone. Lou took on the challenge.

'Good morning,' she said, pressing her face close to the glass, and tapping it lightly with her knuckles.

The name on his neatly pinned plastic strip suggested this was Brian, and he was working hard to appear engrossed in the computer screen beside him.

Lou tapped harder. Brian looked up. Pulling his lips upward followed a beat later.

'Yes, Madam, how can I help you?'

'Hello, Brian,' she said, dipping her head slightly to be sure he could see her reading his name badge. 'We are actually here to find a gentleman who may have worked here.'

Brian puffed out his chest. 'I'm not sure we can help you with a personal matter.'

'Well, how about we show you a photo and you can let me know if he is familiar.'

Lou turned to Mel, who handed her the photo of Peg and Peter she'd removed from the incident board. Lou held it up against the glass. Brian stared at it for a moment. 'I'm sorry Madam, I have no idea who those people are, and even if I did, I couldn't make a comment.'

Lou sighed. She let the paper slide down the glass so she could eyeball Brian.

'We're not asking for his birth certificate. We just need to find someone who remembers him.'

'Madam, as I said, that isn't something we can help you with.'

'Well, Brian, how about you call someone who might be able to help.'

'I'm sorry, but that's not possible.'

Brian turned toward his screen. Lou ground the photo into the glass.

Mel leant over Lou's shoulder, 'Sorry, Brian. We're sorry to bother you with this, but it's a matter of particular importance. Would there be anyone who has worked here since the 90s who we could talk to?'

Nothing except Brian's eyeballs moved. First toward, then away from Mel. After several seconds of silence, Mel tried again. 'Please, Brian, there must be someone?'

Brian started to move backward away from the screen.

'If he takes another step away from this counter, I'm going in,' said Lou through gritted teeth.

Brian took a step backward.

Lou growled. 'You better be going to get someone who can help us mate!'

Brian turned sideways and moved right, toward a closed doorway. Lou followed him along the glass panels. Every pair of eyes followed her. Brian's hand was on the door handle. Lou's was thumping on the glass. 'Listen, dickhead ...' but Brian was disappearing through the door. 'Arsehole!' she yelled as he vanished. The door slid shut behind him.

Then the door to her left opened.

A tall, wiry security guard with a droopy nicotine yellow moustache stepped through it. Lou moved, as if in slow motion, to face him. Mel was sure if they had pistols they'd have drawn them. Lou was half his height, but twice the width. If he took her on, it wasn't her going down.

The guard stood with his legs wide and his arms folded. Lou responded 'What!'

Sharin grabbed the photo that Lou dropped onto the counter and skipped lightly across the pale fake floorboards to stand between them. She held it up toward the guard, who was sixty-five years old, if he was a day.

Mel clapped her hands together.

In tones of drippy honey, Sharin whispered 'Any chance you know the man in this photo? Peter Schneider?' Her tiny face appeared beside the photo, drawing her eyes up through her lashes as she moved a step closer. The man was putty in her hands.

The guard stared down at Sharin and the photo. He had little choice. He couldn't move without looking down and his gaze was caught between Sharin and the floor. He studied the photo.

Sharin watched his eyes flick back and forth across the paper. They finally rested on one spot and remained for a long moment.

'Yep. So, what if I do?'

Sharin threw her arms around his waist. His arms and eyebrows shot up in unison. Lou prised her off and Mel skidded to his side.

'Oh, my God. This is too good to be true. Can you tell us about him?'

'Why?'

'I need to find him.'

'Why?'

'The woman in this photo,' said Mel, reaching for the paper in Sharin's hand and pointing at Peg, 'is my mother. Peter dated her. My mother died about a year after this photo was taken, and he may know something about it. I need to find out what he knew. I need to find him,' she repeated.

The guard ran a finger along his moustache. The finger was just as stained with nicotine. He studied the photo for a time without speaking.

Brian called from the behind the safety of his glass petition. 'We don't give out personal information, Randall.'

Randall never took his eyes off the paper. 'Thank you for the reminder, Brian. I've only worked here for thirty-five years. Think I might know the rules.'

Lou turned to face Brian, who stepped back from the glass.

'Thanks very much, Brian!' she shouted, as she started moving forward, but Sharin grabbed her arm.

Randall leant over them both and took Lou's free arm. 'Time to go ladies. I'll escort you to the door.'

Lou stood rigid. 'Take your hand off me,' she threatened.

He hesitated a moment but did as she asked, although he left it hovering above her wrist. 'You will leave now,' he said firmly. The smug look on Brian's face caught her eye but faded quickly as the last thing he saw before she turned back toward the door was a look that told him he was a dead man if he ever crossed her path.

The paper in Mel's hand slapped against her thigh but she didn't move. Randall herded Sharin and Lou around her. 'Come on,' he said, pulling her into the throng. All four of them shuffled to the door. Instead of leading them through the automatic doors he drew them to a side door that opened conventionally. The door swung out and he opened it pushing out onto the steps ahead of them. He held the door open as they filed through, his body resting into the handle as he looked down the stairs to the road. Mel filed out last, fixing him with a glare. Her last hope was just about to shut the door on them. But as Randall began his move around the door he passed across Mel and said, 'Meet me at the Whipper Street Café at 1p.m.,' before encircling it and entering the building. Mel spun to say something but he was gone. She bit her lip and yahooed internally.

They were on the street before she slipped between Lou and Sharin, hooking her arms through theirs. Lou was painting a colourful picture of what she'd like to do with Brian when Mel interrupted, stopping all three in their tracks.

'He said that?' asked Sharin, surprised. 'Wow, didn't see that coming.'

'Suck shit, B_r_i_a_n!' said Lou.

Mel pulled them both in closer. 'Reckon he knows something. Thirty-five years in one job, gotta have the dirt on the best of them,' she said.

'I would rather eat my young than work in one place for that long,' said Lou.

'Some people don't have a choice.'

'Some people don't have ambition, Mel.'

Mel nodded. 'True, but still, it's working in our favour.'

Sharin lifted her free arm to check her watch. 'We have an hour to kill. Ideas?'

'Let's lunch and wait,' suggested Lou. 'Whipper Street Café sounds uninspiring, but worth a shot, and I need a sit down.'

Mel pulled out her phone and tapped 'Whipper Street Cafe' into Google. It was a five-minute walk - less than a block away. It turned out to look a bit like Randall. Rundown, worn out and shabby. The menu was basic but the smell of espresso and authentic Italian cuisine was heady. Lou fell instantly in love. They ordered, then sat themselves at a table for four, flanked by peeling paint and age-old mildew stains, and waited.

Chapter 41

Right on 1 p.m., Randall sauntered through the door. He squinted against the gloom, but soon found them. Sharin waving wildly, provided him a clue to follow.

On the way to the table, he nodded to the owner who was engaged in making coffee and received a chin wave in response. By the time he was seated at the table with the three women, the owner's wife was setting a bowl of minestrone and a bread roll before him. Clearly, Randall was a regular.

'Thanks so much for this, Randall,' said Mel.

'No problem. Can't stand that prick, Brian. Besides, what's the harm? Peter left years ago. And I only got three months till retirement.'

'So, you remember him then?' she said.

'Yep, nice enough bloke. Quiet. Kept to himself.' He paused to slurp his soup. Mel wanted to rush in with a question but held back. Randall seemed like a man who thought before he spoke.

'Lived with his Mum. Never understood that. Still, only child and all. Not natural for a man though, I reckon. Gotta move on.' He paused again to eat and this time Mel did butt in. 'How long did he work with you and when did he leave?'

'He was already there when I started in '85. Left in '92,' said Randall.

Lou leaned forward 'When in '92?'

'Don't remember exactly. Later in the year. It was after July, left in a hurry.' Randall sopped up some of the soup with his bread roll and sucked the soft dough into his mouth. Part of it hung off his moustache. Thankfully the next spoonful of soup washed it away. Lou was crushing a dry retch back into her throat.

'In a hurry?' said Sharin.

'Yep, embezzlement.'

All three girls exchanged looks with each other.

'Embezzlement? I thought he was a technician?' said Mel.

'Nope. Accountant.'

'Are you sure that's why he left?' she said.

'Mmm. Don't know for sure. But he was definitely fiddlin' the books. Janet - pretty lass, big ...' he took another bite of his bread roll, 'glasses – always wore those big owl glasses, thick lenses, you know the ones?'

'Yep, and what about Janet?' said Mel.

'Well, she was new then and working with Peter in accounts. She did admin, bookkeeping, that sort of thing. Anyway, she was doing what they do at end of the financial year and she found this company that was getting paid. Didn't quite fit the bill. She'd worked in internal audit for some government office before she came to us. Clever little thing. Did some digging, but before they could pin it on him, Peter left. He'd been on holiday which is why Janet had a free run to check everything. He came back on a Monday and was gone by lunchtime. Rumour was, he got wind of what she was up to and just up and left. Never came back. Pretty much disappeared.'

Randall finished his soup.

The girls exchanged more looks.

Finally, Mel asked, 'Would anyone know what happened to him?'

Randall shrugged. 'His Mum?'

'Wonder if she's still alive?' said Sharin.

'Do you have any idea where she lived?' said Lou.

'Nope. Like I said, he was a quiet one. Didn't talk much. Had this weird tick,' said Randall as he bounced his right shoulder up and down to demonstrate. His head dipped each time his shoulder shot up.

Randall dropped the spoon into the bowl, pushed it away, and leaned back in his chair. 'Never would have picked him for a crook though.'

'I don't know, I just can't imagine Peg with him,' said Mel to the others.

'Yeah, it does seem odd. From what you've said of Peg he doesn't sound like her type,' agreed Lou.

'Peg?' said Randall.

'Long story,' said Mel

'And he never mentioned a girlfriend?' asked Lou.

'As I said, didn't talk about himself at all. Only reason I knew he lived with his Mum, was 'coz she dropped his lunch off each day.'

Lou shifted in her seat. 'Jesus, how old was this bloke!'

Randall looked at her sideways. 'That a question?'

'No, but sure. How old was he?'

''Bout my age. Mid-sixties now. If he's still alive. Disappeared, like I said. Might'a topped himself, who knows?'

Mel shook her head. 'Oh, I hope not. I have to find him. But after 27 years he could be dead.'

'Or still alive. Don't give up,' said Sharin, reaching a hand out to rub Mel's.

'Yeah. Maybe. Still, I hope you find him. Cheeky bastard. Wonder what he did with the money? Ask him that for me, if ya find him,' said Randall, leaning toward Mel and giving her a wink.

With that, Randall pushed his chair toward the wall and stood. Mel stood to join him and shake his hand. 'Thanks so much for your help, Randall. I really appreciate it.'

'You're welcome, Lass. Good luck.'

He tipped his head toward the others. 'Ladies, have a nice afternoon,' and was on his way.

Mel sat down.

Lou twisted sideways in her chair and leaned into the peeling paint. 'So, what do you make of that?'

'Well, it confirms Peter worked for Telecom so it's possible the guy Peg met in the café was him. Even if it wasn't, he might know something,' said Sharin.

'But how do we find him? I mean he clearly hasn't been around for a while,' said Lou.

'Yeah. Very convenient,' agreed Mel.

'It is pretty strange that he exits at the time your Mum died,' said Lou.

'And gets busted for fraud at the same time,' said Mel.

'Maybe Peg knew about the money he was nicking and he knocked her off?' suggested Lou.

'Certainly a possibility. But how did he find her? Tanya didn't give him an address and it would've been a year since they'd seen each other,' said Mel.

'Maybe she found him,' said Sharin.

Mel leaned forward. 'What do you mean?' she asked.

'Well, if she did have the dirt on him, maybe she thought she could use that to her advantage. Perhaps she needed money or something?'

Mel sat back and stared at Sharin. 'You mean like blackmail?'

Sharin shrugged.

'Would she do that?' she asked no one in particular. 'God, that would be terrible.'

Sharin peered sideways at Lou. Her face expressed all sorts of regret for suggesting it. Mel leaned forward again. 'It's ok, Shaz. Anything was possible with my mother. I don't want to think she could do that, but maybe she could.'

'Either way,' said Lou, 'she didn't deserve to die for it.'

Mel tapped the table. 'We really need to find this guy.'

'Hang on,' said Lou, 'I thought we were giving this up?'

'We are, but we have one more day,' said Mel, 'so let's head back and start searching.'

Chapter 42

THEY WALKED INTO THE OFFICE TO FIND A BASKET OF flowers on Sharin's desk with a note from Michel. Sharin took the card from a stick in the centre of the bouquet and flipped it back and forth between her fingers.

'Read it,' said Lou.

'Only if you want to,' added Mel.

'Yep,' agreed Lou, leaning into the colourful blooms and sniffing deeply. 'And then tell us why.'

Sharin pulled a face. 'Should there be a 'why'?'

'No one sends this many flowers without a why,' said Lou.

Sharin sighed and read the card, 'I'm sorry. Please call me. Michel.'

'Any kisses?' asked Mel.

'Yep,' said Sharin.

'Call him,' said Lou.

'You don't know the 'why'.'

'Let me guess,' she said lifting one of the irises out of the basket. 'He came over. You cooked a fabulous meal. You chatted, drank wine, flirted. You snogged. But nothing happened. He left. You feel rejected. You haven't answered his calls.'

Sharin tapped the card against her lips. Mel watched on.

'Do you have a camera in my house?'

Lou stuck the iris back between a white stock and a pink peony. 'Nope. Just a solid guess.'

'What is wrong with me?'

'Nothing!' Lou and Mel spoke as one.

'Then what am I doing wrong?'

'Nothing. It'll be him. Who the hell knows what goes on in a man's brain? Just call. Talk it out.'

'Do you want to see him again?' asked Mel.

Sharin returned the card to its place on the plastic stick and tweaked the leaves around it. 'I think so.'

'Then do it,' said Lou.

Sharin picked up her phone to text. She made several attempts before she was satisfied with the one she sent. Lou busied herself editing a project report and Mel made her way to the photocopy room.

She was standing at the photocopier, contemplating the complexities of love, when a waft of pine and sandalwood swirled up her nostrils. She knew, without turning, that William was behind her.

'Hello you,' she said over her shoulder.

'Hey, yourself,' he replied crisply. 'You gonna be long?'

'Nope, just ..... getting.... the.....last... page................now,' and with a flourish, she scooped the pages from the printer tray and swung around to face him. 'All yours.'

'Thank you kindly,' he said.

Mel added pages to the six small piles lined up on the bench beside the printer and began stapling them together. 'Didn't see you around last week. Please tell me you were in some exotic location with sun and sea.'

William leaned against the photocopier and laughed. 'I wish. Nope, I was being tortured by PowerPoint for three days at Deakin. Project management course. Stimulating stuff.'

'Ah. I did one of those once ... and look where it got me,' she said waving her arms above her as she spun slowly on the spot. 'All this glamour and excitement.'

'What, this isn't glamourous and exciting? Clearly, we aren't working in the same department,' said William.

'We won't be working at all soon.'

'Sorry! I keep forgetting. That was crass of me,' said William.

'No it wasn't. At least the department's investing in some of us.'

'Yeah, a few of us are doing it. Jill's there at the moment and there's two others next week.

'Mel, are you ... Oh hi, William.'

'Hi, Shaz, how you doin'?'

'Good now I've seen you,' she said.

'Oh, girl!' he said swatting the air, 'you are too kind!'

Sharin giggled and blushed. The fact that William was gay didn't temper the flirting between them.

'Um, yes Sharin? You wanted me?' said Mel.

'Oh yeah, Lou got a call from her friend in Corrections. She has info.'

William pursed his lips. 'Sounds interesting. This about your Mum's case?'

'I hope so. Piecing together fragments but still fumbling around in the dark.'

'I love a good fumble in the dark,' said William, flicking a rubber band at Sharin, who giggled uncontrollably.

'Good grief,' said Mel. 'You two are incorrigible! I'm 'outa here!'

Sharin reluctantly followed her into the office where Lou was waiting by the incident board. Mel had tacked pictures of the Telecom logo and Peter with Peg back up on the board. Lou was studying the picture of Robert Lang.

'Righto, what do you know Ms Barnes?'

'Not a lot more, but Nathan said that while Lang was in jail, he lay low, built something of a reputation as a leader, and perfected ways to be of use to his mafia mates. Turned to the books. And I don't mean the holy ones. He ventured beyond thuggery and extortion to creative accounting. Became very adept at making money disappear then reappear all nicely washed. Made them a lot of moolah.'

'Laundering and extortion. Very noble,' said Mel.

'Yep. Goes to work in a shirt and tie each day. Still a crook, but dressed up all presentable,' said Lou.

'And there's no evidence of violence since he came out of jail?' asked Sharin.

'No. Squeaky clean by all accounts,' said Lou.

'Maybe Dave has him all wrong. I mean why hide in the shadows for so long and then expose yourself? What could possibly have changed?' asked Sharin.

'It does seem odd,' agreed Mel. 'I mean, Coreman was the one convicted of the four murders in '93. If Lang is actually responsible for those, Peg's and more since, then he's got away with it all this time. Why bring attention to it now?'

'Maybe someone's framing him? Setting him up perhaps?' said Sharin.

'Or he's just getting cocky,' said Lou.

'You know, if the only murders people are aware of are the ones from the early 90s then maybe someone would copy them if they wanted to set him up?' said Sharin.

'Mmm,' agreed Lou, 'shine a light on him and bring him back into the public eye. Opportunity for investigation.'

'Problem is, who would do that, and why?'

'Maybe it's Dave?' suggested Lou.

'That is ridiculous,' said Sharin.

'He wants revenge on Lang. He thinks he got away with his sister's murder. And he knows your Mum's story.'

'No way!' said Sharin.

Mel looked less sure.

'Plenty of fires lit by people in the Fire Department,' continued Lou.

'There is no way it's Dave ... uh uh ... no way!' said Sharin.

Mel chewed the tip of her nail.

'It's not Dave,' said Lou.

Mel still looked uncertain.

'Mel. It is not Dave. I was being facetious,' said Lou.

'Mmmm ... I know. It's just ...'

'Stop. It's not.'

'Maybe it's Peter? Randall said he was embezzling funds. Paying some business. Perhaps he had links with the Honourable Society too. Lang and Peter might'a known each other? Or Coreman for that matter,' said Sharin.

Lou's mouth split into a wide grin. 'My goodness Miss Sharin, you are good at this!'

Sharin laughed. It was the sound of bells tinkling.

'You really are,' agreed Mel. 'And thinking about it, Tanya said Peter liked it rough. Maybe there was more to him than meets the eye?'

'Yeah, got to watch the quiet ones,' said Lou.

Mel sighed and shrugged. 'It's a long shot. But who knows? I mean, he seemed to disappear. Maybe he reappeared?'

Lou took a step back and squinted at the board. 'You know who might know?' she said, 'Angel.'

'Of course!' said Mel 'Can we call her?'

'Sure, why not.'

Lou used the landline on Mel's desk to phone Angel. It went to voicemail. Lou left a message. A few minutes later the phone rang and it was Angel. Lou put her on speaker. She had a high-pitched voice and although she had been in Australia for many years, a thick accent.

'Your number came up private. I don't answer private calls,' she said.

'Me neither,' agreed Lou. 'Forgot, sorry.'

They exchanged a few pleasantries and she introduced Mel and Sharin before asking about Lang and Peter.

'Angel, did you know a man called Peter Schneider? He was

an accountant. Got busted for fraud at his government job. Any connection to Lang that you know of?'

'Or Coreman' Mel added.

Angel was silent for a few seconds. 'Doesn't ring a bell. I can ask around if you like. But I can't get too involved. Don't think Jeremy would like it.'

'Jeremy's her husband,' whispered Lou. 'No problem, anything will be good. Thanks so much, Angel,' she said more loudly.

'Do you think Lang is still likely to kill people?' asked Sharin.

'Absolutely. He has no soul. Evil. Pure evil.'

Sharin clenched her teeth tight together. Lou nudged her.

'He set up Coreman, then beat him brain dead in jail. And they were best mates! Everyone in the game knows he did it. Just can't pin it on him. He has no conscience. A bad man,' said Angel.

'You don't think Coreman was guilty?' asked Lou.

'He was guilty. But not of what Lang said he did. Coreman was a lacky. He was capable of rape. My girls knew how he liked it. But he wasn't a murderer. I could be wrong, but I've seen a lot of men in my time. I've seen every type of man there is,' she said.

Mel pressed her fingers into prayer and raised them to her lips. 'Angel, did you know a man called Dan Hilliard at all?'

She closed her eyes as she waited for the answer. After Angel spoke, she opened them and breathed out slowly.

'Nope. Don't know that name at all. But I can ask around.'

'That would be great. Thanks. And Angel ...' began Mel.

'Yes.'

'I don't suppose you met my mother?'

'Peg. No. But women used all sorts of names if they didn't want to be known. I've seen her photo though, and I don't recognise her.'

Both Sharin and Lou smiled at Mel. The relief was written on her face.

They hung up with promises from Angel to call once she knew something.

'What a woman,' said Mel.

'She sure is,' agreed Sharin.

'If anyone can find something in this mess, she can,' said Lou.

'I hope she doesn't find anything about Dan,' said Mel. 'That would kill me.'

'Have to wait and see,' said Lou. 'Be interesting to see is she finds anything on Peter.'

'There are so many possibilities if she does find a connection. I mean, Lang is into extortion and laundering. Peter is a fraudster. Coreman is a bagman,' said Sharin.

'Dan was a car man,' said Lou, as she raised a hand to stop Mel from intervening, 'And Lang used car yards for money laundering.'

Mel returned her fingers in prayer to her lips. 'No, I asked him about that.'

'And ...?'

'He knew of Lang and Coreman but denied ever being involved with them. He had nothing good to say either.'

'Denial does not equate to truth,' said Lou.

Mel's jaw tensed.

Sharin stretched backward 'I'm sorry, but I don't believe there's a connection there.'

'I agree,' said Mel. She rubbed her eyes then slowly lowered herself onto the edge of the incident desk. 'There are so many threads. So many bloody theories!'

'Certainly are,' agreed Lou.

'It really is beyond us,' said Mel. 'We just have to give what we have to the authorities and be done with it.'

Sharin and Lou rounded the table and wrapped themselves around her. The pop of emails on the computer marked the moments that passed.

'Can we just wait to see what Angel uncovers?' asked Lou.

'Can she do it in a day?'

'Knowing Angel, yep.'

'All right, but Thursday we hand over to Dave. He can take it to the Police by Friday,' said Mel.

Lou lay her head on Mel's shoulder. 'Deal,' she said, 'but it's kind of sad in some ways. I've really enjoyed this.'

'Me too,' agreed Sharin, then added, 'not in a freaky, murder-loving kind of way, though.'

'Speak for yourself!' said Lou, pulling back from them both.

Mel laughed then frowned. 'You don't think they'll see us as interferers, do you? You know, internet warriors who just waste their time?'

'Probably. But who cares? And if Dave adds his part of the story, it'll have more credibility.'

'Oh, and I've nearly finished the map,' said Sharin. 'I'll get it done now.'

'You don't have to,' said Mel.

'No. I will. Won't take long. Still half an hour till five o'clock. All good.'

Sharin started toward her desk, then stopped. 'Umm, sorry Lou, have you finished?'

'Yes, Ma'am. Nothing else to report.'

'Wonder what Dave will make of all this speculation.'

'His reaction will speak volumes,' said Lou.

'Stop!' said Sharin. 'Dave is on our side.'

'Either way. Keen to see what he thinks.'

'Factual speculation – he'll love it!' said Mel.

Chapter 43

At 5 p.m. they left Sharin at her computer and finished for the day.

They'd made the front door when Mel's phone rang. It was Annie. Lou waved as she took the call.

'Hey, love.'

'Hey, Mum. I'm going to Elena's to study. She said I can stay for dinner.'

'OK. I'll pick you up after.'

'No. It's all good. Elena said her Mum will drop me back.'

'That seems unfair. I can come.'

'Mum, its fine. She's right here. Nodding at me. All good.'

Mel paused, weighing up the rejection and gratitude. Gratitude won. She could drink tonight.

'Righto. Tell her thanks heaps.'

'Mum says thanks,' Annie repeated at her end.

'Enjoy yourself. See you tonight.'

They hung up together. Mel mentally calculated the number of hours till Annie was home, and prepared to wait.

Her next call was to Lexie's home to check on her. She wanted to visit but Lexie's carer said she was tired and needed her sleep, however, she promised to call if anything changed. She also offered to call Dan, but Mel said she would do it. She needed answers. She hung up and dialled his number. The phone still went to voice mail.

On the way home, she bought wine. Ricky had dinner prepared for them. He growled when she told him Annie wouldn't be home to eat.

'Eets my famous cassoulet!'

'Her loss big boy. My gain,' she said patting her belly.

'My gain,' said Ricky, patting her arse with one hand.

'Oi, stop it!' she teased pulling him close. He squeezed her butt with both hands.

'You don't want me to do theez?' he asked squeezing some more.

She batted his hands away then moved them to her waist.

'No, I don't. But you can kiss me.'

Which he did. Until the oven timer buzzed.

He gently pulled away. Still holding her waist. 'You huzzy. Taking advantage of me like that.'

She grabbed the tea towel draped over his shoulder and flicked it at him.

'You gonna pay for that,' he said ducking sideways.

'Oh yeah,' she said, flicking him again.

He snatched the tea towel back with one hand and spun her with the other. The cloth licked at her hip as it whipped back and forth. 'Oh yes!'

'Ok, ok stop!' she squealed, spinning to face him.

'Only if you pour wine and set the table,' he said, dangling the tea towel in front of her.

Table set, dinner served, wine consumed, they relaxed on the couch together and waited for Annie. Normally Ricky was asleep by 8 p.m., but tonight he stayed awake.

'Did you call the police yet?' he asked.

'No, Thursday.'

Ricky leaned around and frowned at her.

'The girls wanted to wait. And Dave's in Canberra till then

with his Mum for his sister's anniversary. Didn't want to land this on him while he's there.'

He leaned against the cushions and nodded. Mel dug around the back of the seat for the TV remote control and they settled in quiet companionship to wait.

At 10.30 p.m. the door crunched open and Annie bounded through. Both heads lifted from the couch to watch her. She seemed upbeat for someone who'd been studying.

'Hi, honey. Everything went well?' asked Mel.

'Yep. Great.'

'You meezed cassoulet,' said Ricky.

Annie pouted, 'did you save some?'

'Maybe.'

'Thanks, Dad,' she said as she came to him for a hug.

Mel put her arms out and looked at Annie optimistically.

'Of course, you get one too,' she laughed, hugging her.

'You had a good night,' said Mel.

'Yep. Got lots done.'

'Maths?' said Ricky.

'English. Group assignment.'

'I never did understand group assignments,' said Ricky 'Eets a free ride for someone.'

'Indeed. And that someone would be Dane. Does nothing.'

'How many in your group?' asked Mel.

'Three. El and I do the work. Dane gets the marks.'

'Estupido!' said Ricky.

'We're Estupido! He's the clever one.'

'Ah well, good practice for real life,' said Mel.

'S'pose so,' agreed Annie. 'Anyway, better get some sleep.'

She kissed both parents who watched lovingly as she walked to the stairs.

'Oh. Guess who I saw tonight,' she said, turning back.

'Who?'

'Uncle Eddy.'

'Tonight?' said Mel.

'Yeah. We pulled up at the lights and I saw his car.'

'Eddy never drives in the city. Sure it was him? His car?'

'I didn't see him. Just the car. But there was a woman getting into the driver's seat,' she said, raising her eyebrows.

Ricky and Mel looked at each other.

'A woman?' said Mel.

'Yeah. She looked hot, too. Tall. Blonde hair. Really cool dress.'

'Eddy has a woman!' said Ricky, 'Sly dog.'

Annie giggled. 'I've never seen Uncle Eddy with a woman before.'

'Me neither,' said Mel. 'Maybe he met her at art class?'

'Art class?' said Annie.

'Never mind,' said Mel. 'And you didn't see Eddy?'

'Nope. Maybe he was in the passenger seat. It was pretty dark. The car was on the side road, you know, off Hoddle St. And we were only there a few seconds. The lights changed and Fletcher took off. Didn't see anything after that.'

'Oo eez Fletcher?' asked Ricky sitting up.

'El's brother. He drove me home,' she said.

'I thought El's Mum was driving you?' said Mel, also leaning forward.

'Well, he offered and she was tired. It's all FINE!' she snapped stomping to the stairs.

They watched her climb to the top, before Mel turned to Ricky.

'A woman. Eddy?' she said.

'Good on him. Finally getting a life.'

'Has to be his art class. Remember I told you what Marcus said?'

'Oh right. 'Nude modelling',' he paused. 'Maybe I could do that. I got plenty to draw,' he smirked.

'Oh, my God! You are too much! And it was nude painting anyway.'

'Painting, modelling. Potato, potarto. Either, I make the girls happy!' He said running a hand across his chest.

'Mr Modest!'

'You know you want it,' he continued, as his fingers roamed around his torso.

She hit him with the remote. 'Well take me to bed and give it to me then.'

Chapter 44

MEL AND THE WOLSELEY HAD REKINDLED THEIR friendship, following its return two nights earlier. The repairs gave the old girl a new lease on life and Mel made it to work in fourteen minutes. She and the car slipped effortlessly back into routine.

Sitting in the office, with two dirty cups on one side of her desk and the photo taken at Enid's birthday on the other, was Sharin.

'You look like you've been here all night,' said Mel.

'No, just since 6 a.m.,' said Sharin.

'Are you crazy?'

'Couldn't sleep. Was up late talking to Michel,' said Sharin.

'That's great!'

'Yeah it is, but then my brain wouldn't shut down. Kept thinking about Peter.'

'Peter? Shouldn't you be thinking about Michel?' said Mel.

Sharin twisted the string of beads around her neck. 'Yeah, but we were talking about work and the stuff with Peter and he had some good ideas about how to find him.'

Mel came to stand over her computer screen. 'And?'

'And I'm trying to find him.'

'Shaz. Brilliant. Anything?'

'Searching obituaries. You have to dig a bit,' said Sharin.

'Boom boom!'

'What?'

'Dig a bit,' she repeated with an air nudge of her elbow.

'Oh, dear. I am losing it,' she said, thumping her forehead with the palm of her hand. 'I haven't found him but I'm going to look for Enid and Margaret. They'll list his name if they're there.'

'That is fantastic, Sharin!'

'Thank Michel. He thought of it,' said Sharin.

'Thank you, Michel. I will offer your body as his reward.'

'I wish. He's working this weekend.'

'Bummer,' said Mel.

Sharin sagged a little lower.

'Cheer up. He sent you flowers. He's keen,' said Mel.

'Yes, he did. I hope so,' said Sharin.

'Thanks for your help with all this.'

'No problem. Oh, the map is on your desk by the way.'

'You are the best. I am going to make you coffee.'

Mel left to make coffee and met Lou in the corridor. She returned with three cups.

Lou was standing behind Sharin's desk squinting at the computer screen.

'Perhaps your glasses would help?' said Mel.

She didn't move. 'What? And wreck this stunning visage,' she said.

'Well, of course you have a point there,' said Mel.

'Besides, it requires effort to find them.'

'Why, where are they?' asked Mel.

'In my bag, on my desk,' said Lou.

'What. That half metre from where you're standing? Don't strain yourself, let me get them for you.'

'Bless. You are a pet,' said Lou.

Mel put the coffees down and retrieved the glasses. Lou put them on and stood back. 'Ah, that's better. Thanks.'

Mel rolled her eyes and came to stand beside her.

'What are you looking at?' she asked.

'Enid's obituary. There are messages from Peter and his mum but that was 1993.'

'Christ, she made 102 years!' said Mel.

'Poor cow,' said Lou.

'Poor nothing. That is amazing.'

'So he was alive in '93,' said Lou.

'Yep, looks like it. I'm trying to find something on Margaret. She'd have to be well into her 80s by now,' said Sharin.

'Mmm, but even with her genes, there's a chance she's dead too,' said Lou.

Mel pressed her hands together in prayer, 'I know Karma will get me for wishing her dead, but I wish her dead.'

Lou looked sideways at her. 'Who are you?'

Mell shrugged, 'I know, I feel bad.'

The screen scrolled down as Sharin rolled her hand over the mouse. She clicked one newspaper obituary section after another.

'Bingo!' she squealed.

Mel and Lou leaned in. 'Holy Toledo. 2019. She died this year.'

'Funeral was when?' asked Mel.

Sharin scrolled further.

'Oh, oh look,' she pointed madly, 'it has a note from a nursing home. She must have lived there. They'll know something surely?'

'Shit a brick! I'll get a pen,' said Mel.

Sharin read out the name and Mel wrote it down.

'And there's a message from Peter!' Sharin squealed even louder, jumping up from her seat. Lou jumped back. 'Settle petal!'

Sharin sat down.

'Sorry, sorry, but look. "Love you forever, Mum. Your Peter."' Sharin was vibrating in her seat as she spoke.

'This is too much. Too wonderful much!!' Mel joined in, dancing from foot to foot.

Lou leaned into the screen. 'Funeral was June. Three months ago.'

'We've got a chance to find him,' said Mel slapping her hands together, 'and possibly talk to him!'

"Talk to him?' said Lou as she pulled back from the screen and folded her arms. The air around her shifted.

'What?' asked Mel, slowing her feet to a shuffle.

Lou's face was stern. 'What if he *is* dangerous, Mel? Meeting and talking to him may not be the best idea.'

Mel stopped moving altogether. Sharin turned away from the computer to face them both. Mel folded her arms too.

'If you meet him, you bring him into your life. Closer to you. Closer to Annie. You don't know how he's involved in this. It's not worth the risk,' said Lou.

Mel pressed her arms tighter to her.

'No, but ...' interjected Sharin.

Lou tilted her head toward Sharin.

'No, you're right, sorry.'

'Look. I'm not saying we can't find out where he lives or works or something if that's even possible. But don't meet him, Mel. Just give that info, with the rest of it, to the police as we planned. Let them deal with him.'

Mel took her top lip between her teeth and sucked in some air. She let it all go with a sigh. 'Yep. I know. I know. You're right.'

Lou let her arms loose and reached forward to take Mel's. 'If he is involved, you'll eventually learn everything you need to know. Just don't get it by being in the same room as him.'

Mel's fingers reached up, enfolding Lou's, and she nodded.

Sharin slid the mouse back and forth as she watched them both. She stopped and stood up.

'I have an idea. I'll see you in a while,' she said.

'What idea?' asked Mel.

'Tell you when I get back,' she smiled, reaching for her things.

She left them standing with their hands still encircled.

Chapter 45

Sharin strode into the office later in the day to find Lou at her desk and Mel standing in front of it with her bag over her shoulder.

'Where have you been?' they asked in unison.

'You've been gone for hours. We were starting to worry,' said Lou.

'Oh, my God, I have so much to tell you,' said Sharin, 'and I think it will make your day.'

'Sorry, Shaz, but I'm on my way out. Just got the call that Lexie's been taken to the hospital. I can't stop.'

'Go, go,' she said. 'I can fill you in later.'

Mel blew them both a kiss and hurried out the door.

'Wait!' Lou shouted after her. 'We'll phone and put you on speaker.'

Mel paused. 'Ok, great,' she called back over her shoulder. Lou watched as she pulled the phone from her handbag, then lifted her own phone receiver and dialled.

The ringtone from Mel's phone echoed up the corridor.

'So, where *have* you been?' Lou asked Sharin as the phone connected. They could hear Mel breathing heavily as she rushed to her car.

Sharin dropped her bag and maneuvered her chair to sit opposite Lou.

'I went to the nursing home where Peter's mother lived and did a bit of snooping.'

'Ohh, I love a good snoop,' said Lou. 'What did you find?'

Sharin shuffled her chair a little closer to the table and the phone. They could hear Mel's car door squeak open on the end of the line.

'I found a lovely lady cleaner who's worked there for ages, and she was very helpful.'

'I take it you didn't tell her you were investigating a murder?' said Mel.

'Gosh no! Although I feel a bit bad because I did a lot of pretending and she was such a nice person,' said Sharin, as she fiddled with hair. 'Is that really awful?' she asked.

'Deception and lies,' said Lou. 'I love it.'

'I did give her flowers though,' said Sharin.

'That's ok, then,' said Lou. 'Flowers cancel out lies. Just ask ex-husband number three!'

'So why the cleaning lady?' said Mel, as her car revved in the background.

'Because the cleaner would have been in Margaret's room every day and they are usually the friendliest people on staff,' said Sharin.

Lou smirked, 'look at you go, Detective Cagney.'

Sharin laughed. 'My next career move.'

'So, what did she tell you,' interrupted Mel.

'She said that Margaret had been in the home for a year but passed away in June and that Peter came to visit every day. She said Peter was a real gentleman.'

'Mmm, that's a good thing,' agreed Mel.

'She said he was inconsolable when she died because he'd been living away for so long and only recently came back. I nearly tripped up because I asked where he'd been and she was surprised I didn't know. I just said that Margaret was a friend of my Mum's, and she lives up north. I said that we chat on the phone a lot but Mum has dementia and gets muddled so she wasn't sure where Peter lived. Thankfully she believed me.'

'I have to know; how did you *actually* get her to tell you this stuff?' asked Lou.

Sharin twiddled her hair again. 'I made out I'd come to see Margaret and I couldn't find her room. It was a way to get the conversation going.'

'And how did you get past reception? They know Margaret's dead.'

'Well, I kinda pretended I was there to see someone else. I checked the register as I signed in and said I was going to the same room as the person who signed in before me.'

'You are devious!' said Lou.

Sharin fidgeted in her chair. 'It was for a good cause,' she said.

'Yes it was. Did she tell you where he'd been living all these years?' asked Mel.

'She just said interstate, and that he came home because Margaret was so ill. She then talked a lot about her own family and moving around the country and missing her kids. But, she also told me that he wasn't married, because she said it was lucky he didn't have to move a family at short notice because that can be tricky, and she knew because that happened to her daughter when her husband's company moved head offices. But the really interesting thing...'

'Her daughter's move wasn't interesting?' said Lou.

'Oh stop,' said Sharin. 'It actually was, but she also said that Peter had a daughter he was trying to reconnect with, but she wasn't sure if that happened because she never saw any other family visit Margaret.'

'A daughter?' said Mel.

'Yep. But where the daughter is, who knows?' said Sharin.

'Clearly this guy keeps things close to his chest. Randall said he didn't talk about anything personal and he seemed to be a loner. Maybe he met someone while he was living away, had the daughter, and she moved here?' said Lou.

'Guess we'll never know,' said Mel.

'Did Margaret tell you anything about what Peter's been doing since he got back? I wonder if he transferred with his work?' said Lou.

'No, that was interesting. She said he'd given up the corporate life and took a job as a personal carer for older and disabled people. Worked for a service in Wellington St but she's not sure whether he's still there.'

Mel gasped. 'I think I better pull over,' she said. They heard the car engine ease before she spoke again. 'I know that service. We spoke to them before choosing Lexie's home.'

'Holy crap,' said Lou.

'But he wouldn't have been there then. He's only been back less than a year,' said Sharin.

'And he couldn't know about Lexie, surely?' said Mel. 'I mean he disappeared when Mum died and Lexie didn't have the seizure until she was two and a half. He vanished when she was three months old.'

'He probably didn't even know about Lexie at all, so little chance he'd come across her in his work and even if he did, it wouldn't mean anything,' said Lou.

'Yeah, I think you're right. It scares me though because Lexie is a Hilliard and that isn't a common name. He might put two and two together.'

'Honestly, I don't think you need to worry. He's only been a carer for this last year. And obviously focused on his Mum,' said Sharin.

'But really, why would a man who's been in finance, become a carer?' asked Mel.

'Well, he couldn't work in finance here. Someone might learn about his past,' said Sharin.

'True, but that would have followed him everywhere. And besides, he wasn't charged so there won't be a record,' said Lou.

'Maybe he needed a job with shifts so he could see his Mum more often,' suggested Sharin.

'Maybe. But working for a disability service?' said Mel, 'that just freaks me out.'

'Probably it was more around aged care?' suggested Lou.

Maybe, but I still don't like it,' said Mel, as she eased the car back into traffic. 'I want to know about him, but like you said Lou, I don't want him close to my family.'

'Truly, I don't think you need to worry,' said Lou. 'Lexie lives in a house with carers who are never going to let an unknown person near her. And if he becomes a carer there, you will know about it.'

They could hear the car humming. Mel had made a makeshift hands-free device and the sound of everything around it filtered into the speaker.

'Ok. I need to stop worrying and focus. But it doesn't feel right. Is there anything else she told you?' said Mel.

'I tried to find out where he lives now,' said Sharin.

'Damn, you are good,' said Lou.

'Not that good. I didn't get an answer. She said she didn't know but it couldn't be far from the nursing home 'cause he always rang when he got home and it was never more than fifteen minutes. Margaret would sit with the phone on her lap and wait.'

'Margaret's house perhaps?' said Lou.

'No. Apparently her house was sold to help pay for the nursing home room,' said Sharin.

'You had quite the chat,' said Lou.

'Oh, she was just lovely. I could have chatted all day, but then she had to finish up her shift, so we had to stop. I got her number though and we're going to catch up for coffee sometime.'

Mel whistled into the phone. 'It's fortunate you are on the side of good and not evil, Shaz. I swear you could persuade anyone to do anything.'

'Hear, hear,' agreed Lou.

Sharin held her hands up in defeat. 'Guilty as charged.'

'So where to now?' said Lou.

'Not sure, but I need to leave it to both of you. I'm at the hospital,' said Mel.

'Ok,' said Lou, 'we'll figure something out and let you know.'

'And you'll put it all together? So we can give it to Dave?' asked Mel.

'Yes, of course,' said Sharin, standing to walk over to Mel's desk. The map she'd prepared was where she'd left it. Sharin took it to Lou's desk.

'I've got the map, so we can start to add the likely places where Peter might live,' she said, laying it flat and reaching for a pen. 'The nursing home is here,' she said tapping the map on the 'x' she'd marked. On Albert St in East Melbourne. And if we draw a circle within fifteen minutes of it that takes us to ...' she paused as she drew on the paper, 'to here.'

Lou looked closer at the map. 'That's a lot of 'burbs.'

'It is,' said Sharin, 'but it puts him in the right 'burbs for where this mess is happening.'

Sharin ran her finger around the circle and then to each of the places she'd marked on the map, indicating the locations of where women disappeared and where they reappeared. "We'll get this written up tonight Mel, and send it to you tomorrow,' she said.

'Thanks so much. You two are the best.'

'And don't you forget it,' said Lou.

'Never. Oh, just quickly, have you heard from Angel?' asked Mel.

'I'm meeting her for a drink after work.'

'Great. Can't wait to hear what she has to say,' said Mel.

'If I know Angel, it'll be good,' said Lou.

'I bet,' said Mel. 'See you later.'

'We better get on with it then,' said Lou.

'Righto. Shove over and let's start. I'll dictate, you type,' said Sharin, as Lou hung up the phone.. For the remainder of the afternoon, they gathered the threads of their case and created a story they hoped would make some shred of difference.

Chapter 46

MEL PUSHED THE THIN WHITE BLANKET DOWN OVER her knees and rolled stiffly to the side.

Her hand reached for the one that draped over the edge of the bed and held it, softly rubbing her thumb over the palm.

The hand was clammy and warm. Mel felt for a pulse in the wrist and found it weak and fast. She sat up, pulling herself onto her knees so she could lean further over the bed. The chair she'd slept in creaked and groaned.

Lexie was asleep. Her pale skin was flushed and the tubes up her nose hissed oxygen into her nostrils. As her chest shuddered with each breath, Mel felt her own heartbeat quicken. Every hospital visit became one of greater fear knowing that one day, it would be the last. Lexie's ability to clear her lungs was always difficult and each time she caught pneumonia it became a little more difficult. One day it would be impossible and Mel couldn't bear to think about it. Her eyes filled with tears as she pressed her head close to her sister's cheek to try and hold them in. She nuzzled her face and whispered to her to get better. 'Don't you leave me,' she whispered. In response, she felt a movement against her forehead and the gentle flutter of eyelashes against her skin. She sat back and Lexie's eyes opened, holding her stare for a

232

moment, before closing again. Mel let her tears fall. This frail and beautiful girl was the only link to her mother and their shared past. Mel had given all she could to Lexie, but so often felt she'd failed. She was trying to become an adult and a mother whilst Lexie was just trying to grow up. She'd always included Lexie in her life and Ricky had made her his own from the moment he met her. For Annie, there was never a time without Lexie and she was her everything. In return they had received a love so unconditional it made her ache. Lexie came close to filling the hole in Mel's heart left by Peg.

She was unaware of how long she sat there before a nurse came in and interrupted her thoughts.

'How are you doing?' she asked, touching Mel's shoulder.

The tears still streaked her face but she tried to hide her emotions behind a smile. 'Good thanks.'

The nurse didn't remove her hand. Instead, she squeezed softly. 'It's not easy seeing someone you love struggling like this,' she said.

'No, it's not,' croaked Mel.

'Take a break. I'll look after her. It may not look like it, but she is doing ok. You take a shower and freshen up. Use Lexie's ensuite. And get some brekky.'

Mel agreed and did as she was told. It was a relief to hand over responsibility.

When she came back into the room, she saw the clothes Ricky left for her. He sent a message to her phone, promising to come back after work with Annie. He had a difficult job keeping Annie away, but with one day before school broke for the term holidays, she needed to stay focused. The formal was enough distraction.

Mel phoned work and Dan in succession. Neither answered, so she left messages. She'd been trying to contact Dan for three days without luck and it was driving her mad. She'd tried Sarah too but came up short. She guessed they were with Sarah's mum who lived remotely, but found it hard to believe neither of them could access their phones in that time. Surely they went into town at some stage and she knew there was a phone signal there. She pushed away the thought that something worse had happened.

She texted both Sharin and Lou who responded immediately. Sharin said to check her email and that both she and Lou would come over at lunchtime.

Mel was reading a page of the report that Sharin had attached to the email when Dave texted saying he was on the road and would be back about one p.m., so Mel invited him to join them. She didn't tell him her plan to end the investigation. It could wait till then.

The report Sharin and Lou prepared was comprehensive and the information Angel provided was gold. Everything was ready to hand over to Dave and from there, the police. Mel felt a weight lift at the prospect of relinquishing the information they had found, but her uneasiness about Peter working for a disability service, remained.

She watched Lexie sleep and wondered what he knew of her. She thought about the events of the past twenty-seven years and couldn't think of any that would provide Peter with an opportunity to know of Lexie or what had become of her. He disappeared when Peg died. He hadn't seen her for a year prior to it and he'd been interstate since that time. He'd come back only months ago. But he was a closed book. What was his story?

Over the next few hours Lexie's condition didn't improve, but it didn't get worse. Mel read and reread the report, making mental notes of what she would say to Dave. He would feel let down. They'd come a long way together on this and they both wanted a result. Dave wanted his sister's killer back in jail. Mel just wanted her mother's killer found. And as a by-product, they hoped to save another girl from a fate as horrific as theirs. More importantly for Mel, to protect Annie from harm. But the web of threads they'd uncovered was tangled and to untangle them, needed skills and resources they didn't have. Mel knew too well that the links they'd made were tenuous and the ones the police were working on were unknown to them. But just maybe, they intersected somewhere and a truth would be found.

Around 1 p.m. Lou texted her to meet them downstairs in the cafeteria. They'd found a booth by a potted plant with a minikin of privacy. Mel texted Dave who arrived shortly after. He strode across the room, curly hair bouncing, looking happy.

'Ladies,' he said, taking a seat next to Mel. 'How are you all?'

His mood lightened the atmosphere at the table. Lou answered for them.

'Fair to muddling with lots to discuss.'

Dave rubbed his hands together. 'Exactly what I was hoping. Let's order and get on with it.' Then he quickly added, 'Sorry, Mel, how is Lexie?'

She updated him on Lexie and he updated her on his time in Canberra before they all moved in formation to the counter to order.

Back at the table, which was wiped clean in their absence by an officious man in a navy-blue uniform, they pulled out the papers Lou and Sharin had prepared and divided them between themselves.

'Wow, this is impressive,' Dave said shaking his head. 'You folk have been busy.'

'We have,' agreed Mel.

'Let's start from the top and Dave, just fill us in with anything you've found so we can add it in as we go,' said Sharin.

Lou opened the first page. 'Sharin, start with the map you drew.'

Dave flattened the map on the page in front of him. He pulled his glasses from a case in his pocket and leaned in to study the details more closely.

A shadow fell across the page and the sound of metal spikes on tiles clicked to a halt.

'Angel, you made it!' said Lou climbing to her feet. The chair scraped against the floor as she pushed back to move around the table and embrace her. Angel resembled a beautifully crafted toothpick with her thin hips encased in expensive leather pants, narrow shoulders draped in zebra-striped chiffon and a bow at her décolletage, sitting at right angles over a bust that was the product of a skilled plastic surgeon. Her hair was a river of black satin, her makeup immaculate and the rock on her finger dazzling. It caught in Lou's hair as she reached up to hug her and they both collapsed in laughter as she fought to extract it.

Lou did the introductions then pulled a chair up between herself and Sharin. Mel watched on as Lou, Angel and Sharin squashed together and marveled at how comfortable they looked. She knew instantly she liked Angel.

Dave said very little but was intrigued by the new addition. Lou indicated that Angel had some interesting information and she wanted her to be here for the telling. Dave nodded enthusiastically. 'Great, on with the show then,' he said.

Everyone looked to Sharin.

Chapter 47

'RIGHTO,' SAID SHARIN, LEANING INTO THE TABLE, 'THE map highlights the locations where the girls disappeared and reappeared, including Peggy. Peg was found here at the back of the restaurant off Lygon St, near O'Connor St, Carlton,' she pressed a finger to the page and they all looked to it. 'Kristen was taken from the Café on Rathdowne St and her body found at the back of the Rose St Art Market, Fitzroy. That's two suburbs from where Peg was found. Erin disappeared here in McCutcheon Way and was found in a lane near the TransDev depot in Fitzroy– one suburb from Peg,' she continued pointing in turn to each location. 'Lisa was taken somewhere around the IGA on Victoria Parade and was found here, off Lygon St in Edward St. That is only a few streets from where Peg was found.'

Sharin paused but no one filled it so she went on. 'There are a few things. Firstly, each body is turning up in closer and closer proximity to where Peg was located. And in Lisa's case, the same setting. Why would that be?'

She looked around the faces. They each stared back. Dave shrugged. 'Maybe he was making a point. Leading a trail to Peg?'

Mel nodded. 'Maybe he wasn't getting his message across and is trying to highlight the point?'

Lou ran a finger gnarled with arthritis across the page, taking in all four locations. 'Or maybe, it's coincidence?'

'No such thing as coincidence,' said Dave and Mel together.

Lou smiled. 'Maybe. Maybe not.' She lifted her finger from the page. 'What other thoughts do you have, Sharin?'

'Well, I found out yesterday, that Peter, Peg's friend, lives within fifteen minutes of his Mum's nursing home, which puts him in the suburbs here,' She ran the tip of her forefinger along the line of the circle she'd drawn. 'Half of that circle takes in the areas the women were either taken or found.'

'Sharin, this is great work,' said Dave.

'It really is,' agreed Mel.

Sharin shrugged. 'Thanks, but it doesn't mean it is Peter, only that he lives in and around the area and would know it well.'

'Good point. What else do we know about him?' asked Dave. 'Did you have any luck with the Telecom lead?'

'We did,' said Mel. 'Randall, he's the security guy at Telstra, knew Peter. Said he'd disappeared sometime in July or August '92. He was fiddling the books and been caught out, but before they could do anything he vanished. Kinda interesting 'cause it was around the same time Peg was murdered.'

Dave's head was bobbing up and down as he scratched the tip of his nose. 'Did Randall say what he was like? Any friends or acquaintances? Habits?'

This time Lou spoke. 'Randall only gave us the basics. Said Peter was a really quiet guy. Nice enough. Kept to himself. Lived with his Mum.'

'So ... bland? Boring even?' said Dave.

'Yep, but good on the math,' said Lou.

'Guess if you're gonna embezzle the boss's money, you want to fly under the radar. Dull and invisible works for ya,' said Dave.

'Except for the tick,' said Sharin.

'Oh yeah, that was the only curious thing about him. Had a tick with his shoulder,' said Lou.

'What do you mean?' asked Dave.

Lou imitated the tick that Randall described. Right shoulder flicking up to her ear, head tilting into it.

Dave stretched back. His eyebrows knitted together as he studied the ceiling. He rocked forward, making Sharin, who sat opposite him, jump. 'Sorry, Sharin,' he said, 'just remembered. The waitress who that numb nuts coppa interviewed when Peg died, said she recalled the time the guy left the café because his arm was jerking and it caught her eye. She was talking to a customer and facing the window when he walked behind her to the door. She saw his reflection in the glass and his arm was jerking up and down. She said she turned to look but only saw the back of him as he left. Could well have been him.'

'Jesus!' said Mel folding her hands behind her head. A buzz of excitement was building. They speculated about the Peg and Peter encounter in the café. Why did they meet? What happened afterward?

'It really could be him who did this,' said Mel.

'Or it might not,' warned Lou.

The chatter stopped.

'Just sayin',' continued Lou, 'because we don't know if he caught up with her after she left the café. She left separately. He's definitely a good candidate but anyone could have met her after she left.'

'Yes, but it puts him in the picture back then, and he's around now. More to the point, he's only been back in Melbourne for the past year. And those women have disappeared this year. AND their deaths are similar to Peg's,' said Sharin.

Everyone looked at Lou who tipped her head and raised her hands in surrender. 'I am just trying to keep an open mind here,' she argued.

'And rightly,' agreed Dave. 'It could also be Lang or a copycat.'

'Or it could be both,' said Sharin.

'Meaning?' asked Dave.

'Tell Dave about the Lang connection, Lou,' said Mel.

Lou pointed to Angel and said, 'This is where Angel comes in. Over to you, my dear.'

Angel dutifully took her cue. Her face remained as serene as it had the entire time Sharin was speaking. She spoke without haste or excitement, never succumbing to drama or embellishment.

'I have several very reliable friends and one was able to help. It's still a relatively small industry, thankfully,' she added, smiling at Lou.

'Lucky for us,' agreed Lou.

'Indeed,' said Sharin.

'My friend has a client who is quite elderly now but with whom she has had a long-standing 'relationship',' she said using air quotations. 'He is very open with her so she was able to extract quite a lot from him.'

All four faces pressed toward her and she lowered her voice so as not to be heard across the room. Her friend's candour could have caused her trouble if overheard by the wrong people.

'Peter worked for John Coreman's father as the accountant for his construction firm in the early '80s. He was very clever and helped build Coreman Senior's business in significant ways. Coreman Senior would have kept him in that role but young Peter developed an attraction for a woman who also worked in the office. Unfortunately, she didn't reciprocate his feelings. He was persistent to the point of stalking and when she finally confronted him with the threat of legal action he backed off. But shortly after, dead animals and nasty notes began to appear on her doorstep and although she couldn't prove it was Peter, it was pretty clear it was him. Coreman Senior couldn't ignore the scandal and asked Peter to leave. But he kept him on as a consultant and Peter always did the end-of-financial-year audits. Pretty sure his talents were very useful. My friend's client suggested Coreman Senior was instrumental in securing the job at Telecom for Peter.'

Dave uncurled himself, stretching out in his seat 'Wow! That is some connection. So clearly, he knew John Coreman. And Lang?'

'He had to know Lang because Coreman was always with him and John had a job at his father's firm. Although, how much work he did is anyone's guess. Either way, he would've been in and out of that office a lot. And Lang with him.'

'Maybe Lang tried to get Peter involved in some of his activities? Money laundering, embezzlement?' said Mel.

'And perhaps Peg found out what Peter was up to and he killed her,' suggested Angel.

'Yeah, we wondered that too and any bloke who dumps dead animals on your doorstep has gotta be someone to watch out for,' agreed Lou.

'Or Lang killed her?' suggested Dave.

'Actually, that's a point,' agreed Mel. 'If Peg did know something and Peter was protecting her, Lang might have killed her to remove the risk and warn off Peter.'

'Good theory. And now Peter is seeking revenge,' said Sharin.

'But why now, and not then?' asked Mel.

'Well, Peter had to hightail it out of the state when Janet uncovered his misdemeanors at Telecom,' said Lou.

'And, if Lang did kill Peg, Peter would have been the likely suspect which would have brought all his other doings into the frame,' added Sharin.

'So, he takes off and only comes back because his Mum is sick. Probably thought he'd be safe after all these years and perhaps he's been making plans the whole time,' said Angel.

'It's a wicked web we weave,' said Dave. 'Tell me more about this map, Sharin.'

Sharin slid the map an inch closer to her and took up where she'd left off.

'Well, the nursing home is here in Albert St, which is not that far from the IGA where Lisa worked. My lovely cleaner also told me that Peter worked for a disability service on Wellington St. If you look at the map,' they all bent further over it, 'Wellington St runs close to the bakery, two streets from Otter, and four blocks from Collingwood College, where Erin lived and went to school.'

'We need to find this guy, and that is the place to start,' said Dave.

Lou shot a look at Mel who shrugged. Dave caught them and asked what the matter was.

Before Mel could tell him that she was handing this over and she wouldn't be involved in finding the guy, the buzzer on the table vibrated letting them know their lunches were ready for collection.

'Sorry, Angel, we ordered before you arrived. Would you like something?' said Lou.

'Heavens no, I ate breakfast a few hours ago. I'm good, thanks.'

Lou suspected there hadn't been food past those lips in at least eighteen hours, but she didn't push it.

When the food was retrieved and they'd started eating, Dave returned to the question he'd posed. Mel put her sandwich down before she spoke and a piece of tomato slipped from between the bread and onto the map. 'Shit,' she said, scraping her nail under the slice and flicking it onto the plate. She looked down to the wet patch on the page and noted the spot where it landed.

Her gaze focused out to take in the location. 'Shit,' she said again.

'What's wrong, Mel?' asked Sharin.

Mel stared at the paper. "Maybe we have this all wrong,' she said.

'All wrong, how?' asked Dave.

Mel looked up. 'There is another possibility,' she began. 'A few weeks, ago, Marcus told me he saw Eddy walking along Wellington St, near Macca's and that he had something glittery in his bag. He shoved it down before he climbed into the cab of the truck but Marcus saw it. And he was pretty sure Eddy had lipstick on his face.' She peered closer at the wet spot on the paper. 'And

Macca's is right near the National Storage Units on Wellington St.'

Sharin gasped. 'You mean those self-storage places?'

Mel nodded.

'And then, on Wednesday night, Annie saw Eddy on Hoddle St with a woman. Well, she didn't actually see Eddy, but the woman was getting into his car. Anyway, Marcus told me that Eddy's been doing this art course but lied to Rosa saying it was a business course. The art institute where Lisa studied is on Hoddle St. Maybe Eddy is at the same art institute?'

'Oh, my God,' said Sharin. 'Maybe he met Lisa?'

'And maybe he's met another woman there?' said Dave.

And ...', Mel continued, pushing her plate away and pulling the map closer. 'Eddy's emporium is right here, in Nicholson St,' she said pressing her finger into the page. 'It's almost central to the three locations where the bodies were found.'

Lou lifted her map for a closer look, then turned it to face the others. 'And Rosa's house is close to all the action.'

Mel clasped her fingers together between her knees and rocked forward. 'Surely not,' she said.

'He knows how your Mum died,' said Lou.

'And he would've been old enough to do it,' agreed Dave.

Mel shook her head back and forth. 'No. Surely not. He'd known Peg all his life. This is nuts. He's a dick but not a murderer. Nope. No way. Why would he?'

'Why does anyone?' asked Dave.

'You said he hated you because you outed him. Maybe he wanted to hurt you as badly as he could. Make you feel how he felt,' said Lou.

Mel rocked more. Could he do that? Was he even capable? And why would he start again now? Would he hurt Annie?

'I just can't think this!' she said, 'It would be too awful.'

'It's conceivable,' said Dave.

'Yes, but I've known Eddy all my life. Surely something would slip. And he was distraught at Peg's funeral.'

'An act, maybe?' said Lou.

'I just can't ... could he? I'm so confused. I don't really believe he could do this.'

Sharin leaned over and lifted the map. 'If you hadn't seen this map, Mel, would you suspect him?' she asked.

Mel twisted a piece of bread off her sandwich. Then dropped it onto the plate. 'No. No, I wouldn't. But I've seen it now.'

'There could be a logical explanation for all of it,' said Angel.

'I know ...' She pushed the sandwich away. 'Honestly, this has to stop. My head hurts.' She turned fully to face Dave. 'Look, Dave. I don't want to do this anymore. This is ... I don't know ... too much. I want answers but the more we look, the more we ask ...'

'But it's coming together,' he said.

'Is it?' she said waving her hand over the report. 'Two minutes ago, I thought it was Peter, maybe Lang, now Eddy. Even thought it was you ...'

'What?'

'Yep, exactly...... Next, I'll think it's Ricky!!'

'That's just ridiculous,' said Dave.

'Obviously. But that's where my heads at. I spoke with Shaz and Lou on Tuesday about it and that's why they've put this report together. So it's all in one place. It's not that I don't want something to happen with all this, I do. But I just can't do it anymore, Dave. And with what you have, we could put something significant together for the Police. It's still a day or two before anything is likely to happen and another girl goes missing, so it could be useful.'

'I just don't understand. You've found so much already. We could do so much more,' pleaded Dave.

'But that's the point, Dave, WE don't have time. And. I've got Annie and Lexie to think about. There is so much going on!'

Mel looked around the room, desperate for a diversion to stem the rising tide of anxiety creeping into her chest.

'You can't. Isn't it for Annie we're doing this?' whispered Dave.

Mel sighed. 'And the others. But we can't help the others by ourselves. It's time to hand it over.'

He looked away from Mel and down to his plate. He looked up at Sharin and Lou for help but they didn't give it. He pushed his fork across the plate with force. It clattered onto the edge before falling off.

'We are getting closer,' he said in a flat tone.

'We're getting closer to the time another girl goes missing,' said Sharin.

Dave looked hard at her. 'And this could help.'

'I know, but not in our hands Dave. We need to take it to the Police. This and everything you have,' said Mel.

Dave snorted, pushed back his chair, and folded his arms hard against himself. 'You seriously believe they'll take any notice of this? Really!'

'Why wouldn't they?' asked Lou.

'Because idiot plods like that coppa you met the other day are on the job. That's why!'

'They're not all like that. Not then, not now,' said Sharin.

'That fucker Lang is out there because people didn't do their jobs properly. Your Mum is dead with no idea who did it because they didn't do their fucking jobs. These girls are dead and we're no closer to knowing who it is because they are NOT doing their jobs. Which bit is going to make them do their goddamn jobs?'

'Maybe this bit right here,' said Sharin picking up the report and flicking through it. 'This might give them something that helps. We don't know what they have. They don't know what we have. Perhaps there is one piece of the puzzle in here that puts it all together.'

Dave continued to press his arms closer, tightening his hands around his elbows. He directed his next words to the floor.

'So that's it. The report is it?'

'It's a pretty comprehensive report,' said Lou who hadn't

moved a muscle since Dave erupted. Mel knew she was getting edgy.

He must have sensed it too because he pushed his chair out behind him and stood in one movement. He paused to straighten his leg, picked up the report, and tapped the table. 'Right then.'

He left without turning back. Four pairs of eyes watched as he walked away. Only time would tell what Dave decided to do.

Chapter 48

MEL WANTED TO CALL AFTER HIM AS DAVE WALKED away, but decided there was little point. They'd burdened him with all the responsibility and had to accept whatever followed. It was his call now.

'Well, that was predictable,' said Lou.

'He's just disappointed. He'll get over it,' said Mel.

'Do you think he'll talk to us again?' asked Sharin.

'He's a man. Needs time to realise you're right. Give him a day. He'll be ok,' said Angel.

'So now what?' asked Mel.

'Dunno. Guess we're done,' said Lou.

'Do you think he'll take it further?' asked Sharin.

'Who knows? He doesn't have much faith in the police,' said Mel.

'He better,' said Lou, 'that was a lot of work wasted if he doesn't.'

'We could take it ourselves,' suggested Sharin.

'We could, but Dave can add so much extra. Besides, they'd take him more seriously than us,' said Mel.

'That's us done then,' said Lou.

'Yep,' agreed Mel.

'I think we need cake,' said Lou.

'Great idea,' agreed Sharin. 'Let me go get us some.'

Angel shook her head profusely. 'No, no, not for me thanks.'

Sharin looked at her in the manner of a nurse responding to someone refusing a blood transfusion, but left without a comment.

'You ok, Mel?' Lou said.

'I dunno. Yes. No. This all seems stupid somehow. Like a game. Except it's not.'

'No, it's not. And what we've found might help,' said Lou.

'Maybe.'

'Mel,' said Lou and paused.

'Yeah.'

'You don't really suspect Eddy, do you?'

Mel shifted in her chair and sighed. 'I don't know. Not really. I just ... he has been acting weird lately. More weird than usual I mean. It's ridiculous though. I do know that. That's why I need to stop this. I'm losing all perspective. We are no closer to knowing who did this and some poor woman is looking at losing her life in the next twenty-four hours if the stats are correct. The sooner the police figure out who it is, the safer we'll all be.'

Sharin returned with cakes for three. A sponge with jam and cream; a hazelnut gateau and a piece of hummingbird cake. She set them down, correctly guessing the taste preferences of each woman and they ate in silence.

As Sharin licked the last dollop of jam-streaked cream from her fork she said to Mel, 'with everything that's going on, do you still want to go to the casino on Saturday?'

'You still up to your old tricks?' Angel elbowed Lou.

'Tricks is such a tacky word, Angel,' said Lou, elbowing her back.

Angel laughed. 'You were always one of the best, Lou.'

'With this crew, I still am,' she said.

Mel watched the delight flow easily between them. They'd shared and lost a husband but found each other in the process.

Mel finished her mouthful of hummingbird cake before answering. 'Yes, I'm up for the casino, but depends on Lexie. If she's worse, I'll stay at the hospital but if nothing changes, I will need the distraction to stop myself fretting.'

'Distraction! I think you've had plenty of that already,' said Lou.

'Yes. But this is a good distraction. Something fun.'

'You don't think Annie's formal will be fun?' said Sharin.

'God no! All those stuck-up snobs prancing about like peacocks trying to impress each other. It might be the girls' night but guaranteed it'll be mothers on parade.'

'I know what you mean! I went to my niece's formal a few years back and holy moly! Some of the dresses the Mums wore were over the top. Talk about competing! I felt like such a frump.'

'You could never look like a frump, Shaz.'

'Oh, next to them, I was frumpy. One chick wore an Armani tuxedo pants suit! Mind you, her daughter looked like a super-model so she had to work hard to keep up, but lordy, it was like being at the Oscars!'

'Melly, you can borrow my blue Kaftan if you like?' suggested Lou.

Mel crushed her face into a grimace 'Now that would make a statement!'

'Haven't seen you in that for a while,' added Sharin.

'Nah, decided the all-black look works better for me.'

'You do look good in black,' agreed Mel.

'Thanks. So, what *will* you be wearing?' asked Lou.

'A black dress as it happens. Nothing flash. Annie's the star here and God she looks fabulous in that gown. So beautiful.'

'We want a lot of photos,' said Sharin.

'Oh, you'll get them.'

'And what are we all wearing on Saturday then?' asked Sharin.

'Black pantsuit,' said Lou.

'Black dress,' laughed Mel.

'Oh dear, me too!' giggled Sharin.

'Black is back!' said Angel.

'We needed understated, yet elegant. We've got it,' said Lou.

'No problem there,' agreed Sharin.

'I can pick you both up,' said Lou.

'Not sure I can sit with my legs around my ears in a dress,' complained Sharin.

'No need, I'll take Trev's hunk of junk.'

'The mighty beast. Will he be up for that?' said Angel.

'Does he have a choice?' said Lou.

'Good point,' agreed Angel.

'Ok, pick you up about 11 a.m. Mel and 11.30 a.m. Sharin?'

'Yep. That should work. Ricky leaves for golf at ten.'

'You haven't told him?'

Mel raised her eyebrows. 'You know I can't,' she said.

'Mmmm. And Annie won't blab?' said Sharin.

'Won't be there. Staying over at Elena's. Although I worry about that. I think she might have a thing for Elena's brother. And when he sees her in that dress, well ...'

'He'll lose his 'nads if Ricky finds out,' said Lou.

'Yes he will,' agreed Mel.

They all laughed. The atmosphere was lighter and Mel felt, for a moment, better than she had in days.

The phone buzzed in her pocket, and instantly the feeling of anxiety returned as she opened the case. 'It's Ricky. He and Annie are coming to see Lexie now. Got off early,' she said reading the screen. 'I better go up.'

Sharin and Lou left for the office, and Angel for home. Mel headed back to Lexie's room. She found Lexie propped up in bed. Several pillows billowed around her making her look even tinier than she was. Her thin dark hair was stringy from sweat on her forehead. She was still flushed and the cough that hacked out of her made the sheets shake. Mel stood by the bed and stroked the hair back from Lexie's face. Lexie watched her. She licked her lips which were beginning to crack. Mel reached over the bedside table and filled a half-empty glass with water, straightening the plastic straw as she did. She slipped her hand behind Lexie's head and gently lifted her a few inches off the pillow so she could drink through the straw. When she'd finished she found a tube of lip balm and ran it over Lexie's lips, which Lexie again licked. She smiled weakly. It tasted of strawberry. Lexie's favourite.

Mel could feel the pain in her heart when it feels like the life is being squeezed out. As a distraction, she busied herself with tucking in sheets and straightening blankets. She found the TV remote and scrolled through channels until she found one that played bosa nova jazz. It was their favourite music. When Mel was helping Dan survive the months after Peg's death, they'd spent many hours swaying around the lounge room to it, in the early hours of the morning when Lexie was a baby and before she'd found her circadian rhythm. Mel wanted more than anything to pick up her sister and dance her around the room again. Perhaps in another life, they would.

Ricky and Annie arrived. So did the doctor. They discussed Lexie's condition and how long she would likely be in hospital. She was beginning to respond to the antibiotics but it would take a while. The doctor felt she would do well. Mel felt herself relax and realised the intensity of the tension she'd been holding.

Annie and Ricky gave Lexie lots of hugs and kisses before taking Mel home. It was 4 p.m. and not too early for wine. While Ricky poured two glasses, Mel curled up in his recliner and told him about the report Lou and Sharin had prepared. She forwarded him a copy to read and sipped at the wine while he made dinner. By the time it was cooked she was sound asleep and the glass sat half empty on the table beside her.

Chapter 49

ON FRIDAY MORNING THE SUN ROSE THROUGH A bright blue sky, whilst a chill wind clipped the edges off an otherwise perfect day. A call to the hospital told Mel that Lexie's temperature had dropped and she'd slept better during the night. Even the Wolseley made her morning cheery by starting the first time and purring smoothly through every change of light on her way to work.

Mel rushed down the corridor with too many things on her mind. She catapulted past the photocopy room and registered a nanosecond too late that a body was moving out of it. Their shoulders collided and both bounced sideways.

'Shit!' exclaimed the person as they ricocheted into the doorway.

'Sorry, I didn't see you coming out,' exclaimed Mel, extending both hands to catch the person.

Mel noticed the cast on her arm before she realized it was Jill.

'Oh,' she said, holding Jill steady. 'I am so sorry. I didn't see you. Just too many things on my mind. Is your arm ok?'

Jill stood in the doorway visibly shaken. It took a moment for her to answer as the look of surprise slowly eased from her face. 'It's ok. I should have been paying attention too,' she said.

They stood motionless for a moment longer and Mel released her. 'No, it's my fault. I am so sorry Jill. But *is* your arm ok?'

Jill rubbed the cast. 'No, I think it's broken,' she laughed.

Mel laughed too. 'So, what happened?'

'I tripped on a loose carpet square. Yesterday. I was at a course and it happened at lunchtime.'

'Nasty.'

'Yep. And no, I wasn't drinking!' she added.

'Might have been better if you were,' said Mel.

'True,' agreed Jill. 'Anyway, it got me out of the course. Although, to be fair, it wasn't that bad.'

'I have heard that,' said Mel.

'Oh, and how is Lexie? I ran into Deidre at the hospital and she said Lexie was in there.'

'That's nice she visited,' said Mel. 'She's not well but is stable according to the doctor. I have to admit, I panic every time. Until she's out of there and home I can't relax.'

'No. But seeing Deidre would have cheered her up I imagine,' said Jill.

'I'm sure it would have,' said Mel. She really liked this woman.

'Oh, and she said she met Lexie's dad.'

'What?' said Mel. 'Dan?'

'She didn't mention his name,' said Jill.

Fragments of phone messages, unanswered voice mails, and the last conversation with Dan crashed together in her mind.

'I've been trying to get hold of him for three days. Why didn't he call?' asked Mel.

Jill shrugged just as her smart watch beeped. She flipped it up, read it, and apologised she had to go. Mel watched her walk away with a barrage of unanswered questions hanging in the air.

Chapter 50

At 10.05 a.m. that morning, Mel logged off her computer, collected her bag, and left the office with Lou to attend a workshop.

'I need to phone Dan. I'll explain ...' she finished as she lifted the phone to her ear.

It rang the usual five times before the now familiar message kicked in 'Dan. Can't answer. Please leave a message.' At the tone, Mel left a message.

'What the hell is going on!' she said to Lou as she hung up.

'Ahh, you're tell'n the story here.'

'I just ... I'm ... I just don't fucking know what's going on,' said Mel.

Lou stopped walking. Mel stopped beside her. 'Take a breath and start again,' said Lou.

Mel took a deep breath as commanded, 'I saw Jill and she said she saw Deidre, that's one of Lexie's carers, at the hospital last night.'

'Why was Jill at the hospital?' asked Lou.

'Broken arm. But she told Jill she'd met Lexie's dad there.'

Lou's eyebrow crept up her forehead, 'And he didn't call you?'

'No,' said Mel. 'And I still can't get hold of him. I don't know what the hell is going on.'

Mel stared at Lou as if she'd find the answer there. Lou shrugged, 'That's odd.'

'It is. Why wouldn't he call?'

'No idea, but can you get up there today? Ask a nurse. Wait for him to visit?' said Lou.

'I can't. The formal,' said Mel.

'Ah, of course.'

'I'll just have to keep calling. But I tell you what, he's in so much trouble when I get hold of him. What's wrong with him? He's never been like this before,' said Mel.

The workshop finished at noon. By then Mel had checked her phone a dozen times and left two more messages, but the phone continued to deny her an answer.

At 12.45 p.m. she collected Annie from school and the whole afternoon disappeared in a frenzy of appointments as Annie worked her way through makeup, hair, and nails, until finally at 5.15 p.m. she was dressed and standing outside on the patio with a corsage at her wrist and a nervous Lucas by her side. Ricky kept glaring at him. Thankfully, Annie was oblivious.

They celebrated with champagne and photos before heading to the group gathering at a local parkland, for more photos. Lucas, along with six friends, had organised a stretch limousine that was waiting on the road when they arrived.

The group of eight, made their way to a bridge that traversed a small but picturesque lake at one end of the park. The sun was beginning to wane, turning the sky pink, and its reflection was amplified in the still waters of the lake, allowing for a photo that was breathtaking. The sunlight, weak as it was, fluttered in patterns around Annie, as it caressed the fabric of her gown.

Lucas and Annie moved to one side of the bridge, for individual photos. Both Mel and Lucas's Mum snapped away as Ricky and Lucas's dad became acquainted. The crowds roiled around the park as families convened and people posed. When a hand slid around her waist, Mel jumped. Rosa tucked herself under Mel's arm and hugged her close.

'Ello, Darrrrling.'

'Rosa!' Mel and Annie exclaimed at the same time.

Lucas stood awkwardly as Annie dropped her arm from around his waist and moved as quickly as three-inch heels would allow, toward them. She rushed in to kiss Rosa before diverting to the left.

'Uncle Eddy!' she squealed.

For the briefest moment, Mel had the urge to leap into her path. The image of Eddy creeping around dark streets in the middle of the night made her tense.

Rosa felt it. 'All right darrrrling?'

Mel relaxed. 'Yep.'

'She looks like a gooddess my boooootiful Annie,' she said.

Annie grinned at Rosa as she hugged Eddy. Mel scrutinised every second that followed. Watched as he enfolded her; gently stroked his hands down her back, inclined his head low to meet the top of hers. For the first time in her life, she questioned this familiar scene. Is it affection or something else?

His hand slid, imperceptibly along the line of the zipper to the small of her back. He kissed her hair. Did he linger there longer than was paternal?

Some deep unknown gripped her gut. She felt her arm loosen around Rosa's shoulder just as Annie pulled away from Eddy. Mel observed as Annie looked up into Eddy's face. It was full of the love and affection Annie had known from this man all her life. He and Mel may have worked tirelessly at their disgust for one another, but Eddy had only ever shown adoration for Annie. Now she wondered if this love was safe.

At that moment, the space between her and Eddy was blocked by two figures distracting her from her thoughts.

'Look who I found loitering in the park!' said Ricky.

'Hey, Marcus,' greeted Mel.

Rosa stepped to the side, as Marcus leaned in to kiss Mel on the cheek, before turning to Annie. 'You look amazing,' he said.

Annie blushed and beamed, swirling on the spot. It served to add an exclamation mark to his comment.

'And this must be the very fortunate Lucas,' he smiled, walking forward to shake his hand. Mel marveled how some people could so simply put others at ease.

Lucas shot a sideways glance at Ricky, hoping this might improve his credibility. It didn't. No man alive was good enough for his one and only daughter.

Everyone gathered to celebrate Annie. She took it in, completely unaffected by the adulation and attention. She was clueless about her impact on others. These were the people she loved. The people who loved her. This wasn't about her but all of them collectively. She slid her hand into the crook of Lucas's arm and led him toward their group of friends. She waved for everyone to follow, and they again assumed their position, posing and photographing.

At 6.30 p.m. the last photos of the groups waving from their cars were taken and the crowd dispersed.

'You all heading out for dinner?' asked Ricky.

'Oh, Darrrrrling. Why pay for dinner when we eat like kings at home?'

Ricky laughed, 'At your home for sure.'

'Ohhh, Darrrrlinng,' Rosa said reaching up to squeeze his cheeks. 'But tonight,' she continued, 'it is dinner at my sister's place.'

'That'll be lovely for you all,' said Mel.

'Oh no, Darrrlinnnng, just me. These two,' she said flinging her thumb in their direction, 'are off and out.'

Mel looked at Marcus. 'Back to the farm?'

'Later tonight. Have to fix up a wine shipment that's been held up on the docks.'

'Of course,' said Mel.

'And Eddy?' asked Ricky.

Mel realised she was leaning in and corrected herself.

'Ahh, going out,' he said.

'Anywhere interesting?' asked Mel.

Eddy's hesitation made Mel suspicious and if they'd been alone, he'd refuse to answer. But a social gathering provided pressure to respond.

'Umm, just the movies. With friends.'

'Movie. What are you seeing?' asked Mel.

'Does it matter?' asked Eddy.

'Just curious,' said Mel.

Ricky pressed closer to Mel, who stiffened.

'The new Tarantino film. Want to come along?' he added sarcastically.

Ricky replied before Mel could. 'Thanks for the offer, but we're required for yet more photos at the Hilton. You know the 'official ones.' Cost a week's salary for a single A4 print!'

'But Ricky, they're professional!' said Marcus.

'Ah yes. Taken on a digital camera like the one in Mel's hand here. But I guess we do get to stand in front of a motley screen with a few hot lights.'

'Something money just can't buy!' agreed Marcus.

They walked together to their cars before taking leave of each other. But for the remainder of the evening, Mel's mind wandered between Eddy's night out and Dan's unanswered phone.

Chapter 51

THE ALARM ON RICKY'S SIDE OF THE BED WAS LOUD and incessant. Mel patted her hand across the bed to where Ricky should be, but the sheets were bare. She opened her eyes and pulled herself onto her elbows.

She looked around the room, which was still dark. He wasn't in the room and the alarm kept buzzing. She dragged herself across the bed, reached up, and fumbled for the button. Two attempts and the blessed thing shut down.

She dragged herself back across the cool cotton and flopped onto the pillow. The next time she opened her eyes, it was in response to warm breath on her cheek and fingers sweeping over her hip. 'I have a cuppa tea for you.'

'Mmmmmm,' she murmured back.

'I'll leave it here,' he said, sliding it onto her bedside table.

'Ta.'

'I'm goin' now. My mistress the golf clubs, she waits,' he whispered into her ear before he kissed her.

She waved him away.

He'd almost reached the door when she mumbled through the pillow. 'What time is it?'

'Eets 9 a.m..'

Mel sat bolt upright. 'Shit!.'

'What?'

'Ah, nothing. Just didn't realise I'd slept so long,' said Mel.

'And you keep sleeping,' said Ricky.

'Yep,' she said obediently, falling back onto the bed.

She waited at least five minutes after the front door closed to be sure he was gone, before getting up and running a shower.

As she ate breakfast, she texted Annie at her friend's house and again phoned Dan. Neither responded. The third of her calls was to the hospital. Lexie was doing well. Mel asked if Lexie's dad visited but the nurse was unable to tell her. She said she would visit later that afternoon and hung up.

For an hour Mel took time to do her hair and makeup. Elegant but understated. She pressed the simple black linen dress and sprayed it with a fixing spray that promised, on the label, to 'prevent linen from creasing'. Finally, she stepped into the black suede sling-backs, completing the look with a marquisate ring and the simple pearl studs Gran gave her on her twenty-first birthday. She always wore them to the casino. They were her lucky charm.

On the dot of 11 a.m., Lou honked the horn. Trev's hulking mountain of a car honked heavy and loud. Mel cringed.

As she stepped up into the cab, she was glad of the wide runner board and the handles placed at two heights by the car door. She swung herself onto the seat next to Lou, who sat on a booster cushion with the chair pulled up close to the wheel. She was smiling widely.

'You love this car, admit it,' said Mel.

'Yep. All this power!' She said revving the engine.

Mel cringed again.

Lou laughed, revved, and honked.

'Stop it!'

Lou laughed hard. Everything wobbled. It was glorious.

'Ok, Bonny. Drive on,' said Mel.

Lou flung the truck into reverse, rebounding down the driveway and over the curb. The mailbox skimmed past the front fender as Mel closed her eyes.

Lou laughed again. She rammed the gears into second and took off down the road, all that power being harnessed.

When Mel opened her eyes and allowed herself to rest back in the seat, she took a good look at Lou. 'You look great,' she said.

'Thanks. So do you,' said Lou, taking a sideways glance.

Lou wore a black pantsuit. The top was jersey, cut wide across the neckline. It draped in handkerchief folds to her knees. The pants she wore underneath were polished cotton, fitted to the ankle. She too wore minimal jewellery, but she'd taken time on her hair and makeup. Lou, dressed up and behind the wheel of his monster motor had, Lou confirmed, left Trevor with a hard-on.

They made it to Sharin's just before 11.30 a.m.. So far, the day was shaping up nicely.

Sharin teetered out of the house on patent black stilettos. Her long auburn hair was piled on top of her head, secured with a diamante-encrusted clip and her black silky dress clung to her curves. Lou looked at Mel. 'Every camera will be on her looking like that.'

'And every pair of eyes,' agreed Mel.

'Could she look any more stunning?'

'Nope and she is so damn unaware of how good she looks,' said Mel.

'Criminal,' said Lou.

'A curse,' agreed Mel.

Sharin struggled onto the runner board and into the back seat of the dual cab. Her dress had wriggled its way midway up her thighs by the time she slid into the seat. 'Helloooo,' she called.

'Howdy, cowgirl,' said Lou.

'OOH, I am sooooo looking forward to this.'

'Are we ready to win?' asked Mel.

'Yes, we are!' the others chorused.

The trip into the city was slowed by the usual Saturday traffic. Mel relayed the events of the night before and handed her phone around to show pictures of Annie. She'd used her phone and the camera so as not to miss a thing.

Lou asked if Mel had heard from Dan and they filled Sharin in about the unfolding hospital visit. Mel said she'd head to the hospital later in the day.

Sharin spoke to Michel the night before and he promised to see her the following week. He was pleased he'd been able to help find Peter's mum.

'Have you heard from Dave?' asked Sharin.

'Nope,' said Mel.

'Wonder if he did go to the police,' said Sharin.

'Bloody well hope so after all the work we put in!' said Lou.

'Hey, speaking of that. No news on any missing girls?' asked Mel.

'Haven't heard anything,' said Lou.

'No, thank goodness,' said Sharin.

'Let's pretend for a few hours that nothing is wrong in the world.'

'Casinos are good for that,' said Lou.

Soon after twelve, they pulled into the carpark. Lou parked as far from other cars as she could. Not because she was worried they'd hit her. But because she might hit them. She could barely see over the bonnet, let alone the back. Mel checked her phone one last time and switched it to silent. If anything happened in the next two hours it was too bad.

The girls climbed down from the cabin, adjusted themselves, and made for the entrance.

There were people everywhere. Women in fascinators and fancy hats; men in suits and more flash and cash than they'd seen in one room for quite some time. Spring carnival was on full display.

The room itself was a carnival. Gold and bronze offset by swirls of pink and blue teased the senses, as light shone like 'God rays' from the ceiling. The noise and movement twirled around them, providing the cover they were hoping for. Amongst the crowd they could be lost. Invisible long enough to get the job done.

First Lou and Sharin went to the bar, ordered a drink, and found a booth. They sipped and chatted for a while before one of them left for the toilet. On the way back, she stopped at the cashier, changed her money for chips, and headed to the booth. The other one took her turn at the cashier and returned to the table. They then wandered around the poker machines, dropping a chip in here and there, before finally making it to the tables.

Mel, on the other hand, delayed her entry by walking the long way around the casino. She ignored the others and walked straight to the cashier, exchanged her cash, and strode with purpose to the gaming room where she took a seat at a busy table.

Today, Sharin was playing. Mel was spotting and Lou was watching the crowd, cameras, and security.

Mel chose a table with two empty seats across from one another. They needed the rest of the table to be full or at least near full, so they were sitting well apart.

Sharin and Lou stopped at the roulette wheel and took a turn each. They had a brief discussion, with Sharin pointing over to the Blackjack table and Lou pointing toward the bar.

Sharin walked to the table Mel was at and sat down.

Lou wandered around looking interested but aloof. When she'd ambled around the room twice, she found a vantage point close enough for Mel to see her but far enough to be out of the way.

She ordered another drink and made herself comfortable.

The croupier dealt. The cards landed. The women counted. Mel played to lose, played to win, played to lose again. Small amounts, anonymous. Sharin played to win. Larger amounts. Less anonymous, but fast and frequent enough that they could win well and leave early.

Mel counted. Twisted an earring. Rolled the ring around her

finger. Smoothed the lipstick across her lips. All signals that Sharin would read. All signals that would confirm or correct her counting.

Each time Mel glanced at Lou, she saw nothing. No sign that anything was amiss. Lou continued to sip her drink and look bored.

The fifteenth hand of their day was being dealt when Sharin looked around. She hadn't lifted her head until then. Mel focused on counting. She tapped the table. The croupier moved around the table, working her way one person at a time to Sharin, who hadn't looked back at the table. She appeared, instead, to be sliding down her stool. For a moment Mel felt alarmed, particularly when she realised Sharin was not only sliding down her seat but rolling to the side. Deliberately.

Mel looked to Lou who was upright and poised to move. Someone they needed to avoid was close.

Mel pretended to stretch, and glanced about. There was no obvious security she could see. No Posse of management walking toward them. Nothing that screamed authority. She looked back at Sharin who by now was head level with the tabletop.

'Is everything ok, Madam?' asked the croupier.

'Umm, yes,' mumbled Sharin. She tapped the table and was dealt another two cards. Mel twisted her earring but Sharin wasn't looking at her. She rolled her ring. Still no response. Mel was well aware that Sharin was five points over blackjack and the game was lost, but Sharin seemed oblivious.

Sharin continued to fold herself in such a way that she nudged the player next to her with the top of her hair bun.

Over her head Mel saw Lou on her feet, gliding as nonchalantly as she could toward the table. When she reached her and tapped her shoulder, Sharin nearly jumped out of her skin.

Lou leaned alongside her and whispered, 'What are you doing?'

Without turning to face her Sharin whispered back. 'We have to go.'

'Why?'

'Let's just go,' she hissed, sliding off the stool. She smiled sweetly at the croupier, still ducking low, and announced her end to the game. She scraped her chips into her handbag and slunk away from the table, pushing Lou ahead of her.

Mel remained at the table, forcing her face into a mask. She played two more rounds, which she lost, gathered her chips, and hastily vacated her place. As she did, she noticed the croupier's hand slide under the table. That was a sure sign to get out as quickly as possible.

At the cashier, she looked around but couldn't see Lou or Sharin. She took the little cash she'd won and opened her bag to deposit it. Her phone was alight and vibrating. It was Lou.

'Meet us at the car,' she said and rang off. There were two other missed calls, but she decided she'd look at them in the car. For the moment she just needed to go.

Mel checked behind her once more as she left. Nobody followed. She sighed and realised she was holding her breath.

She arrived at the car to find Lou and Sharin huddled inside. Sharin was almost prone on the back seat.

'What happened?' she asked opening the back door.

'Get in,' summoned Lou.

Mel closed the back then opened the front door and clambered in.

'Shaz, what's wrong? Are you sick?' said Mel.

'No. I saw Michel!'

'Michelle? Who's she?' asked Mel.

'No! Meechel,' said Sharin.

'Oh! Is that bad?' asked Mel.

'Yes!'

'Why?'

'He's in security! I just didn't know it was here!' said Sharin.

'What?'

'Black suit, shirt too crisp, curly wire in his ear,' said Sharin.

'You could see that?' asked Mel.

'Not at first. I saw him crossing the floor between the craps table and thought, 'what's he doing here?' Then I thought, 'he's supposed to be working'. THEN it hit me. He does work. Here. And then I saw the curly wire.'

'I never saw it,' said Lou.

'I wouldn't either except he has a tattoo on his neck below his ear. It's a circle with a star in it. And it doesn't have a tail!'

'Jesus, Shaz. What if you're wrong? You were on a roll!'

'Mel! It was a wire and I'm right!'

'Ok, sorry. I just meant, maybe he was here for pleasure, not business,' said Mel.

'Oh well, that makes it so much better!' said Sharin.

'No, I mean ...'

'I think it best to stop there, Mel,' said Lou, leaning back over the seat to stroke Sharin's hair.

'You're right. I'm a douchebag. Sorry, Shazzy,' and she too leaned over to pat Sharin.

Outside the car, a patron walked past with his head bent low. The air conditioner in the car whirred as tiny particles of dust filtered across the windscreen and onto the dashboard.

'What should we do now?' asked Sharin.

'Guess we head for home,' said Lou.

'You, ok?' Mel asked Sharin.

She nodded, adjusting herself to sit upright. Mel and Lou shifted around in their seats.

Lou cranked the key in the steering wheel column and the engine roared to life. Lou set the gears in motion and pulled slowly out of the carpark. She turned on the radio for a subdued drive to Sharin's. Mel opened her phone to check her messages.

The first message was from Annie. '*Hi, Mum. El and her Mum dropped me home. Change of plans. My phone is nearly dead. Forgot my charger. I'm going to ride to the hospital to see Lexie. See you home later.*'

Mel checked the time Annie had rung. 12.15 p.m..

The next message was from Dan. *'Sorry I missed your calls, Mel, phone me.'*

'Finally! Dan's left a message,' she relayed to the others. 'Permission to phone?' she asked.

'Permission granted,' said Lou. She turned the radio down and Mel made the call.

Chapter 52

DAN ANSWERED IMMEDIATELY.

'Where have you been, Dan? I've been calling for days,' said Mel.

'Sorry, Mel, I know you're upset, but so much has happened. How's Lexie?' he asked.

'You should know that. You were at the hospital. Why didn't you let me know you were here?'

'What? I'm in Townsville. Sarah's mum died,' said Dan.

'Townsville? But Deidre said she saw you at the hospital, here?'

'Mel, I am in Townsville. Apart from here, I've been on the property trying to keep the cattle from disappearing. I haven't been home in a week, let alone Melbourne ... and who's Deidre?'

Mel stared at the windscreen trying to understand what he was saying. 'Umm, she's Lexie's carer. One of them. She's fairly new.'

'I don't know her. Why would she say she saw me?' asked Dan.

'Dunno. A woman I work with saw her at the hospital on Thursday night and said she met Lexie's dad.'

'Well, it wasn't me. She must have been confused about who it was.'

'I don't understand?' said Mel.

'Me neither. But I've been here all week. I came up last Monday. Sarah's mum's been getting worse and there was some trouble with the cattle. Anyway, on Thursday she had a heart attack and was airlifted to Townsville. Sarah went with her but I stayed. Eight cows disappeared last week and there's been some rustling further up north. I was out until Friday night. When I got in, Sarah called to say her mum had died. I'm here with them now.'

'Oh, I'm so sorry, Dan. Give Sarah my love.' She shook her head at Lou.

'Thanks, darl. I'll tell her.'

Mel could hear Dan relaying the message to Sarah.

'When's the funeral?' asked Mel.

'Next Friday. But I'm booking a ticket for Tuesday to come down and see Lexie. All right if I stay a night or two?'

Mel smiled before she realised. 'We'd love it.'

'Have to be back Thursday, so won't trouble you for more than two nights.'

'You're no trouble. Can't wait to see you. Lexie will be so happy.'

'I am really sorry, Mel. I don't say it enough but I am grateful for all you do for Lexie. And me,' he added.

Mel felt the tiny crush of her heart. 'It's all good,' she said.

'I'll email you the flight details. Gotto go now. Sorry, love.'

'Yep, sure. 'Course. See ya Tuesday.'

Mel hung up. Her face moved through happy, relieved, and then confused. 'That was Dan,' she said.

'Yes, it was,' agreed Lou. 'So, not the dad Deidre saw?'

'No. Not the dad.'

'What happened?' asked Sharin, leaning over the front seat.

Mel filled her in. Sharin sat back in her seat. Lou looked up into the rear-vision mirror and watched Sharin as the cogs turned in her head. 'What are you thinking, Miss Sharin?' she asked.

'I'm thinking, perhaps the dad is Peter.'

Mel spun around so fast her neck clicked 'What? Why?'

'He and Peg were together before Dan. Immediately before Dan, and a little less than a year before Peg died. And Lexie was three months old. And my new friend said that Peter was hoping to reunite with his daughter now that he was back.'

'And the daughter is Lexie?' said Lou.

'You think he could be Lexie's dad?' said Mel. 'But surely Dan is?'

'Maybe not. It's not implausible. Maybe Peter found out about the baby and that's why they met up again. Wanted to know for sure. Wanted to be part of her life.' said Sharin.

'Ghost from the past,' murmured Mel.

'And Peg wouldn't let him,' said Lou.

'So he killed her,' added Mel slowly as if everything was finally falling into place. She looked at Lou, 'Let's go.'

'To the hospital?' finished Lou.

'Yes, please.'

Mel turned back to face Sharin. 'You are a freaking genius,' she said.

Sharin grinned and blew Mel a kiss.

Mel caught it and blew one back.

They drove in silence. Several weeks of investigation, information, and speculation floated around the car.

Chapter 53

AT THE HOSPITAL, LOU DROPPED MEL AT THE DOOR and left to park the car with Sharin.

Mel made her way to Lexie's room and looked in. Apart from Lexie, it was empty. She went in, kissed Lexie, and promised to come back shortly. She left to find the nurse and reception staff.

'Excuse me,' she said approaching the nurses' station, 'could you tell me if anyone has visited Lexie today?'

'And you are?' asked a male nurse in dark green scrubs.

'Her sister.'

'Ah, ok,' he said. 'Well, there were two people in her room earlier. The young woman looked a lot like you actually,'

'Annie,' she replied.

The nurse shook his head. 'I didn't catch any names.'

'And who was the other person?' she asked, as the tingle of fear began to spread through her.

'A man. He and Annie were deep in conversation when I came in.'

'They were?' asked Mel trying to keep calm. 'What were they saying?'

'Didn't catch it. Was only in there a few minutes. Checking the IV drip. Busy time of day.'

'Of course. What did the man look like?'

'Dunno. Big bloke, bald, glasses. Ordinary, I guess. Why?' he asked.

Mel gripped the counter. The tingle became a throb.

'Some guy claimed he was Lexie's dad. We're trying to find out who he is,' said Mel.

'Maybe Annie can tell you?'

'Course. Thanks.'

Mel pulled out her phone and walked to a corner of the corridor. She rang Annie's number. The phone rang out. She left a message and phoned again. The phone rang out again. Mel's heart pounded in her chest. She tried a third time. Nothing.

She phoned Ricky. 'I can't get hold of Annie!'

'She's at El's,' he said.

'No, she's not.'

Mel explained what happened. 'Ricky, she was here talking with some guy in Lexie's room and he matches Peter's description. I don't like it. She's not here and she's not answering her phone.'

'Eets, ok, I have a tracker on her phone. I'll find her and call you back.'

Mel leaned against the grey-white of the walls. She paced back and forth across the corridor. Finally, the phone rang.

'Did you find her?' she asked.

'At home,' said Ricky.

'Thank goodness! You spoke to her?'

'No. She didn't answer. But her phone's there.'

'Then why isn't she answering?'

'Calm down, Mel. I don't know. I'm nearly home now. I'll call you soon,' he said and hung up.

Mel paced more. Lou and Sharin found her. 'We spoke with the woman at reception. Peter *was* here.'

'You know for sure?'

'Yep. Sharin had the report we gave Dave, on her phone.

Showed the photo of Peg and Peter at Enid's 100th. She said he looked older but that it was him.'

'Fuck. Annie was talking with him in Lexie's room.'

'Where are they now?' asked Lou.

'No idea. Annie isn't answering her phone. Ricky tracked it to home. He's nearly there. He'll phone me.'

They waited together. Uniforms moved about the halls. An elderly lady on a walker shuffled past them before turning and shuffling back. The doorway to the stairwell opened and closed.

Finally, the phone rang. Mel answered before the first ring faded.

'She's not here. The phone is on the charger,' said Ricky.

'Shit!'

'How did she get to the hospital?' he asked.

'She rode.'

Mel and Ricky were thinking the same dreaded thoughts at the same time.

'Ricky, what if she's had an accident? What if she's with him?' her voice couldn't conceal her panic as it rose an octave.

'I'm calling the police.'

'Ok. Ricky, what if ...'

'Stop, Mel. We don't know anything yet,' and he hung up.

Mel burst into tears.

Lou and Sharin enveloped her and they rocked together. 'We have to get you home,' said Lou.

Mel shook uncontrollably, half carried to the car by her friends. 'If he is killing women then the timing is right. It's a month. She is probably with him. What the FUCK was she thinking?'

Mel sobbed harder. Snot and tears mingled as they ran down her face. Sharin dug a tissue from her bra and wiped Mel's cheeks.

'Calm down,' ordered Lou. She was authoritative but not unkind. She spun Mel toward her, taking her face in both hands. 'We don't know for sure what is happening. He may not be the killer. Sure, he's involved somehow, but we don't know how. You need to stay in control, Mel. Annie is going to need you and we all need to figure out how to find her. Let's just get home and go from there.'

Mel hung onto every word like a lifeline. Control. She needed it now. She took a deep breath, hiccupped it out and nodded.

The car ride was short but felt like an eternity. Ricky was in the driveway before the car had stopped. He took in the fancy clothes and shoes and knew immediately where they'd been. He said nothing, but took Mel in his arms and hugged her tight. She let every ounce of fear flood from her in giant waves. Tears soaked his shirt. Then she heard Lou's words in her ear and stopped.

'I called the police,' said Ricky. 'They are on the way.'

'They took it seriously?'

He nodded solemnly.

As if by saying the name they conjured them up. A police car pulled in behind Lou's and two police officers, one male and one female, climbed out. Lou mentally scanned her car for drugs. She was pretty sure the tiny stash of hash in the glove box was used a week or so earlier. She pressed herself against the car door and smiled sympathetically as they walked past her.

They were gathered in the kitchen when Mel's phone rang. It was a number Mel didn't recognise and her heart stood still as she read it.

'I don't know the number,' she said to the room.

'Answer and put it on speaker,' said the female officer, who'd identified herself as Kate.

Mel pressed the green button on her phone. 'Hello,' she said tentatively.

'Mum, it's me.'

'Annie!' Ricky and Mel yelled together.

'What's wrong?' asked Annie.

'Where are you?' said Mel.

'At the cemetery.'

'What?' said Ricky.

'Long story but I'm at Melbourne cemetery with this guy

called Peter. I met him at the hospital, and you won't believe this, but he is Lexie's dad. Dan is not her real dad. Wow, Mum, it's incredible but ...'

'Annie, you don't know anything about Peter. Is he with you?' asked Mel.

'Yep.'

Mel's eyes widened and she gestured wildly to Ricky.

'Annie, is there anyone else with you, and what's this number?' asked Ricky.

'I'm in the caretaker's office, with the caretaker. I need Peg's date of birth and death to get her grave location.'

'What?'

'Mum, what is wrong?'

'You need to get home.'

'Annie, this is Officer Kate Connor. Are you safe?'

'Who Connor? I'm confused.'

'Your parents called us. They were concerned you were missing.'

'Oh My God! Mum!'

'Stop. You have no idea what is going on. How did you get to the cemetery?' said Mel.

'Rode.'

'Do not get in his car or move from that office. Do you understand?'

'Mum, what's wrong?'

'I can't explain. Don't say anything. Give him the number to Peg's grave and you stay in that office.'

'Mum, I'm fine.'

'Annie, do what your mother says,' said Ricky.

'Ok. But I need birth and death dates.'

'Born November 18th, 1957, and died July 12th, 1992, but she's in 9th Ave.'

'Great. Thanks.'

'DON'T leave that office!'

'Ok, *OK*, got it.'

They hung up.

Mel dropped her face into her hands.

'Want to tell me a bit more about Peter?' asked Daryl, the male officer.

Mel looked at Shaz and Lou who'd hung back in the lounge. They stepped forward and the three of them filled the others in on what they knew.

Both officers looked at each other and Daryl took out his walkie-talkie. 'I'll call in a car to attend the cemetery.'

Daryl stepped outside while Kate provided more detail as to what would happen.

'We're taking all this as speculation. But a car will attend the cemetery to follow up on Annie. An officer will question Peter about Annie's situation, but as we have no other information, we can't pursue your concerns at this time. But they're noted.' Everyone nodded in unison.

'We gave all our documentation to Dave Ferguson. He's a journalist. He was going to pass it on,' said Lou.

'I can't comment on that. But I'll follow up,' replied Kate.

'Can we go to the cemetery too?' asked Ricky.

'Yes, but follow advice from the officers who attend.'

'Of course,' said Mel.

Kate joined Daryl at the door and they left together. Lou and Sharin hugged Mel goodbye, insisting she call later.

Ricky and Mel took his car on the longest ride of their lives, to Melbourne cemetery. Ricky held Mel's hand all the way there.

The car hadn't stopped before Mel tried to leap out. Ricky slammed his foot on the brake as he saw her door opening and she fell forward against the window. As the car pulled up, she straightened up, jumped out and ran toward the caretaker's office. A police car was already there.

Chapter 54

RICKY PARKED AS MEL REACHED THE DOOR. SHE stopped, took a deep breath to calm herself, and pushed the door open.

The room was wall-to-wall marble tiles and standing in the middle of it was a furious Annie, two police officers, and the caretaker. Mel pushed past them all, snatching Annie into an embrace.

'You scared the life out of me,' she said into the top of Annie's head.

Annie pushed back a little and looked up into her mother's face. 'This is sooooo embarrassing!'

'I promise I'll explain everything, Annie,' she said, holding her tighter.

Annie wriggled free. 'Mum!'

One of the officers spoke to Mel and informed her of what was happening. Two officers were dispatched to Peggy's grave to find Peter. Ricky marched through the door and Annie hurried to him. She wrapped her arms around his waist and pressed her head into his chest. He stroked her hair. Mel felt a pinch of jealousy, but let it go instantly. The two people she cared most about were standing safe and sound a few metres from her. She smiled and Ricky smiled back.

To one side a gnarly old man with a wise face stood watching. He looked like he'd seen everything there was to see in this world, and probably the next. He remained expressionless throughout but spoke to the room in a rich voice. 'You got a good girl there. Smart one.'

Annie turned to look at him. He nodded at her and turned back to his desk. Mel felt immensely proud. Whatever had happened, she'd handled it well.

'We've got Annie's statement. If we need more, we'll be in contact,' said the Officer, handing Mel a card. She took it, glimpsed over it, and tucked it into her palm.

'Will you let us know what happens with Peter?' asked Mel.

'Our liaison officer will be in touch.'

It didn't answer her question, but Mel felt she couldn't push it. In all honesty, she wanted to meet him. She needed to know who he was. But now was not the time. If he was committing the atrocities she thought he was, then getting him off the streets was all that mattered. She knew she'd learn more in time.

'I need to put my bike in the car,' said Annie, as they left the building, Ricky walking ahead of them both.

The sun was starting to fade, casting a golden glow across the graves. It soaked into the green of the trees and the neatly mowed lawn, turning their colour to lime. The cool and calm felt intense after the heated adrenaline and Mel paused to soak it in. Somewhere above her, she heard the night call of a bird. It was sweet and sharp. Far into the distance, another called back. Life flourished amongst death. She thought of her mother, lying buried in the ground. For the first time in her life, she wasn't repulsed. It was peaceful here. Peg was at peace. Something she hadn't had in life.

Ricky came back toward her. He took her hand and led her to the place where Annie left her bike, which she unlocked as they watched.

Until they were in the car, no one spoke. Once the seatbelts were on though, everyone started.

'So, what's going on?' asked Annie. She crossed her arms and legs tight.

Mel didn't hold anything back. She told Annie everything she'd found out, stopping only at the details of the injuries both Peg and the others received.

'He didn't seem like that kind of person,' said Annie, when she'd finished.

'They never do,' said Ricky.

'But he really didn't, Dad.'

'What did he tell you?' asked Mel.

Annie uncrossed her legs and arms. Her face relaxed and she leaned forward with the seatbelt straining against her shoulder. She slid closer to the middle seat. Mel turned as far as she could to look at her.

'He loved Peg. He said they were together for about three months before Peg went to Melbourne. He called into her home one day and she just wasn't there. He didn't know where she'd gone, and he tried to find her but couldn't. She never contacted him again. Anyway, about a year later he was shopping in Carlton and saw her. She was shopping with Lexie and he just went up to her. He said she was really stressed and annoyed, even pulling a blanket over the pram so he couldn't look in. She wanted to leave but he insisted she talk to him. She told him she was married and they had a baby and she didn't want to see Peter again. But he wanted to know why she had up and left like she did. She got angry and asked him to leave her alone. In the end, he did, but he wasn't happy.'

'Clearly he did find her again. Did he say if he met her in the café?'

'Yep. He kept going to the shopping centre hoping to see her, and one day he did.'

'And that's not stalkerish?' said Mel.

'Well, yeah, but I guess he just wanted answers.'

'Mmmm, well.'

'Anyway,' Annie continued, 'he saw her feeding Lexie and her little arms were uncovered. He saw that birthmark on her arm and hand. He has one the same.'

Mel shifted to fully face Annie. 'Seriously!'

'Yep.'

Mel stared at Annie, remembering the dark wine birthmark that was so vivid against Lexie's pale skin.

'So, he confronted Peg,' said Annie.

Mel scowled.

'Not like that Mum. He just approached her.'

'Right.'

'He came out and said he thought Lexie was his because he'd looked up the birth notice and he'd worked out the dates. The birthmark just sealed it for him. She was pretty flustered and didn't want to talk to him at the shops, so she agreed to meet and talk later. I think her reaction gave her away. He pretty much knew then. He made her promise to call him.'

'I wonder why she did. She could have just avoided him,' said Mel.

'Well, he did say, and I think he was a bit of a bastard for it, but he said he'd tell her husband if she didn't meet him.'

'Fuck'n arsehole!'

Annie waved a hand at Mel to stop her. 'He said he felt bad about that, but he was desperate. He really loved her.'

'Funny way of showing it!' said Mel.

'And, she met him?' asked Ricky.

'Yes. They met at a café in Lygon St. The night she died.'

Mel felt her skin crawl. This creep knew everything but never come forward. She knew now, he had to be guilty. The fact he told her daughter made her skin crawl more.

'Why did he never report that to the police?' asked Mel.

'He said he was scared to. He knew he'd be a suspect and he was in trouble over some fraud he'd been accused of, so he just took off.'

'Prick!' spat Mel.

'Yep, prick all right' agreed Ricky.

Annie rolled her eyes. 'He isn't like that!'

'How do you know!' snapped Mel. 'You spent one afternoon with him. He can tell you what he likes and I am sure he believes it! Psychopaths don't have a conscience!'

Annie threw herself back into the seat and thumped her arms across her chest again.

For the remainder of the trip there was hostile silence. But once home Ricky took Annie into the living room and sat her down.

Mel went upstairs to the bedroom to change, so Annie and Ricky were alone. But she left the door open and threw on the closest things she could find. When she was dressed she crept to the top of the stairs and listened.

'Annie, what else did Peter tell you?' Ricky was asking.

'He told me that Peg met him and they talked. They were both angry. Peter wanted to know for sure if Lexie was his, and Peg wanted him to leave her alone, but she finally admitted Lexie was his. He agreed not to tell Dan if she could find a way for him to get to know Lexie as an uncle or friend of the family.'

'Did he meet Dan?' asked Ricky.

'No, they never met. But I think he would have figured out where Peg and Dan lived. He'd have found Dan to tell him.'

'So, Peg agreed?'

'Yep, but she didn't want to. He said she agreed then went to the loo and disappeared. He never saw her again.'

Ricky slid his hands under his thighs and stared up at the ceiling. Annie watched him.

Finally, Ricky spoke. 'When did he find Lexie again?'

'Well, he's only been back in Victoria since the beginning of the year. His mum was sick.'

'I knew that.'

'Did you?' Annie looked confused.

'Part of the investigation your mum's been doing,' he said.

'Oh.'

'We know he came back to see her but she died not so long ago. He's been living interstate since Peg died,' said Ricky.

'Yeah. Well, when he got back, he needed work, and he couldn't do accounting, so he took a personal care role. He'd been helping his mum so it worked for him. He ended up working with kids with disabilities and he met a carer who looked after Lexie. He didn't know for sure it was his Lexie, but her name is unusual, and he asked questions. He found out only recently where she lived. He called and they said she was in hospital. That's how he found her.'

Ricky shook his head. 'How the universe works is a mystery.'

'Pretty weird luck,' said Mel.

Annie and Ricky looked up as she stepped off the bottom step, wearing a loose white t-shirt, faded blue jeans, and bare feet. Her long blonde hair fell around her shoulders as she moved. Looking back to his daughter, Ricky felt that tie that binds a parent inextricably to their child, and the love of a woman you can't forget, and knew he would have done the same as Peter.

But would he have killed for that? He didn't know.

Chapter 55

THAT NIGHT, ANNIE FELL ASLEEP ON THE LOUNGE WITH her head on Ricky's lap. When she was gently snoring as her body relaxed into the deep sleep of exhaustion, Ricky and Mel talked. They went over everything that had happened that day, the past weeks, and the past years. They supposed and speculated. The opportunity for Peter to kill Peg was evident. But would he? And why start again now? The other idea that his foray into fraud linked him with Robert Lang was tenuous at best, but possible. Had Lang killed Peg as revenge for something Peter did or perhaps didn't do? Did he do it to frame Peter? Did Lang know Peter was back and set up the recent string of murders to open up old investigations or did Peter set them up to snare Lang? Or was there, as Lou kept insisting, no link at all?

They talked and waited for the phone to ring.

Finally, around 9 p.m. the Police Liaison Officer phoned. She apologised for not calling earlier and informed them that Peter had been questioned and no further action was being taken. His explanation matched Annie's, and he was regretful he'd caused angst to the family.

Mel asked if the information they'd given Dave was reviewed

or discussed with Peter. She said she knew nothing about it. Mel began to explain how important it was, but the liaison officer fobbed her off. Mel's agitation was obvious as she pressed her concerns, which only served to annoy the officer, who made it clear she was not interested and that the matter was dealt with. There was a mutual slamming down of phones as the call ended.

When Mel finally calmed down enough to go to bed, she spent the night tossing and turning, snatching sleep between broken dreams and fetid thoughts.

She woke late. Ricky left a note saying he and Annie were going to buy croissants. Mel dragged her headache and weariness to the kitchen and boiled the kettle for coffee. Using the coffee machine took effort and concentration so she dug out her old silver plunger and poured coffee grounds into it. When the water boiled, she sloshed it over the coffee and waited for it to brew.

The radio was playing. Sunday was jazz day. She couldn't remember how it became a Sunday staple, but for as long as Annie had been with them, jazz music carried them through the day. As the final notes of 'round midnight' shimmied to a close, the news came on. Mel flopped into Ricky's recliner to listen.

'Police are concerned for the whereabouts of a teenager reported missing early this morning. Nineteen-year-old Bree Baxter was last seen at Collingwood train station at 11.15 p.m. last night. She did not return home and her family alerted authorities this morning.

Bree worked in a health food store on Cambridge St. She is described as 168 cm tall, slight build, with blue eyes and blonde hair. She was wearing black pants and a white lace top. Police believe the disappearance may be linked to another late on Friday night, when a young woman was grabbed from behind on Davies St, near Collingwood station. She didn't see her attacker but described him as at least 180 cm tall and wearing black clothing. He pressed a chemical soaked cloth to her face, but she managed to free herself and scream for help, before being pushed to the ground. Her attacker fled the scene. Anyone with information is asked to call Crime Stoppers.'

By the time the report was over, Mel was on her feet and dialling Crime Stoppers. She knew she sounded like a lunatic, and the voice on the end of the line did little to dissuade that opinion, but she was determined to be heard. She was giving her name and address when Ricky and Annie came through the door.

'Who was that?' asked Ricky, laying a paper bag of fresh croissants on the bench and dropping the newspaper alongside it. 'Ah, you made coffee?' he said pointing to the pot.

'The police and yes,' snapped Mel, tossing the phone onto the counter.

Ricky dropped his hand to his side and sighed. 'Why am I getting growled at?'

Mel folded the front of her dressing gown in on itself and stared down at her wrist, as she held it closed. 'Sorry,' she mumbled.

'What happened, Mum?' asked Annie, as she reached for coffee cups. She poured coffee, adding spoons of sugar as Mel explained.

'That's four girls now,' said Ricky.

'Yep, four.'

Annie had her back to them both. She added milk to the cups before turning. 'And you called the police to tell them it's Peter?'

'I did.'

Annie handed each of her parents a coffee 'It's not him, Mum.'

'Annie! For God's sake, why?' said Mel, but Ricky stopped her. 'Lose the tone!'

Mel spun away, sending a wave of coffee over the edge of the cup. 'Fuck!'

'Leave it!' snapped Ricky.

She stormed off toward the stairs. Ricky rinsed the dishcloth and cleaned up the spilled coffee. Annie followed her mother up the stairs to her room.

Mel crawled onto her bed and hugged the coffee cup. Annie stood in her doorway. 'It's not Peter.'

'Right.'

'He loved her. And he loves Lexie. I believe him. Looking at him yesterday when he was watching Lexie was just ... I don't know. Real. He said that since he'd found Lexie, he feels complete. When he saw me, he looked shocked – like he'd seen a ghost. He said how much I look like Peg. Everything he said about her was beautiful. He knew she didn't love him, but he'd never felt that way before. All he wanted was a family and Lexie is his family.'

'Lexie will never be his,' said Mel.

'Mum!'

'She's Dan's.'

'Peg told Peter that Lexie was his,' said Annie.

'So *HE* says. But even if she is, he is not her DAD!'

Annie came into the room and sat on the bed. Mel sipped the coffee but wouldn't look at her.

'Why are you so against him?'

Mel sipped some more and stared at the bottom of her cup. Annie waited. Finally, she spoke. 'Someone killed my mother in 1992. And someone is killing young women who look like my mother, in 2019. The one person in both pictures is Peter. I don't know how he is connected to these latest deaths, but it cannot be a coincidence that he vanishes after my mother dies, then shows up 27 years later and girls start dying again. And now, another woman, who looks like my mother, has disappeared. And he was let go last night. Tell me how he can be innocent?'

Annie ran her hand back and forth across the velvet bedspread. Brushed one way, bright and crisp, brushed the other, dull and dark. 'I don't know, Mum. What you say makes sense. But I just have a gut feeling.'

Mel reached a hand to hover over Annie's. She let it fall and wrap around the fingers she'd held since her birth. 'I don't believe him.'

Annie wrapped her fingers in her mother's and gently squeezed. Then she released them and stood up. 'I'll heat the croissants. Come when you're ready.'

Mel finished the coffee, gently placed the cup on her bedside table, and slid down under the covers. She pulled Ricky's pillow over her head and breathed in her warm breath. She let her mind go blank, staring into the dark of the down until sleep overcame her.

Chapter 56

WHEN MEL CAME DOWNSTAIRS, THE HOUSE WAS AGAIN quiet and empty. The croissant Annie had heated for her still sat on baking paper in the oven. It was soggy and cold. Mel threw it in the bin and poured another coffee.

She checked her phone. Ricky and Annie had sent a photo of themselves with Rosa standing next to a big bunch of flowers. Eddy stood behind Annie with his arm around her shoulders. The message read. 'Dropping the dress bag back. Be home with fish and chips. Rxx.'

Mel texted back 'K', but then felt bad, and sent another one with a heart emoji.

An hour and a half later they were home. Mel managed to sleep most of the day away and was feeling better for it.

She laid the table and poured wine ready for dinner. It was early for a meal, but she was hungry.

Ricky ripped open the paper and scooped fish and lemon onto each plate. He set tongs in the middle of the chips so everyone could help themselves before setting about squeezing litres of sauce onto his plate.

'For an Italian, you sure like ketchup,' said Mel.

'Si,' he said smiling. 'Eets tomato.'

They ate and chatted. Eddy had shown them the photos he'd taken of Annie before the formal and promised to send them to Ricky. Ricky was impressed. He said Eddy captured Annie at her best and his use of light really enhanced the images. Ricky felt he was truly talented. Mel scoffed but secretly couldn't wait to see the photos.

Annie said that Rosa had visited her sister, who she felt was getting way too friendly with the neighbour. Rosa did not approve. He'd invited Maria to go dancing one night and the theatre another, and she thought he was moving far too quickly. Given he was in his seventies, Ricky suggested it was probably wise to make his feelings known sooner rather than later. Rosa was not impressed.

'But I bet she forgave you,' said Mel.

'It's Dad. Rosa would forgive him anything!', said Annie.

'Ah, what can I say? *Lei mi ama*,' said Ricky.

'She loves me,' repeated Mel, translating for Annie, who then hurled a chip at her dad. 'She does though,' said Annie.

'And who's *Rosa's* admirer?' asked Mel.

Ricky knitted his eyebrows together. 'What do you mean?'

'In the photo you sent. There was a big bunch of flowers.'

'Oh yes. From Marcus. He stayed an extra night. In lieu of rent.'

'As if Rosa would ever charge extra rent.'

'I know, but it was thoughtful,' said Ricky.

'It was,' agreed Annie and Mel together.

With dinner and the wine finished they settled in the lounge room to watch a movie. Ricky deliberately avoided the news and found two movies to watch back to back. For three hours they forgot about the world outside.

Chapter 57

ALL THE GIRLS WERE IN EARLY ON MONDAY. SHARIN and Lou insisted on hearing every detail of Saturday afternoon's events. Mel had texted them the brief version on Sunday but it wasn't enough.

For half an hour they rehashed all the old information. Sharin misted up when discussing the latest disappearance and all three felt somehow responsible.

'If only we'd worked it out,' said Sharin.

'If only we could be sure Dave took the information to the police,' said Lou.

'I wonder what he did do with it,' said Sharin.

'Shall I call him?' asked Mel.

'Go on,' said Lou.

Mel dialled his number and waited. When he answered, she put the phone on speaker. 'Hi Dave.'

'Hi Mel.'

'You're on speaker so don't diss anyone, but we're wondering what happened with the police? Any response to the info?'

'I'm taking it today.'

'What! Dave!'

'I know. I thought I needed more time. I shouldn't have held off. I know that and I feel worse than you can make me feel. Truly, I'm taking it in today. Just adding my final pages now.'

The three women looked from one to the other. Lou shook her head.

'You still there?' asked Dave.

'Just gobsmacked. It might have helped stop this,' said Lou.

'And it might not have,' he said defensively. 'But I'm taking it in any way. Given this guy's track record she will still be alive.'

Sharin shivered. 'But in what condition?'

'I know, Shaz. I feel like shit. I'm going in this morning.'

Mel felt bad for him. 'Just so you know, we have a lot more on Peter.'

Mel heard Dave shift in his chair. 'Tell me.'

Mel relayed the details of Saturday and the information Annie told her. She omitted to mention that Annie thought he was innocent. Mel still didn't believe it and she wanted him in the frame when Dave gave his report to the police.

Dave hung up after promising to let them know how his information was received. They hoped, but weren't optimistic, that it would be acted upon.

The next call was to the hospital. Mel followed up with the staff who informed her that Lexie would be going home the next day. Mel asked them not to leave Peter alone with Lexie, if he showed up again. She couldn't demand he not be allowed to see her, but she painted a vivid picture of why she wanted him watched. The duty nurse said she'd do her best. Mel said she'd visit later in the day. Secretly she hoped to cross paths with Peter. She sure as churches wasn't letting him near Lexie, but she also wanted answers.

The rest of the day dragged by. An official letter from HR pinged into each inbox. It was their thanks and goodbye letter. No golden watches for them. Sharin left the room shortly after.

'You want my cigarettes?' Lou called after her.

The back of Sharin's head shook from side to side but she gave a little wave.

'She'll be all right,' said Lou after she'd gone.

'I know. But it will take her a while to get over this.'

'We'll have to start our own business together,' said Lou.

'Like what ... grant writing?' asked Mel.

'Why not?' said Lou.

'I can see the banner now,' said Mel, arcing her arm across the space in front of her. 'Duds do dollars!'

Lou laughed, 'Or how about, 'Grants by Goddesses'.'

'Ohh, I much prefer that one,' said Mel.

Lou rocked back in her chair. 'Or maybe we form a detective agency, what 'ya reckon?' She looked excited.

'Yeah, right.'

'Detectives without Guns!'

'Not a great track record, Lou.'

Lou pouted. 'Go on, kill my vibe bitch.'

This time Mel laughed.

Sharin walked in. Her eyes were red-rimmed. Lou heaved herself out of the chair, walked over to her, and wrapped an arm around her shoulders. Sharin sniffled into it.

'You'll be ok,' said Lou.

Sharin nodded.

Mel stood up and grabbed her purse. 'Let's go out.'

They stayed out until 4 p.m. then called it quits for the day. Mel left for the hospital and arrived at 4.30 p.m. No one, except Lexie, was in the room. She'd checked with the staff but Peter hadn't made an appearance.

Mel sat with Lexie and told her that Dan was coming to visit and how exciting it would be to see him. Lexie expressed her happiness in sounds that were created deep in her chest but burst out in sing-song patterns of low and high-toned trills. Her body squirmed from side to side. Mel giggled with her. Lexie's joy was infectious.

Mel leaned in and kissed her on both cheeks. 'I am so relieved you are better,' she said, hugging her close.

When she sat down again Lexie reached for her hand and

raised it to her cheek. Mel felt the full force of mother protection. If Peter had walked in at that moment, he wouldn't have walked out.

The phone beeped in her pocket. Mel lifted it out to see it was a text from Annie. 'Hi, Mum. Riding to Rosa's. Lost my bracelet yesterday. It's there. Be home after.'

Mel texted back. 'I could drive if you wait.'

The text came straight back 'All good Mum. I'll ride.'

Mel sighed and texted, 'Ok. Straight home after.'

A smiley emoji came back.

'I worry about that girl, Lexie.'

Lexie held her gaze, eyes full of a wisdom she couldn't express with words. Mel stood up and kissed her again. 'I'll see you tomorrow sweetheart.'

Lexie touched then stroked Mel's face, as if to say, it will be ok. Mel left with the belief it would be.

The Wolseley drove home like a dream. Mel patted the steering wheel and promised to give it the full car detail treatment before Christmas. Her gift for a job well done. On the way, she picked up milk and bread and planned what to cook for dinner. Tonight was going to be easy. Chicken Kiev with potato bake and salad.

She was still thinking about dinner when she arrived home. She dropped her things on the kitchen bench, set the oven to 180 degrees, turned on the TV, and went upstairs to change.

When she came back down the 6.00 p.m. edition of the news was on. She put the Kievs in the oven and set about peeling potatoes. At the end of the news was a short segment on the murders terrifying women all over the city. A re-enactment of Lisa Harding's last hours was about to play. Mel put down the peeler, wiped her hands on a tea towel and headed into the lounge room to watch.

The photo of Lisa standing between her friends at a party the night she disappeared was the first image to be appear. The pretty face, big smile, and glittery dress just served to enhance the darkness that hung over her death.

The voiceover described the last hours before her disappearance, and the photo faded, replaced by a reporter standing outside a nightclub in Swanston St. Lights from two large lamps shone on a mannequin wearing the clothes Lisa wore that night. The camera panned in on the dress, as a wavy pattern created by lengths of pale gold sequins glinted in the light. The image scanned up to the blank stare of a mannequin whose face was painted in the same makeup Lisa had worn on the day. Bronze eyeshadow, black eyeliner, frosted lips, and swipes of bronze gold powder on each cheek. Powder that glittered like gold dust. Mel leaned in closer. The camera moved upward to the pile of blonde hair loosely woven together in a bun. It scanned around from front to back and there, holding the bun in place, was a long narrow clip with a pattern in diamantes along its edge and 3 strands of pale yellow flowers dangling from its end.

Mel dropped the tea towel and gasped. She pressed closer to the TV screen. The clip was unique. And she'd seen it before.

Chapter 58

THE WOLSELEY SPED ALONG STATE ROUTE 45 IN EXCESS of the speed limit. She made it to Rosa's well under her personal best.

Annie's bike was nowhere to be seen. Mel texted her. No reply.

She parked the car out the front and raced toward the door, then backtracked to look down the side of the building in case Annie's bike was there. She used the light of her phone to shine through the darkness between the building and the industrial panelled fence, but saw nothing except the bonnet of a car at the back of the building.

The night was unseasonably warm and the entrance way was blocked only by the screen door. A lamp was on in the hallway casting shadows on the wall, but no one was visible.

Mel rang the doorbell. She waited impatiently and rang again. She had the key Rosa gave her many years before, but she never let herself in uninvited.

Finally, she heard a noise from the top of the stairs. 'Who is it?'

It wasn't Rosa's voice, but Eddy's. Mel swore under her breath.

'It's Mel. Can you let me in please?'

Eddy hesitated, making Mel twitch with annoyance. 'Right now isn't a good time,' he said.

'Open the door, Eddy. Where is Rosa?'

'Out.'

'When is she back?'

'Later.'

'Where's Annie?'

'She left.'

Mel thumped a hand against the wall. 'Open the door, Eddy,' she said again.

She took the handle and began shaking the door.

'Fuck off Mel!' he yelled down the stairs.

Mel thumped the door again. She fumbled in her bag, swearing and cursing as she struggled to find the key. Eddy realised what she was doing and started down the stairs, but as he grabbed the door handle, she crushed the key into the lock and opened it.

Eddy was trying to hold the door shut, reaching with one hand as he stood on the bottom step, mostly out of view.

Mel slammed her body against the door as the lock gave way to the key and pulled hard. The door flung open, pulling Eddy along with it. He crashed against the wall before falling heavily into the hall.

Mel stood in the open doorway with the door handle still in her hand and a triangle of light cutting Eddy in half as he lay sprawled across the floor.

He stared up at her. Eyes open as wide as his mouth. A mouth lined with palest pink lipstick. A sheath of long blonde hair cascading around him. He snatched at the gown he was wearing, pulling it tight around him, and sunk back onto the floor, but not before Mel took in the cream lace of the camisole that hung loosely over his torso.

'Fuck you,' he spat as she stared back at him.

'Where is Annie?!' She repeated.

'She left.'

'When?'

'Twenty minutes ago.'

Mel closed the door and dug about in her bag for the phone she'd tossed into it earlier.

She rang Annie.

'Hi, Mum. Where are you?'

'Where are you?' replied Mel.

'Home. The Kievs are cooked.'

Mel leaned against the door as her chin dropped to her chest. She pushed back the hair that fell over her face with her free hand.

'Great. Can you put on the potatoes and make a salad, please? I'll be home soon. Start dinner without me if I am late.'

'Where are you?'

'Rosa's.'

'Mum!'

'It's all good, Annie. See ya soon.'

She hung up before Annie could say more.

'I told you,' said Eddy, pulling himself to his feet. He slid the back of his hand across his lips, smearing the lipstick with it. The light from the lamp on the hallway table shone across his face and tiny flakes of gold glitter sparkled on his cheek.

'Are you here alone?'

'None of your business. You have no right to be in here.'

'Are ... you ... alone?' she said.

'Why?'

'Is Marcus here?' she asked.

'No!'

'Where is he?'

'How do I know?'

'His car is out the back.'

'So.'

'When's he back?'

'How the Hell do I know!'

'Well, clearly you weren't expecting him soon,' she said waving her hands at his attire, 'or maybe you were?'

'Piss off.'

Mel adjusted herself so she was standing at her full height. She didn't move from the door. 'You know I don't give a shit about you dressing up. So what? You know what I hate. The fact you hide it. You're a liar. You sneak around and pretend to be something you're not.'

Eddy tied the gown he was wearing tighter at the waist and folded his arms around himself. 'I know exactly who I am. I pretend so my family isn't ashamed of me. I pretend so my mother can hold her head up. If that's the price I pay - then for her, it's worth it!'

'It's the 21st century, Eddy. People are out of the closet. People accept men wearing women's clothes. People love people for who they are, not who they pretend to be.'

'Not in this family.'

Mel shook her head, 'Jesus, Eddy.' But her memory of the day his brothers beat him mercilessly for showing who he was filled her mind.

'Just go home, Mel.'

Mel shifted on the spot. Eddy didn't move.

'I need to see in Marcus's car.'

'Why? Is he a pretender too?'

'I just need to see in it.'

'How? It's locked,' he said.

'It's got windows, hasn't it?'

'You're going to break in?'

Mel tapped the phone against her leg. 'No Eddy, I am not breaking in.' She held up the phone, tapped on the light, and fluttered it across his face. He blinked against the light, holding a hand up to block it. 'Just having a look,' she said.

'Either you tell me why, or I'll phone him,' threatened Eddy.

Mel lowered the phone. Eddy watched her expression vacillate between telling him and calling his bluff. Her ability to trust her judgment was shattered. She still didn't know if Eddy was inno-

cent or not. She realised she also didn't truly know his relationship with Marcus.

'First tell me where you got the glitter on your face.'

Eddy ran his fingers across his cheek then rubbed the gold
dust off them with his thumb. 'Why?' he asked.

Mel knew he had no reason to tell her, and she couldn't make
him. She couldn't explain without accusation so she chose to
bargain.

'Please, Eddy, I just need to know and then I can tell you why
I want to look in the car.'

Eddy continued to roll his thumb over his fingers, massaging
the gold glitter away until only a few specks remained. 'It's mine.
It was given to me for some creative work I'm doing.'

Mel was surprised. Not because of the explanation, but
because he told her. 'At Art school?'

Eddy pulled back. 'How do you know that?'

'Marcus told me. Said you painted nudes.'

Eddy looked offended. 'I don't paint. I model.'

The warm glow of the light in the room softened the harsh
edges of the walls. Mel felt a gentle breeze on her back and realised
she hadn't been aware of anything but Eddy since she'd arrived.
She hadn't taken her eyes off him the whole time but now, she
actually saw him. The colour of his gown accentuated the olive
brown of his skin whilst the Kohl pencil, artfully applied, drew
out the hazel green of his eyes. His body, long and lithe, was
accentuated by the languid silk of his robe. She thought but
didn't say it, that he'd be a beautiful model. Instead, she nodded.

'And why do you have a lock-up?' She was taking a punt but
she needed to see his reaction.

'What the hell?'

'I know you have a lock-up.'

'Really. Wow. How?'

'Just tell me. Please.'

'It's none of your goddamn business.'

'Does Marcus know about it?'

'No!'

'Eddy, just tell me. We don't have time for this.'

'For what?'

'I'll show you. But tell me.'

Eddy shook his head.

'Ok then,' she said. 'Damn you. I need to see that car and,' she hesitated as he began to interrupt, 'the reason is that he has a silver clip in there and I think it belonged to one of the girls who was murdered.'

Eddy frowned then laughed out loud. 'You have got to be joking. You've seriously lost your mind!'

Mel stepped toward him. 'Then let's have a look and see how mad I am.'

Eddy hesitated before taking a step up onto the staircase. 'Why should I help you? Why wouldn't I help Marcus instead? He's been a whole lot nicer to me than you ever have.'

Mel pressed herself back against the door. It was coarse against her bowed neck. She looked up into Eddy's face. 'I know. But I don't think Marcus is who he says he is.'

'And what evidence do you have?'

'Well, that fucking clip, if you'd let me see it!'

Eddy clapped his hands at her. 'Not sure that will do it, Mel.'

Mel allowed a moment she didn't have to pass between them. She knew it would hurt him but she needed his help, so she said, 'Well, how about the fact that he is the one who told me you were acting weird the night he gave you a lift from Art school? And, that you are lying to Rosa about what you do at night.'

Eddy blushed. Mel continued. 'He also said he knows what you watch on your Instagram.'

Eddy didn't move. Mel could see his mind working over the past months, sifting through opportunities when Marcus might have seen it.

'What did he tell you?'

'Enough.'

'It's not illegal,' said Eddy.

'I know. And it's no one's business. But he didn't need to tell me. I think he is playing us. Sharing secrets. Planting seeds.'

Eddy took another step up. 'Why?'

'I have no idea, but I have a terrible feeling he's involved in the death of these girls,' said Mel.

'And you thought I was involved too?'

Mel pressed her lips into a thin line. 'I'm sorry, Eddy. I've been chasing shadows since my mum died and lately it's just been out of control. I think I suspect everyone.'

Eddy shook his head. 'I don't know how you could think that of me.'

Mel bowed her head again, but this time in shame. 'I am so sorry, Eddy.'

Eddy gripped the rail of the staircase with two hands. His eyes followed the line of the wall up to the ceiling and across to the door. 'I am a lot of things, Mel, but not that. How you could even think it …' his voice trailed off.

Mel rushed forward. The movement surprised her as much as it did Eddy. She leaped up the step to him and threw her arms around his neck. 'I am so, so sorry, Eddy,' she said pulling him close.

Eddy stood rigid. The shock of her left him with his arms wide open. Gradually he encircled her with them and held her close. For endless seconds, years melted away. Finally, she pulled back.

'Please help me, Eddy, I need to see that car.'

Eddy explored her face with his gaze. Finally, he gave her what she wanted. 'Ok, but I need to put some clothes on.' She laughed and stepped back down the step, letting him go 'Well can it be done in a hurry? Please?' she begged.

At the top of the stairs, he paused. 'The lock-up. Where else could I keep my dresses?' he said.

Chapter 59

WITHIN MINUTES, EDDY WAS BACK. THEY LOCKED THE heavy front door behind the screen and headed out the back. Marcus's car was parked close to the side fence so Mel started on the passenger side. She held her light up and aimed it toward the console between the seats, just under the dashboard. It was dark and the light reflected off the window. 'Bugger, I can't quite see,' she said.

Eddy tried to peer under her arm. Mel moved the light around but still couldn't get a clear view of the console. Eddy was in her way which annoyed her.

'If you're going to get your boof-head in the way, can you see anything when I shine this in?' she said.

Eddy strained. 'I don't know what I'm looking for but something is catching the light,' he said.

Mel pushed him aside and tried to see. Something was glinting but the detail was impossible to see. 'We need to get in there.'

'No way, Mel.'

'There must be some way.'

'Not in these cars. It's not a Wolseley – a coat hanger won't open the door.'

She knew he was right but she was getting desperate. 'I'll have to break the window.'

'What the!'

'He won't know who did it. I'll use a rock or something. Make it look like vandals.'

'Right. No CCTV camera's here!'

'They're never in laneways,' said Mel. But she looked up anyway, taking in the street lights and power poles along the lane. She couldn't be entirely sure that was true.

'This is important, Eddy. I need something heavy.'

'This is nuts,' he said, scanning about for a suitable object. He found a broken brick against the fence at the back of the lane and handed it to her.

'Stand back,' she said lifting her hand high. She was about to hurl it as hard as she could but stopped. She turned to Eddy. 'Do these things have automatic alarms if they get broken into?'

Eddy shrugged. 'No idea, but we'll find out.'

Mel lifted her arm again, pulling it far back behind her right shoulder before forcing it forward with all her strength. She'd been a soft-baller in high school and she could throw a ball.

The brick crashed through the window at speed, splintering and cracking it apart.

Mel and Eddy stood motionless in the dark, waiting for the sound of an alarm. It didn't come. Mel dashed for the door, wrapping her hand around the bottom of her shirt before reaching through the glass for the lock. She'd seen enough crime shows to know you never leave prints.

Eddy stayed in the dark, watching up the lane in case anyone came. Mel crawled into the car, fumbling around in the console until she felt the small piece of metal against her covered fingers.

She pulled it out and extricated herself from the car. Mel handed Eddy her phone. 'Switch the light on, let's have a look at this.'

When the light was on and the clip held up to it, Mel gasped. Little shards of light bounced off the diamantes that impregnated the length of the silver clip and swirled around the lengths of pale yellow flowers on its end.

'Is it?' asked Eddy.

'Yep, it is.'

'Fuck.'

'I know.'

'We have to call the police.'

'What if there's more stuff? In his room? Have you been in there?' asked Mel.

'No. He keeps it locked.'

'What if ...?'

'No way, we'd know,' he said.

'When's he due back?'

'Tonight sometime.'

'He took the van?'

Eddy thought for a moment. 'Yep. Must have. The car's been here all weekend.'

'He didn't leave till Saturday though, right?'

'Yes., 'coz the shipment of wine didn't get cleared Friday night.'

'Do you know that for sure?' asked Mel.

'That's what he told us.'

'That girl was attacked Friday night, but she got away. They think it's related to Bree's disappearance on Saturday.'

'We need to call the police,' said Eddy.

Mel took her phone back from him and started to dial as they headed toward the back door which was resting shut, but not closed against the door frame.

Mel was just connecting as Eddy pushed open the door and stepped up onto the doorstep and into a booted foot.

'Eddy, what are you doing out here? Oh, Hi Mel?'

Mel let the phone hang at her ear as the voice answered at the end of it 'Police, Fire or Ambulance?'

Eddy looked up into Marcus's face. 'Ah, hi Marcus,' stammered Eddy.

The person on the end of the phone repeated. 'Police, Fire or Ambulance?'

Mel just mumbled 'Ummm' into the phone.

Marcus looked over their heads and saw glass on the ground twinkling in the hall light.

'Jesus! My car!'

'Yeah,' said Eddy. 'Mel was just calling the police.'

'Police,' repeated Mel into the phone.

Marcus gently maneuvered Eddy aside as he eased past and through the door. Eddy looked wildly at Mel who grimaced and spoke into the phone. Mel was still clutching the clip in her hand, the lengths of flowers sticking out between her thumb and forefinger as Marcus pressed past her. He was looking down at the ground and the glass as she gently wiggled the flowery tassels with her thumb to catch the loose ends.

He stopped just past Mel's shoulder.

Mel's eyes followed his. They both stared at the tip of the clip in her hand and the evidence that would not be hidden.

Mel stopped speaking into the phone. Eddy moved too late as Marcus snatched at Mel's hand. He grabbed at her with such force that the phone slipped from her grasp and hit the ground.

He wrenched her hand back and pain seared up her arm, right before the snap that made her scream. Marcus punched her in the face, sending her flying backward toward the fence. Eddy screamed her name and ran for her. Marcus caught him around the neck and hurled him to the ground. Mel lay where she was, dazed and confused. She could see Eddy struggling against Marcus but failing. She felt around for something to use to stop him. Her head pounded from the punch and a warmth oozed into her mouth. She tasted metal and the thick viscosity of blood. She dragged herself closer to the fence, flailing around for something hard, strong. Finally, the rough skin of a brick grazed her palm and she grabbed it with both hands.

Eddy was on the ground with Marcus's hands at his throat. He was scratching and hitting but making little impact. Mel struggled to her feet and scrambled forward at Marcus. Her vision was doubled and she felt nauseous. She swung at Marcus and missed, wobbled but managed to remain upright. The brick slipped from her hand and she lurched forward to grab it. But he was quicker. He let Eddy fall as he lunged for the brick.

He stood up and smiled down at Mel as he lifted it to strike her.

She ducked just in time, but her unsteadiness sent her reeling and she fell against the fence. Marcus moved swiftly toward her. She hated herself for doing it but she cowered and covered her head. She thought of Annie and Ricky and how she'd miss them. She felt the movement of air rush past but the blow didn't land on her. It landed on the fence. The crash rocked the fence and shook the ground. Through her arms and blurred vision, she saw Marcus on the ground next to her, his head rammed into the fence. At his feet was Eddy, hanging on for dear life. He'd managed to roll onto his belly and catch Marcus's feet as he'd made the move for Mel.

Eddy lay face first on the ground coughing. 'Call the police, Mel,' he croaked. He didn't let go of Marcus's legs.

Mel crawled to the phone. It had hit the ground but not disconnected from the police. When Mel spoke into the phone, the operator assured her the police were on their way. In the distance, a siren wailed.

Chapter 60

SHARIN AND LOU MADE IT TO THE HOSPITAL TOGETHER as soon as they were allowed, two days later. Lou was far too impressed with the black eye and bruised face Mel presented to them when they arrived. Sharin was horrified.

Ricky stayed the previous two nights in her room but left so the girls could talk. Annie took him for a walk. She'd spent the nights since the incident, with Rosa, who was still being sedated.

'So, it was Marcus,' said Lou.

'Yep. A freaking serial killer,' said Mel.

'He seemed so nice. And so good looking!'

'Evil doesn't always look like evil, Shaz.'

'Amen to that!' said Mel.

'Well, we were right about revenge. Those poor girls,' said Lou.

'His poor fiancée.'

'Did she cheat on him?' asked Shaz.

'No, she left him. Well, tried to. He killed her. Wasn't going to be humiliated by another woman. Started finding look-alike girls to replace her. Blonde and blue-eyed.'

'My heart breaks for those girls. Didn't stand a chance. He met each of them along the route he did his wine deliveries. Places he bought lunch. He fantasised they loved him and he loved them. But, when they were locked up in his house and terrified for their lives, there was no love on display. Just like his fiancée. So he killed them. Then he found a new girl. Cycled over and over,' said Mel.

'Beast,' said Lou.

'Worse,' said Sharin.

'Who'd of thought a hairclip would seal your fate?'

'I know. But he took souvenirs from all of them, so he was going to get caught out sometime,' said Mel.

'How many would have died before then? Four was too many,' said Lou.

They sat quietly and thought about each of the girls who'd died. Young women whose fate was sealed by their genetics and the fact that destiny placed them in his path.

'Thank goodness they found Bree alive,' said Mel.

'Dave filled you in on everything?' asked Lou.

'Yep. Visited last night.'

'How'd he get in here last night?!'

'Sweet-talked his way in I imagine,' grinned Mel.

'All that bouncy hair and hobble,' said Sharin.

'They probably thought he was a patient!' said Lou.

'Ha! Probably.'

'It is incredible how Marcus could move those girls between the city and his farm without being found out,' said Lou, suddenly sombre.

'And keep them alive while he was away. They must have been petrified.'

'You know, when I heard, I was sure he'd kept them at the Wine Warehouse,' said Sharin.

'Would have been the obvious choice. But probably too many people coming and going.'

'Well, no one was ever going to hear those girls in the cellar under his home,' said Mel.

'Yep, especially so far from other farmhouses,' said Lou.

'I thought he lived with his parents on the property?' said Sharin.

'He did. But separate houses. His parents respected his privacy and didn't visit without an invitation. So those girls were never going to be found.'

'And no one was looking for missing Melbourne girls in Avoca,' said Lou.

'Did Dave tell you he strangled them where he dumped them?' asked Mel.

'He did,' said Lou, 'But he beat and raped them at the farm. Then drugged them and put them in a wine crate lined with plastic to bring them back here. Imagine if they'd woken up. Be like waking in your own coffin.'

Sharin scrunched a portion of the sheet where her hand rested. Her knuckles turned white. 'I don't get it,' she said. 'How do people do these things, then carry on like everything is normal?'

'Psychos Sharin,' replied Lou. 'Total insane psychos.'

'It makes me physically sick to think of it,' said Mel. 'And I know I shouldn't feel relief, but that is all I feel because Annie didn't get hurt. God, when I think of him with her ...' she shook herself at the thought.

'Is Annie doing ok?' asked Sharin.

'I think she's still spinning out about it. Probably put her off men for life.'

'There are good ones out there,' said Sharin.

'Yep, there are. Speaking of that, is Michel still in the picture?'

'Just,' grinned Sharin 'But we have a lot to sort out. It *was* him at the casino, and he *is* security. For several casinos on the east coast.'

'Which explains the interstate travel,' said Lou.

'Exactly. And ... his dates with me were part of his security checks.'

'No way!'

'Yep. We'd been flagged.'

'Bullshit!' said Mel.

'How exciting,' said Lou as she held up her hand to high-five the others, 'we have a reputation.'

'So, was it luck he found you?' asked Mel.

'Nope. Apparently, they do a lot of searching on people like us. My social media screams single. So that's how he connected with me.'

'What does it mean now you know?' asked Mel.

Sharin bunched her fists together and propped her chin on them. 'Well, he was supposed to just find out everything he could, but he kinda fell for me,' she said, battering her lashes.

Lou gave her a shove. 'Of course, he did.'

'See we knew he was hooked.'

'Yep, and that's why he was so slow to make a move on me. Really wanted to but wasn't supposed to.'

'And, what now?'

'We're going to give it a go. Since it's all in the open.'

'That is fantastic!' said Mel.

'The security man and the crim,' laughed Lou. Then she added, 'Maybe he has a gun?'

'And I can learn to use it. Be a researcher with a gun!' said Sharin.

'That officially makes you a detective,' said Lou.

Sharin tossed her head from side to side, 'I guess it does.'

The door opened and a stout woman with a trolley poked her head in. 'Afternoon tea?' she said.

Mel shook her head. 'No thanks, I'm fine.'

The woman nodded and quietly shut the door.

'No tea. Are you sure you're all right?' asked Lou.

'Must be dying!' said Mel.

'Speaking of which, how's Eddy?' asked Sharin.

Eddy was treated for severe bruising, a broken rib, and damaged windpipe. He couldn't speak because everything was swollen.

'Doing OK. Have to say, I saw another side to him. He saved my life you know.'

Both girls nodded. 'You friends again then?' asked Lou.

'Wouldn't go that far,' said Mel. Then smiled to herself. 'Maybe.'

The room was quiet. Mel frowned and looked serious. 'You know you were right, Lou. None of this was related to Peg's murder.'

Lou tilted her head to one side. 'To be fair, it was. He copied it. Right down to the broken thigh and cutting their hair. And for poor Lisa, where he left her.'

Mel looked out of the window. Branches of a tree swayed slowly back and forth, shifting the sunlight from one end of her bed to the other. 'Yes, but he didn't murder Mum and he has no connection to anyone we suspect may have,' she said softly, looking back at the girls.

Lou touched her arm. 'He may not answer the question of your mum, but the others might.'

'Lang and Coreman, perhaps. Peter, maybe. But not Dan,' she said looking straight at Lou.

Lou laughed. 'I know, I know,' she said brushing the air with her hands.

As if on cue, a head of grey hair peered through the window in the door and smiled. Mel gasped and pulled herself up onto the pillows with her good hand. The other was in a brace where Marcus snapped it. She waved, beckoning to him.

Sharin jumped up and raced to the door, pulling it wide so Dan could push Lexie and her wheelchair through it.

'Oh wow! It is so good to see you!' said Mel.

'You look like crap,' said Dan.

'Better than you.'

'True,' he said and leaned down to kiss her on the forehead. Dan was a big man. Age had stooped him and the lines on his face were deep, but his smile still crinkled the corners of his eyes. Mel looked into those eyes and wished for all the world they belonged to Lexie, who sat nursing a bunch of pink lilies in her lap, but knew in her heart they didn't. In the end, it didn't matter, because the way Lexie looked at him was in every way complete. He was hers, and she was his.

Dan took the flowers from Lexie's lap and handed them to Mel, who sniffed their heady perfume and caressed their leaves. She dropped her hand down the side of the bed and reached for Lexie who lifted it gently to her face. She stroked the back of Mel's hand along her cheek before laying it in her lap and holding it until they left.

When everyone was gone, Mel slid down into the bedclothes and pulled the pillow over her head. She breathed in the warm air of her breath and stared into the down until sleep overcame her. This time her sleep was unbroken, filled with the scent of lilies.

Sometime on that day her phone rang. It was on silent and the message went to message bank. It was Dave.

'Hey, Mel. I spoke to Peter. Asked him about Lang and Coreman. Told him what we know. Have to say, if only we had this information all those years ago. Anyway, he confirmed he knew them and they did meet Peg. Coreman's father's company held an End of Financial Year party at the end of July every year and Peter took Peg to the last one he attended which was in 1991. Coreman was there, of course, and Lang, who took a very keen interest in Peg, as it happens. Peter was wary of Lang. Really wary. Lang previously tried to recruit him but he'd refused. That was the last weekend they spent together before Peg went back to Melbourne. We know she moved in with Dan, but Peter didn't. He thought she'd just disappeared. He was worried and tried to find her because he didn't trust Lang. Or Coreman for that matter. He tried for weeks but no one could tell him anything about where she was. He gave up until he did find her the year later. He was so relieved, but she didn't want anything to do with him. He admitted he did persist in

seeing her. He said they met at the café and talked. Mostly about Lexie. She got angry and left and he never saw her again. He read about her death in the paper.

Thing is Mel, I believe him. We got the autopsy report this morning. Confirms what we know. Skin on her chest was ripped. It has to be Lang. I just know it. We need to talk. Call me.'

Chapter 61

PETER KNELT AT PEG'S GRAVE, DIGGING A SMALL HOLE in the corner of her plot. In his hand was a blue velvet pouch. He hummed quietly to himself as he dug. When he finished, he sat back and drew apart the gold braid at the neck of the bag.

He pushed a finger deep into the pouch and lifted out a band of silver. It had today's date etched into it and the words 'I love you'. He held the ring over his left thumb then slowly, chanting, moved it from forefinger to ring finger. 'Father, Son and Holy Ghost.' On 'Amen', he slid the ring onto his finger. Finally.

For minutes he stood perfectly still, feeling the weight of the ring on his hand and the cool metal against his skin. He had waited so long.

He brought the ring to his lips. Kissed it, then slid it off and dropped it into the pouch. It clinked against the smaller gold band also etched with the words 'I love you.' And a date. But not the same date.

He smiled as he tightened the braid around the pouch once more, then dropped it into the hole. As he covered it with dirt, he whispered to her. 'We're a family forever now, my love'.

The End

About the Author

Claire Harrison is a weekend writer supported by weekday employment in the public service. She lives in Brisbane, Australia, near the ocean with her husband. A mother of two and a (young) grandmother of one, she balances family life with her creative pursuits.

When not working or writing she travels, reads, hikes, cooks, watches movies and spends time with friends and family.

She loves stories that thrill, chill and keep you guessing. Inspired to read by a father who was an avid consumer of books, she started writing short stories and outlines for novels at a young age. It took a lot of years and a redundancy to kick the ideas into pages of prose, but eventually, those pages came together as a manuscript. And now, with Next Chapter, a book. And so, the journey continues.........

To learn more about Claire Harrison and discover more Next Chapter authors, visit our website at www.nextchapter.pub.

Printed in Dunstable, United Kingdom

71199894R00184